THE
DROWNED
WOODS

THE DROWNED WOODS

EMILY LLOYD-JONES

LITTLE, BROWN AND COMPANY

New York Boston

Cover art © 2022 by SPIDER.MONEY (Wansiya Visupakanjana). Marble background © Artlusy/Shutterstock.com; brown paper texture © Krasovski Dmitri/Shutterstock.com; gold foil © detchana wangkheeree/Shutterstock.com. Cover design by Jenny Kimura.
Cover copyright © 2022 by Hachette Book Group, Inc.

Little, Brown and Company
Hachette Book Group
1290 Avenue of the Americas, New York, NY 10104
Visit us at LBYR.com

First Edition: August 2022

Little, Brown and Company is a division of Hachette Book Group, Inc. The Little, Brown name and logo are trademarks of Hachette Book Group, Inc.

Decorative flourishes © mashakotcur/Shutterstock.com; grunge background © Krasovski Dmitri/Shutterstock.com.

Library of Congress Cataloging-in-Publication Data
Names: Lloyd-Jones, Emily, author.
Title: The drowned woods / Emily Lloyd-Jones.
Description: First edition. | New York ; Boston : Little, Brown and Company, 2022. | Audience: Ages 14 and up. | Summary: "Mer, the last living water diviner in the isles of Wales, seeks revenge against the prince who used her powers for his own evil ends." —Provided by publisher.
Identifiers: LCCN 2021039629 | ISBN 9780759556317 (hardcover) | ISBN 9780759556331 (ebook)
Subjects: CYAC: Witches—Fiction. | Magic—Fiction. | Blessing and cursing—Fiction. | Fantasy. | LCGFT: Novels. | Fantasy fiction.
Classification: LCC PZ7.L77877 Dr 2022 | DDC [Fic]—dc23
LC record available at https://lccn.loc.gov/2021039629

ISBNs: 978-0-7595-5631-7 (hardcover), 978-0-7595-5633-1 (ebook), 978-0-316-50572-7 (OwlCrate)

Printed in the United States of America

LSC-C

Printing 1, 2022

*To Brittney—who read some of my first
stories, followed me into an old copper
mine, and never drop-kicked me out of
a second-story window*

THE FARMER HAD *four ordinary children, which was why the magic of the fifth came as a surprise.*

The daughter was born with hair too dark to be golden but too light to be brown. She was a clear-eyed little thing who sat quietly in her mam's arms. That night, the farmer brought the child outside. Omen-seeking was unpredictable and the results often vague—putting snails beneath a basin in hopes the trails of slime would spell out a beloved's name; grass taken from beneath holly trees; knotted yarn trailing from windows to see what might be caught.

There were more certain ways to test for magic, but the farmer could not afford a hedgewitch.

It was said that in the cities magic had been tamped out. The tylwyth teg had been banished by iron on every street corner, by roads made of rock instead of packed earth, and by the sheer prevalence of humans. But in the wild country, the expanse of rolling hills and old forests seemed to invite the unexpected. Parents brought their babes out to meet the night—and see what awaited them. The farmer had heard tales of a neighboring village where a newborn had been visited by a flock of ravens. That lad had grown up to sow such death upon the battlefield that several princes sought his services—until a poisoner slipped something into the lad's cup of ale.

The farmer waited with his newborn daughter, but there were no flocks of birds nor strange colors in the sunset. He was about to take the babe indoors when a friendly call stopped him. A weaver from the village had come to deliver a gift of a blanket for the new babe. She cooed over the small child, and in those moments before the farmer could ask her inside, rain began to fall.

It was the thick, misty rains that often sank upon the lands. The farmer raised his arm to shield his daughter, but then he realized there was no need.

The rain did not touch him. It fell—and then seemed to hit some invisible roof, sloughing away without splashing upon him or the babe. The weaver, who stood an arm's length away, was flecked with rainwater. Her gaze fell on the babe and she drew in a sharp breath. "Take her inside," she told the farmer, her voice low. "Take her inside and do not tell anyone."

The farmer was startled. "What?"

"If the prince finds out what she is," said the weaver, her face drawn tight, "he will want her."

"Why?" asked the farmer.

The weaver shook her head. "Do not let her swim. Keep her away from rivers and creeks."

The farmer was frightened by the weaver's sharp words, so he agreed. He never spoke of the encounter with the weaver, instead treating the babe as if nothing had happened.

And for a time, all was well.

At first glance, the farmer's fifth daughter looked an ordinary child: She played with her siblings, helped herd the chickens into the barn, threw clods of dirt at passing foxes, and chatted with those who came to buy crops from her father. The farmer could not afford to keep a strong child indoors and unseen—he had need of another pair of hands.

But as time wore on, it became clear why the weaver had been so troubled.

Rain never touched the girl. She could stand in a thunderstorm and remain utterly dry. She found small streams in the woods, tracing them to their sources with as little thought as finding her way home. She charmed her siblings with dancing mud puddles. She froze small pools of water so that they could slide across the ice. She played in creeks, directing the ebb and flow of the water to her whims. When the summer became overlong, she brought water up through the soil to the dry crops. Her father tried to stop her, told her that such magics were dangerous, but the girl reveled in her power.

She was a headstrong girl whose fingers were gentle when taking eggs from beneath the warm hens—but if she saw cruelty, her temper flared to life. When she found a handful of older children kicking a stray dog, she picked up a stick and tried to drive them off. They laughed and tossed her to the ground, and she committed their faces to memory. For a month afterward, the dirt outside of their front doors was churning, sucking mud that stained their boots.

And when she was eight years old, she saved a child.

The winter rains had lashed the lands for weeks on end, leaving the river a churning, muddied mess. The child was little more than a babe, toddling too far out of his mother's grip. He slipped on the mud, slid into greedy waters that pulled him away too quickly for his parents to save him. The boy was yanked downstream, too frightened to utter a cry.

It was the farmer's daughter who heard the shouting of the parents. She ran barefoot to the river. She felt the raw power of the seething water up through the soles of her feet as she raced toward the overrun banks. Ignoring the warnings of the other villagers, the girl stepped into the river. The froth and foam calmed around her, going unnaturally still. The girl hastened to the boy, pulling him into her arms. She was barely old enough to carry him to safety, but she did it. And the moment her feet left the river, it returned to rushing and pushing at its banks.

The boy's parents were grateful and thanked her again and again, but those who had seen began to whisper among themselves.

Magic.

There was magic in that girl.

Whispers traveled all the way to the nearest city and to the ears of the ruling prince. The prince of Cantre'r Gwaelod was young, come into his throne when his father took ill. But he knew what the rumors meant—diviners were rare but not unheard of. His father had kept a diviner of metal, using magic to weld signet rings to his most trusted servants. When the prince heard tales of a girl who tamed a river, he sent his spymaster for her.

One afternoon, the farmer returned from his fields with dirt-crusted nails and a sweat-dampened brow. He caught sight of a strange man in his yard, and without even speaking a word, the farmer understood. The spymaster wore clothes finer than anyone in the village, bore a signet ring welded to his left index finger, and carried several knives at his belt. The farmer could no more have challenged him than he could have shouted down a storm.

A purse of coins exchanged hands—gold to soothe the sting of the loss.

The girl kicked and struggled, but the spymaster paid her no heed. He carried her to a horse and galloped away. The girl threw one last look at her home before they rode into the forest.

The spymaster was wary, knowing that he had to get the girl to the prince's castell, behind siege walls and iron-clad guards. He rode his steed hard, keeping off the well-worn roads. But whispers of a water diviner had spread past the borders of Cantre'r Gwaelod, to the ears of royals who would not see such a girl fall into the wrong hands. That is to say, any hands but their own.

On the second day of travel, an arrow slammed into an oak tree. The spymaster cursed and urged his horse on, racing through the thick forest foliage, hoping to lose his pursuers. The girl pressed her face into the horse's mane, squeezing her eyes closed.

She never saw the arrow that felled the horse.

The girl and spymaster crashed into the undergrowth—the former falling harmlessly into a patch of moss while the latter cracked his head against a tree. He lay there, trying to recover his senses, while their attacker slid off his own mount. He wore the colors of a neighboring cantref and there were blade scars across both hands. He drew a hunting knife from his belt and made for the girl.

The girl saw him coming. She tripped on a tree root and fell. Her heart hammered in her chest, and she called for her father and mother, for the strange spymaster, for anyone—

But no one came.

And she realized no one would come.

Her fingers curled into the moss, into the familiar dampness of rain-soaked earth—and a thought occurred to her.

The girl had used her magic to care for plants, to amuse her siblings, and to aid her family. Water had seemed a gentle magic, a trickle of power.

Now, gazing at her attacker, the girl looked at him and saw everything. Veins flowed like rivers through him; every gusting breath carried droplets of spittle; his eyes were damp after the hard ride.

The girl raised her hand, moss still tangled around her fingers, and called to her magic.

It was more difficult than affecting a stream or puddle. The iron in his blood dragged at the magic. But she gritted her teeth and called every drop of water she could find, forcing it into his lungs.

A terrible gasping sound emerged from the man's lips. The knife hit the dirt, falling harmlessly to the ground. He clutched at his chest, at his throat, trying to breathe.

Perhaps she should have released the magic.

But the girl was angry. No one had protected her, not like they were supposed to. Her parents had given her into the care of a spymaster and even he couldn't protect her.

She would have to protect herself.

So she did.

It was the spymaster who found her afterward. She sat beside a corpse, her face almost as pale as the dead man's. But she did not cry, nor did she protest when the spymaster bundled her in a cloak, murmuring quiet reassurances. She didn't listen.

It was that day the girl learned that water could save a life—or take it.

It was a lesson she wouldn't forget.

The Diviner

CHAPTER 1

THE THIRD TIME a customer grabbed her, Mer considered drowning him.

It was an idle thought—the way a gardener might have pruned a weed or a painter covered a smudge. It would be a simple thing; a twitch of her fingers could have drawn the ale from his mouth into his lungs. Everyone would say it was a shame that Rhys had choked on his own tongue.

But someone might realize how strange it was for a man to drown on dry land.

It was that chance that stayed Mer's hand.

That and killing him would be wrong. On principle.

She yanked her arm free. "Rhys," she said, her voice icy, "I told you to wait. I'll have your order in a moment."

Rhys gazed at her from across the bar. He slouched over his drink, eyes glazed. He had broken blood vessels at the corners of his nose, sunspots flecked along his cheeks, and a mean cunning in his eyes. Mer had known men like him before—dissatisfied with their lot in life, so they snarled at those who had little recourse. "'M been waitin' for hours," he said.

"You haven't finished your last drink yet," she replied, glancing down. Rhys followed her gaze, squinting at the tankard between his hands.

The Scythe and Boot was always bustling during the evening hours. Many a crop-cutter or traveler would stop by the tavern for a cup of ale and a bit of gossip before ambling home. Mer nimbly carried several drinks to a table of off-duty soldiers, keeping her head down and gaze averted. "Sorry for the wait," she said quietly.

"Think nothing of it, lass." The one who spoke was a woman; she had the calloused hands of someone who'd spent years holding a sword. "You look as though you could use a cup yourself."

Mer wiped the sweat from her brow with a forearm, then touched her fingers to her hair to make sure it was still in place. She kept her hair long, carefully arranged so that it covered the corner of her left eye.

The air was thick with steam and the scent of lamb cawl. It was served in chipped bowls, most of them scavenged from abandoned homes. More and more of those who lived near the borders of Gwaelod were fleeing, leaving behind that which they could not carry. *More for us*, Carys had once said. She was a sturdy woman with thick forearms and hair cropped short. No one quite knew how she had managed to take ownership of the tavern, but none dared question her.

Mer had arrived three months ago with only a few coins in her purse and blisters on her heel. She came to the Scythe and Boot looking to rent one of the upstairs rooms for a night. She'd stayed for three before Carys asked her if she had naught elsewhere to go—and when Mer couldn't answer, Carys pushed two full tankards of ale into Mer's hands and said, "Table in the far right corner."

Mer had stayed. She served drinks and swept floors. Her pay wasn't much, but she was given an upstairs room as compensation. The Scythe and Boot had once been a barn, and the rough wooden walls were still studded with metal hooks for tack and hinges where stall doors had penned in animals. The place smelled of damp hay, and when the wind howled in from the west, the building made odd whistling sounds. But Mer liked it. The tavern felt like the closest thing she'd had to a home in years.

Or it would have felt like a home, if not for the drunkards.

Rhys reached for her a fourth time and Mer ducked out of his grasp, resisting the urge to seize his wrist and bend it back.

"All right, all right," she said, taking his tankard and carrying it to one of the full casks. She refilled it, then slid it back to him.

Rhys gave her a watery glare. "'Bout time. You're paid to serve this swill."

"Don't let Carys hear you say that," said Mer. She grabbed an old cloth rag and began wiping down the bar, her gaze sweeping across the tavern. There were the soldiers, a group of merchants, and two men dicing in the far corner. Everyone had food and drinks, and they looked content. She had a moment to catch her breath.

Mer walked into the kitchens. At once, the smell of fat on the griddle made her stomach ache with hunger. A young man stood in the small kitchen, sleeves rolled up around his elbows and dark hair gone curly in the steam. Elgar was quiet and kept to himself, but he could throw together a meal out of nothing but a handful of flour and leftover vegetables.

"What are you making?" Mer said, setting her tray down.

"Leek and oat cakes," said Elgar. He picked up a bowl, full of batter, and began to pour dollops onto the hot griddle stone. "You think they'll sell?"

"I think we'll have customers starting fights over them," she said.

Elgar threw her a shy smile over his shoulder.

"Shall I bring them out now?" asked Mer.

Elgar nodded. "They're best warm. Oh, and I left you a plate on the table—over there. A few of the cakes, and some of the lamb bones I used for the cawl. I thought you might want them."

"You think I like to gnaw bones?" asked Mer, leaning against the counter.

"I saw you feeding that dog near Hedd's farm," said Elgar, flushing.

It was true—she had been bringing scraps to an old sheepdog that lived in the barn nearby. The family that used to live there had been taken by illness, and no one seemed to remember the sweet sheepdog. Mer had seen the hound wandering the fields, and the next time she had taken a walk, Mer brought scraps of meat too gristly for the stew. The dog would only take the food if Mer put it on the ground and backed away. Since then, Mer had visited every day to bring more. Every time, the dog had become a little friendlier, and Mer hoped that soon the sheepdog might allow her close.

Mer liked animals. There was a simplicity to them, an innocence she never found in people.

"Why not take the hound for yourself?" asked Elgar. "No one would mind. Even Carys would agree, although she'd probably spend a good fortnight blustering on about it."

Mer let out a breath. "I—I am not suited to take care of a dog."

"You are taking care of her," said Elgar, pointing a wooden spoon at her.

"Not forever," said Mer. "Just until…" She had to run again. "…someone else takes a liking to her."

Elgar shrugged. This was something she liked about him: He didn't ask too many questions. Maybe because he was afraid of people prying into his own life.

Mer carried a tray of the fresh oat cakes into the dining room. At once, a few of the regulars turned their heads toward the smell of warm food. She walked to one of the tables, prepared to tell the customers the cost and how delicious the cakes would be—

The tavern door opened. Mer felt it, even if she couldn't hear the creak of old hinges above the din of chatter. There was a gust of cold air that carried the scents of mist and rain. Mer put the tray down as she glanced up to see where the newcomer would sit.

Her heart gave a horrible lurch.

The man who stood in the doorway had dark blond hair fading to a pale gray. His ears were too large and his mouth was all in his lower lip. Even so, he had a sharp focus and confidence that drew people to him. He wasn't handsome but he didn't need to be.

It was a face she had not seen in four years.

Renfrew.

Keeping her gaze averted, Mer murmured to the table, "Enjoy the cakes, compliments of the Scythe and Boot." She set the oat cakes down, and before any of them could comment, she turned so that her back was to the door and hastily made for the stairs. The hayloft had been divided into rooms for rent. She kept a key tied to her wrist and she used it to unlock her door, peering inside.

Her room was empty. No soldiers awaited her. Shoulders sagging with relief, Mer stepped inside and shut the door behind her.

It was a simple room: an old bed frame with a straw mattress suspended on ropes, a single candle, and a sack with the rest of her belongings. She had never unpacked it; unpacking was a luxury Mer could not afford. She swung her pack over one shoulder.

She couldn't go back downstairs—she would have to leave through the window. She took a steadying breath. Outside was a rain-slick roof and a cloud-heavy sky. The drop from the roof to the ground would be a steep one, but she could make it. The windows weren't glass—merely a wooden panel that could be opened on sunny days.

Mer unlatched the window and began to push it open.

But it wouldn't budge.

Mer rammed her shoulder against the wood. It hurt, but the window still wouldn't open. As if it had been jammed shut from the outside. Which meant—

A clicking sound came from the door behind her. She whirled, heart hammering against her ribs. Renfrew had planned this. He had known she would try to flee out a window, so he must have scaled the roof and jammed every single window shut before he allowed himself to be seen. It was the methodical attention to detail that made the old spymaster so good at his work.

And she'd played right into his hands.

The door swung open and Renfrew stood there, a lockpick's wrench between his fingers.

"I thought I taught you better than this," he said, gently chiding. "Always have at least two methods of escape."

Before he had finished the sentence, Mer's hand was at the back of her belt. Her fingers found the hilt of a knife—she'd spent months training with them, learning the heft and balance of the steel. She threw it as hard as she could.

The blade sank into the wood of the doorway, only a finger's width from one of Renfrew's ears. He did not so much as flinch. He reached over and began to pry the knife free. "You missed."

Mer didn't bother to reply. She hadn't meant for the knife to hit him. A distraction, nothing more.

His heavy leather boots had been doused with rainwater. Her hand reached out—and in the same moment, she closed her eyes and called to her power.

To divine a thing, one must find it within themselves. She remembered those words from an old book in the prince's library. It was not just rhetoric. To control water, a diviner needed to pull from that ocean within themselves. If she used too much of her magic, it left her parched and with a throbbing headache. All divining had a price, and she'd heard of how others had suffered—metal diviners weak from little iron in their blood; fire diviners chilled to the bone; wind diviners who died for lack of breath.

At least water was simple to replenish. All she had to do was drink it.

She froze Renfrew's boots to the floor. He tried to lift one of his feet but couldn't.

"I thought *I* taught you better," Mer said coldly. "If you wish to confront me, you'd best dry your boots first."

She reached down, picking up her pack. She didn't have much—firesteel, a knife, a few clothes, a water flask, and coin. That was all a person needed, and the rest could be bought or stolen. She would smash her window open.

"Mer," said Renfrew, and then he did something that made her go still. He *laughed*. A warm chuckle, the kind that came up through the belly and could not be forced. "I have missed you."

Gazing into Renfrew's face made her feel like a child again: torn between a simmering resentment and a yearning for approval. He was the only father she'd known since she was eight. And despite herself, she felt that old tether behind her ribs, a tug of memory that made her want to soften toward him. But she couldn't afford that. Not if she wanted to keep her freedom.

"I'm not going back," she told him, even as her heart pounded. Saying the words was a risk; part of her wanted to pretend that Renfrew's arrival didn't mean what she knew it did. "I'll die before I go back to the prince's service."

"Will you kill me?" asked Renfrew idly.

Mer hesitated only a moment. "No. But I will hold you in place while I run."

Renfrew exhaled. "Look at me properly before you make any hasty decisions."

It felt like a trick, but Mer's gaze swept over the man. He wore tattered clothing, but that was no surprise. He could not wear his spymaster finery in this small town, not if he wished to go unseen.

And that's when she saw the missing finger. It was his left index finger, the foremost upon his dominant hand. It had always been the finger that had borne the heavy signet ring, the one that marked him as belonging to Prince Garanhir. The prince's father had paid a hefty sum to a metal diviner to have his rings welded to the fingers of his inner circle. The only way to remove it would be to—

Remove the finger.

It made her breath catch. That finger had been cut off and cauterized recently—within the last year, at the earliest. Mer knew how slowly burn scars healed.

"You see," said Renfrew, voice still soft, "you are not the only person who has cut ties."

It could not be true. Renfrew had served the royals of Gwaelod all his life. He had been shadow and knife, poison and steel. He would be sent into the field by the prince, only to return with bruised knuckles and dark hollows beneath his eyes. Entire wars had been averted because the right throat had been cut or the correct sheaf of parchment stolen.

There were those who said that Renfrew did not have a heart.

That only someone who did not care could commit such atrocities. The truth was simpler and more frightening: He did such things *because* he cared.

A person with a knife was one thing. A person with a knife and a cause could topple kingdoms.

"You're lying to me," she said.

Renfrew shook his head. "I have never lied to you."

And that was true. There were times when Mer had wished he would lie, to smooth over the harsher edges of their lives. But that did not mean he told her everything. "If you're telling the truth," Mer said, "then tell me this. Did you know?" The words came out low and harsh.

Renfrew tilted his head in silent question.

"What the prince was using my power for," Mer said, unable to keep the throb of hurt from her voice. "When I was sent into the field. Did you know?"

There was a long pause. Renfrew suddenly looked ten years older. "No," he said. "I did not know."

All the air left her lungs. Something deep within her unclenched— a muscle she'd been holding tight for years. If he hadn't known—

She still couldn't trust him. But she could probably let him go.

Mer released her grip on the magic. The ice crusting his boots melted, water draining into the cracks of the floor. Renfrew lifted his foot, shaking the last of the water away.

"If you didn't come to drag me back to the prince," said Mer, "then why are you here?"

One corner of Renfrew's mouth twitched. "I missed you."

"And?" she prompted.

"And I need someone with your abilities," he said.

She crossed her arms, felt her expression hardening. She should have known this wasn't solely about seeing her—Renfrew never did anything without at least two motives.

"I have a job," said Renfrew. "One last job. It will pay handsomely enough for you to do what you could not manage here."

"Serve drinks?"

"Disappear," he said. "With enough coin, you could go anywhere in the isles, build yourself a fortress if you liked. Sail to the continent."

"How do you know I'm running?" she asked.

"Because it is the only thing you can do," he said. "Run or die. Garanhir made sure of that when he—" His fingers reached out, but Mer took a step back before he could touch her hair.

She wanted to deny his words, but they rang true. The prince had all but ensured she would live the life of a hunted rabbit.

Mer had small dreams. She dreamed of a house, of a place that could be wholly *hers*. A place where she could grow things, tend to things. Maybe it would be a short walk from a village, so she could buy what she needed on her own. When she couldn't sleep, she would spend hours imagining what the cottage would look like and what she would do with it.

Even as she craved that home, she knew it wasn't a place she was looking for.

She wanted safety. She wanted to wrap it around herself like a warm cloak.

"One last job," Renfrew repeated softly. "And you can buy your way to freedom."

Mer considered him. "I don't use my powers, not anymore."

It was mostly true—charming the dampness from her socks didn't count.

"You managed to capture me rather handily," said Renfrew.

"Yes, well," said Mer, "you're the exception." She licked her lips; she tasted the salt of her own sweat. If she closed her eyes, she could sense all the water in this room—not only here but below in the tavern: the ale sloshing in tankards, the brine of sweat, the slight droplets in the air, the fog of the windows.

Water was everywhere, if one knew how to find it.

"Why me?" she said quietly, leaning forward. "There's another up north. I heard he was offering his services to—"

"Dead," said Renfrew. "Found with both his purse strings and throat cut."

She hadn't heard that. "Then what about the woman south of—"

"Also dead," said Renfrew, without even waiting for a name. "An illness—or that was how the poison made it look. A cough that wouldn't leave her. And before you suggest the elderly man living near the docks down south, he suffered what appeared to be an attack of the heart."

It felt as though someone had wrapped an iron band around her chest. There were only three others like her.

"Garanhir has been busy in your absence," Renfrew murmured. "If he could not have a water diviner, he wished to ensure that no one else would."

That band around Mer's lungs seemed to cinch even tighter. "He's been hunting them?"

The look that Renfrew gave her was calm and unwavering. "You're the last."

She had to put her hand against the wall to steady herself. The last—she was the last living water diviner in the isles.

Which meant she was all the more valuable. She would be hunted by Garanhir and his rivals alike, because if she were to side with another kingdom, it could change the balance of power. She would never be safe here, never be safe anywhere. Even if Renfrew was right about this job paying well, there wasn't time to take it.

She had to run. Tonight.

"I can't," she said. "Renfrew—I'm sorry, but—"

"Mererid," he said. Her name rolled off his tongue, soft and familiar. "Do not apologize. That's the one thing I wish I could have taught you. Never apologize for what you have to do."

She looked at him. He was father and not-father, friend and enemy, and the one person in the world she'd most wanted to please.

"I have to run," she said. "If Garanhir is truly as desperate as you say, I can't stay. I wish you well, but I cannot help you."

Renfrew inclined his head in a nod. "I understand, dear child." Then he took a step back, so the way through the door was clear. "Take care."

She was taken aback for a heartbeat; she half expected him to argue further. But he merely stood there, accepting her choice.

Gratitude tangled up with resentment—she didn't want to be thankful toward him nor owe him in any way. Chin held high, her pack slung over her shoulder, she walked past him and into the narrow stairway. She hurried, taking them two at a time, not daring to look over her shoulder. If she looked, her heart might soften. Her steps might slow. She could not afford that. The only reason she'd survived this long was that she'd left sentiment behind.

She pushed through the old canvas cloth that hung at the bottom of the stairs. Keeping her head down, she strode for the front door. Maybe if she was quick about it, she could slip out with only a few of the regulars seeing.

A hand caught her around the elbow.

Mer's pack slipped from her shoulder, thudded against her hip. She turned her head, fully expecting to see Renfrew behind her.

It was Rhys. His face was red with drink and anger, and he looked about as friendly as a wild boar. "Where've you been?" he snarled. The words rubbed against one another, barely distinguishable. "Needed a drink."

"Get off of me, Rhys," said Mer, trying to yank her arm free.

"S'posed to serve." The man was surprisingly strong and he gave a hard pull. She stumbled back, caught off balance. She couldn't break his grip, not while holding on to her pack. She twisted her arm, craning his wrist at a painful angle. Any other man would have cried out and released her, but the drink must have dulled Rhys's senses.

"Leave off!" There was a yank, and then Mer found herself freed. Elgar had come up behind them both, holding a rolling pin.

Rhys blinked a few times, touching the back of his head, then glared at Elgar. "Cheeky little—" He fumbled at his belt and came up with a knife. All the folk carried knives around here. One never knew when they might need to whittle or pry open a bottle. This knife looked old, sharpened to a thin edge.

Rhys was drunk and furious—and Mer knew those two things never boded well. There had been a few brawls in the tavern, but not one involving blades.

Elgar brandished the rolling pin like a sword. "Get out, Rhys, or—"

"I'll not have a cook speaking to me like that." Rhys's face reddened with anger. He lunged forward.

A knife like that could slide up between Elgar's ribs. He was a good sort, a kind friend who'd given Mer table scraps for that dog and always asked after her.

Old instincts flared to life.

Mer dropped to a crouch to duck beneath the knife, slammed her fist into Rhys's elbow, and then drove her shoulder into his gut.

Disarm, disable, escape.

It had been her first lesson in fighting, and it came back as easily as breathing.

Rhys fell to the floor, wheezing. The knife skittered away and another patron picked it up. Mer pushed the hair from her eyes as she sat back, grinning. She turned to glance at Elgar, to make sure he was all right.

But the smile died on her lips.

Because the tavern had gone utterly silent. It was the kind of heavy quiet that hung around graveyards. And then Mer realized what she had done. She had pushed her hair back from her left cheek.

She knew what they saw: the ugly kiss of hot iron against the corner of her left eye. The brand bore the same emblem that had marked Renfrew's signet ring—that of the royal family of Gwaelod.

She felt as though *she* had been the one encased in ice this time. Cold stole through her belly, up into her arms. There were too many people in here, too many obstacles. She'd been taught to slip in and out of danger the way a needle threaded cloth—she was a tool, not a blunt instrument.

She kicked a chair at the nearest soldier. It hit him at the knees and he fell into the man behind him, causing both to stagger against the bar. It drew the eyes of the other patrons, made them look at the new commotion rather than the young woman crouching on the floor. Mer used the distraction to scurry to her feet and dart toward the front door.

She made it three steps before someone grabbed for her.

Mer tried to break free, but then lightning cracked through her skull. She was on the floor again, staring up at the ceiling. She'd been struck from behind, she realized belatedly. The thought was distant, coming to her as if through thick water. One of the soldiers had struck her with the pommel of his sword, brought her down before she could fight back. Before she could summon even the smallest bit of power.

A second soldier reached down, pushing Mer's hair back. He let out a hiss.

"She's got the prince's mark on her. We've got an escaped prisoner here, lads."

"No." Mer barely managed to speak the word. It hurt; her jaw ached and her skull throbbed. But then another soldier was hauling her upright, taking her pack and pulling Mer's arms tight behind her.

It was every nightmare she'd woken from in a cold sweat. The sense of entrapment, of helplessness, was galling and terrifying and made her want to spit like an angry cat. She couldn't be taken back to the prince, *she couldn't*. She tugged at the water in the air, tried to pull it around herself. If she could just call up a mist, it might startle them long enough for her to escape.

Iron closed around her wrists—and her connection to the magic *snapped*.

Mer staggered, twisting to look over her shoulder. Iron. The man holding her had iron worked into the knuckles of his gloves. Cold iron pulled the magic from her like leeches drained blood. She could not use her magic so long as he held her.

"Come on," snapped one of the soldiers. It was the woman, the one Mer had smiled at when she had served drinks. It had been such a friendly interaction, and yet here they were.

Mer looked about desperately. She half expected to see Renfrew coming to save her, but there was no sign of the spymaster. He would have slipped out the moment he heard the commotion; he had as much to lose as Mer.

All the faces staring back at her were mixtures of astonishment, disgust, and confusion. Rhys just looked irritated, like he knew he wouldn't be getting another drink any time soon.

The only kind face belonged to Elgar. "Mer?" he said.

There was no time to apologize to him or Carys. To tell them she was grateful for even this short time when she'd had something close to a home.

"Take care of the dog at Hedd's farm!" She threw the words at Elgar over her shoulder. Before she could utter more, she was dragged from the tavern into the cold night.

CHAPTER 2

MER WAS EIGHT years old when she was given into Renfrew's care.

She'd been a slip of a child, with unruly gold-brown hair and muddied feet. Her nights were sleepless, filled with memories of a hunter chasing her through the woods and of her father's face when he gazed at her one last time. It had been an eight-day ride to the prince's castell in Caer Wyddno, and Mer remembered those days of hoofbeats and the blur of green countryside. Her journey ended when the bare soles of her feet touched cold, clean stone and she found herself gazing into the face of a prince.

She had heard of princes. Her mam and da told stories when they weren't too tired by the end of the day. Mer had always thought princes were a little like the otherfolk—something not quite real, not quite touchable, caged within the boundaries of word and myth.

But Prince Garanhir looked like any other man. He had dark

hair and his features were sleek as a ferret. He was surprisingly young, come into his power when his father took ill. Garanhir had given Mer a cursory examination, discovered she was little more than a child, and instructed the servants to take her. The prince had no room in his life for children—he filled up his days in a war room, a heavy oaken table laden with tiny carved figures and maps. Once Mer was old enough to be made into one of those figurines, powerful enough to be a piece on the board, then he would take notice of her.

The servants dressed her in stiff, uncomfortable clothing and shoes that felt wrong on her feet, and gave her a room that was only hers. Solitude was a luxury she'd once craved, but now she longed for the presence of her siblings, for her mother and father, for anything warm and familiar.

Mer did not sleep well in the castell. The rumble of the nearby ocean kept her awake and she flinched every time a servant passed her door. She took to wandering at night, when there were neither servants to force her into shoes nor nobles to ask her awkward questions. Mer slipped through the corridors like a tiny wraith, wearing nightdresses stained at the hem with courtyard dirt.

One night, she found herself standing before the door to the prince's war room.

It was forbidden, locked, far beyond her reach.

Something had awoken inside her that day in the woods—a fury so potent that she had left a man dead upon the ground. And now, that same anger sparked to life. All these people at the castell weren't her family and they could not tell her where and where not to go.

So Mer had placed her hand upon the door and let her power sink into the wood.

All wood had water in it. And in this castell—built into a sea cliff, full of mists and spray and salt—Mer had no lack of water to work with.

She called to the small droplets clinging to the floor, to the walls, even to her own bare feet. The water sank into the wood, expanding it. Water did that—she knew because at home, her front door had always stuck in the rainy seasons. But now, she could use that to her advantage. She listened to the creak and whine as the fine grains of oak were forced apart. Mer then called all the water out from the door, straining the wood even further. Something cracked.

Mer grabbed the knob and pushed as hard as she could. The door sagged, scraping over the floor, but it opened.

She stepped inside. The room smelled of candle wax and parchment, and her footsteps were muffled by a soft rug. It was a beautiful room—draped with tapestries embroidered with the lineage of royal families and artwork depicting heroes slaying dragons. Mer gaped at the study; no wonder the prince spent so much time in here. She would, too, if she had such a room. She walked farther inside, transfixed by the wealth and beauty.

A voice rang out. "It is lovely."

Mer's heart lurched with fear. She turned so swiftly that she nearly fell over, preparing to rush for the door before someone caught her. But a hand snagged in her dress and she found herself pumping her short legs and getting nowhere, caught like a rabbit in a snare.

She looked up and saw him.

It was the man who'd brought her to the castell, who'd taken her from her family. Renfrew. The prince's spymaster.

He did not look like a spymaster. He had rather plain features and big ears. But his eyes were sharp and keen as a hawk, and his mouth was upturned in a smile.

"That door was locked, was it not?" he asked.

Mer considered lying, but her mother had told her never to lie. She gave a decisive nod.

"Ah," said Renfrew thoughtfully, but not as if he spoke to her. "I thought so." He cleared his throat, and this time he was most definitely speaking to Mer. "You found your way in—but how were you planning to escape?" He released her and Mer stood there, arms at her sides, cheeks flushed with defeat.

"Same door," she said.

He *tsk*ed a few times. "That was your one mistake. Never leave the same way you came in. You should have at least two points of escape."

Mer looked at him in confusion; she'd expected to be punished for sneaking into the war room. But Renfrew seemed to approve of her boldness. He squatted down before her, so that their eyes were nearly at the same height. "I wanted to see what was in here," she said, lifting her chin stubbornly.

"Do you know what those maps mean?" he asked. "Or those notes? Can you read?"

She shook her head.

"Do you wish to learn?" he asked.

Mer squirmed, unsure of herself. She didn't care about the maps or notes—but Renfrew was offering her something. And even if she was too young to understand what his teaching would entail, she had wanted to belong to someone. Her parents had given her up and the prince did not care for her. This spymaster was the only one who had taken notice.

"Yes," she said.

And that was how Mer's education had begun.

Water dripped from the bars of the prison wagon.

Mer listened to the rhythm of the soft *plunk-plunk*. If not for the manacles around her wrists, she could have used that water—forcing it into the planks of the wagon, cracking the wood.

But pure iron rendered her just as helpless as everyone else.

There were many words for what Mer could do.

The nobility called such people *diviners*. Mer had always scoffed a little at that term; she could do much more than simply divine the presence of water. City men and traders preferred to call people like Mer *dowsers*. Which was slightly more accurate. She could dowse a person if she wanted to—in both senses of the word.

But then there were those who lived nearest the wilds. Who still kept the old ways and the old tales. When they heard of someone like Mer, they would cast a look in the direction of the eastern mountains.

Other-touched.

Magic was not a human trait. It was *other*; it was something to be feared and wondered at. Anyone who found themselves with the gift was viewed with equal parts distrust and avarice. It was said that some of the otherfolk walked through human lands and when the mood struck them, they would touch the swollen belly of a pregnant mother—gifting that child with magic. Or perhaps it was simply a bit of luck, a slip of fate that certain people found themselves with the gift.

Mer leaned back against the side of the wagon, trying to keep her breathing steady. They'd be leaving in the morning. Mer had overheard the soldiers. They wanted a good night's rest, so only one of them stayed behind to guard the wagon. But one was enough. None would be enough, as her talent was negated by the presence of iron against her skin.

She had to get free. She couldn't let herself be taken back to Prince Garanhir—she hadn't lied to Renfrew when she said she would rather die.

Mer's fingernails bit into her palms.

The night was a cold one. Summer was only for the afternoon hours, when the sun would break through the gray clouds. Autumn was damp and cold and *hers*—but it was beyond her reach.

She tried to call for her power. All she got was a sharp pain through her skull. She winced, glared down at the manacles, and then exhaled hard. It could be worse. The first time she had escaped Garanhir, it had been much worse. Despair had dragged at her every step and she hadn't slept a single night without dreaming of—

Bodies strewn about a well, soldiers feeding the corpses down into the water.

—all that she'd been responsible for.

There had been days she'd considered not rising from her bed, to just let the exhaustion have her. Let the winds and the rain and the ache in her belly lull her into a dreamless sleep.

In the end, it was not bravery that saved her. It was sheer stubbornness.

People wanted her dead.

And in her contrary heart, that made her want to live.

Grimacing, Mer tugged on the chains again. If she had a piece of metal, she might be able to pick the cuffs—

There was a soft sound outside.

She never would have heard it if she had not been trained to listen. There was a footfall that did not belong to a soldier—there was no telltale clank of armor nor a whisper of chain-mail links rubbing against one another.

Mer's breaths came faster, her body attuned to the sudden absence of noise. The guard standing outside had gone utterly quiet: no grumblings, no shuffling of his feet, nothing at all.

She shifted, using her legs to press her back up against the wagon's wall. It was all she could do to ready herself.

The wagon door swung open.

And Renfrew stepped inside.

Mer let the tension fall from her shoulders. "Renfrew."

"Mererid," he said chidingly. "Look at you. All trussed up like some hen that's stopped laying and ready for the stew."

"Not quite ready," she replied.

"I thought not." Renfrew had to duck a little as he walked into the wagon. He settled on the bench across from her like it was a comfortable chair and not the place many a prisoner had been chained. "How have they treated you?"

"As well as to be expected," she said. "No water nor food. I'm to be taken to the prince."

"Yes," he replied. "Yes, you would be. As would I, if I hadn't left the guard outside . . . indisposed."

She wondered how he had done it—perhaps a choke or a drugged cloth to the nose. Renfrew had many skills at his disposal—and while death was among them, it was not his only tool.

This would have been easier if it were.

"Are you here to kill me, then?" she asked. "It would be a mercy."

"I know it would," said Renfrew, and his voice was all compassion and understanding. It made her hackles rise. "The prince would bind you to his service. You are merely a tool to be used or discarded at his leisure. And I fear I was the whetstone used to sharpen you."

She blinked a few times, startled speechless. Of all the things she thought Renfrew might say to her, a half apology was not among them. Renfrew did not apologize; he was whisper and steel, poison and shadow. He did terrible things and knew no regret. She wasn't even sure if he was capable of feeling it.

"Why?" she finally said. "Why did you come here?"

"To your inn or to this wagon?"

"Both," she said.

A faint smile tugged at one corner of his mouth. "I came for the reasons I told you. Because you are the last—and because I have need."

"Of a water diviner?" she said.

"Of you," he said. "You were the best. Even when you were barely taller than my knee, you were the most talented, the—"

"If you think to earn my loyalty through compliments," she said, "I should warn you, it won't work."

He laughed. It was sharp and quiet. "I know. And I do not seek your loyalty—only your skills." All the mirth vanished from his face. He set elbows to knees and leaned forward. "I have a job."

"You said that before," Mer replied. "But you never said what—"

"We are going to break the prince's power."

All the words died on her lips.

She tried to draw in a breath, but even that wouldn't come. It took three tries before she could inhale, and a fourth before she could utter a word. "Are you jesting?"

"I am not," he replied. "I am utterly sincere. Prince Garanhir has stood untested long enough."

"That's not possible," she said. "The prince—he cannot be overthrown."

"Why?" said Renfrew, in the same tone he'd used when teaching her lessons.

Mer stared at him incredulously. "Because the walls of Gwaelod are impenetrable. They are magicked, other-touched as much as I am. A bargain from King Arawn himself, who traded with Garanhir's great-grandfather."

"And what if I told you," said Renfrew, "that I had found a way to thwart those walls?"

"I'd say you were reaching, even for you." Mer shifted, her chains grinding against one another as she tried to adjust her posture. Her legs were aching with cold. "Armies have tried to breach those walls, to climb them, to tunnel under them. Nothing has worked."

"There is a well," said Renfrew quietly. "It is the heart of the magic that feeds into those walls. It has been hidden within Gwaelod for over a hundred years. It has kept those lands safe—and without its magic, the kingdom would lose that protection."

"A well," said Mer, unable to hide her skepticism. "That's what feeds the magic? If it's so simple, then why hasn't anyone tried to take the magic?"

"Because Garanhir's family has guarded the secret. And people *have* tried," said Renfrew. "But none have succeeded."

"Oh." She licked her dry lips. "I get the feeling you're about to say, 'I plan to be the first.'"

"I will be," said Renfrew. "Because I have one thing those others did not."

All the pieces fell into place. And Mer finally understood why Renfrew had gone to such lengths to find her.

A well. A magical *well*.

"You have a water diviner," she said quietly.

Renfrew's eyes gleamed. "I don't know. Do I?"

She felt entrapped by his words, as if their entire exchange had been an elaborately woven web. He could ensnare her just as easily as these physical chains.

She thought of returning to Caer Wyddno and her stomach clenched.

"This is the moment," said Mer, "that you will make your bargain. My release traded for my services."

Renfrew shook his head. "No, Mererid. I will release you from those chains whether or not you choose to aid me. Should you run, I will not stop you. But if you decide to join my cause..." His eyes flashed like blue fire. "Within the Well are treasures. Come with me. We'll steal the magic, the gold, and you will have enough coin to settle far beyond the reach of Gwaelod."

She wanted to argue. This all seemed far-fetched, straining credulity. Prince Garanhir and his kin had ruled for over a hundred years from the safety of Caer Wyddno. It was difficult to imagine anyone ever unseating the prince from his throne.

We are the agents of order, Renfrew had always told her. *We restore things to how they should be. We win wars with the least amount of spilled blood. A soldier would have to hack his way through hundreds of enemies to reach a noble, but we can do so with forged papers, a quick smile, and a dose of poison—and only one life lost.*

There had been a time when she'd believed in him.

And looking into his face, she wanted to believe in him again.

"If I do this," she said. "One last job—then it is truly the last. I will not work for you again. And I'll need enough coin to escape."

A fierce victory flashed through Renfrew's eyes, but he did not smile. It looked more like a grim triumph. "Agreed," he said quietly.

"So are we to journey to Caer Wyddno?"

"Not quite yet," said Renfrew. "First, I intend to hire a little muscle. A former spymaster and a diviner are all well and good, but if we are to survive this, we'll need a few strong arms."

"Might be easier to hire the help if these were gone." She rattled the shackles, ready to be done with the bite of iron.

Renfrew's smile, when it finally came, had the curve of a wicked blade. He reached into his pocket and withdrew a stolen ring of keys.

CHAPTER 3

F ANE'S MOUTH WAS full of blood.

One of his teeth had cut into his lower lip. He kept licking at the small cut, tongue flickering across the wound before he remembered to leave it be. He knew that if he smiled, his teeth would be smeared with crimson—which was precisely why he bared his teeth at his opponent.

The woman hesitated for all of a heartbeat, then she attacked.

Her fists slammed into his ribs with startling swiftness, driving Fane to his knees. Then one of her legs wrapped around his throat and he was on the ground, struggling for breath.

A cry rang out and the tight grip around his throat loosened. Fane drew in a breath and coughed. He spat blood on the packed earth of the floor.

"—And the round goes to Blodeuyn!" The crier standing atop

an overturned crate bellowed the words with no small amount of glee. Of course he'd be cheerful; he would take a fraction of the betting coin, no matter who won. The surrounding crowds yelled and cheered in equal measure—some stood and some were sitting on makeshift benches or the dirt floor.

Blodeuyn turned to gaze at Fane. She had hair so pale it looked like mountain snow. When she held out a hand, Fane took it. She helped haul him to his feet. "Good match," he said, nodding respectfully to her.

He rather liked her. She'd been the first one to speak to him when he arrived two weeks ago with little coin and even fewer friends. She had bought him a few meals at a local tavern, tried to pry stories of the wild country out of him. And she had been the one to suggest this match when his losing streak ensured that few would consider fighting him. He was not seen as a worthy challenge.

Blodeuyn shook her head. "You look like a hound after a fresh kill," she said. "Come. I'll buy you something to wash your mouth." She pushed through the crowds, toward the wall. A decade ago, this building must have once been a meetinghouse for the city of Pentref yr Eigion—but it had been repurposed for the fights. The air was thick with the smells of damp wood and sweat. There was a man selling day-old oggies and cups of drink to spectators and fighters alike. Blodeuyn tossed the man a coin and picked up two of the cups. She handed one to Fane and he took a swig. It wasn't ale—it was water laced with honey and mint. They found a place by the wall to stand, away from the cheering crowds. The noise was painfully loud—jeers and encouragements, curses and songs. And even above that, Fane could feel the hum of iron. Iron permeated this place: in the knives tucked away within sleeves and boots, in the studs of the walls, in rings and belts, in the scattering of counterfeit coins, and in the blood that had splattered the dirt floor. The dried blood was softer, a whisper of old injury and hurt. The fresh blood had a sharper sound, like the cry of ravens that followed soldiers into battle.

It all came together in a discordant song and Fane closed his eyes.

After years of living in a forest, he had not realized how loud the iron of a human city would be—and he would have walked away, if he could. But he needed to be here.

The next two fighters were stepping into the ring. There were always at least two fights happening at once, and coin changed hands quickly as the contestants entered and left the rings.

The fights were illegal in this cantref as any coin made from wagers was supposed to be taxed. But such fights cropped up all over the lands, despite attempts to quash them. They were a diversion for folk who yearned for the chance at a better life and did not mind risking their wages. And those who came to fight could earn a fair amount if they took to betting on themselves and did not lose.

And if they did not die.

The danger only seemed to add to the festive air. An older woman played the pipe and tabor, and people chatted happily at the fringes of the fights.

Fane glanced at Blodeuyn. "Thank you," he said. "For the drink."

She gave him a speculative look. "I thought I owed you something, since you threw that fight."

Surprise flickered through him, but Fane did not let it touch his expression. "Why would I do such a thing?"

"That is what I was going to ask you," she replied. "You didn't hit me. Didn't even try—I mean, I know you made a show of it. You raised your fists and threw punches at the air, but I know a diversion when I see one." Her mouth pressed thin. "Is it because I'm a woman? Because I've no problem thrashing you again."

Fane shook his head. "No, no. Nothing of the sort, I assure you." That much was true, at least.

Blodeuyn drained her cup in a few swallows. "You haven't won once," she said. "You've been losing matches and coin since you showed up here."

"Perhaps I'm not as good a fighter as everyone else," said Fane.

Blodeuyn tapped a finger against her empty cup. "You know what I think? It's a swindle. You're going to keep losing fights until the odds are so stacked against you that no one else will bet on you. You'll wager everything on yourself. And then you're going to finally fight back and walk away with a full purse before moving on to the next village."

Fane let out a startled laugh. He had anticipated many problems with this job, but being scrutinized by a fellow fighter had not entered his mind. In his experience, people did not question their own victories—they were either too greedy or too grateful. "You make me sound like some kind of master criminal, Lady Blodeuyn."

She cut him a sharp look. "You're here for some purpose. If it's not to win fights, then what is it?"

"Perhaps I like the company," he said, smiling.

"Perhaps you enjoy being beaten," she replied, with a nod at his bruised face.

"Perhaps I wish I could be," he said, with more honesty than he'd intended.

Blodeuyn stared at him for a few heartbeats and Fane let out a breath. He was used to speaking with double-edged words, to using truths as both shield and weapon. Humans did not speak in such a manner—they either lied or they didn't. He'd spent too many years in Annwvyn to sound human anymore. And while he could feign normality for a time, these two weeks among the fighters were beginning to dissolve that illusion.

Blodeuyn opened her mouth. She could prove to be a problem if she chose to make herself one, and he hoped she wouldn't. Then there was a shout from the man standing atop the crate. "—Challenger! None has defeated the Blaidd of Hafn Glawog."

Blodeuyn's head snapped up. Her posture shifted from relaxed and friendly to something harder and more dangerous.

"Finally," she breathed. "I thought he would never come."

It took him a few heartbeats to understand what she meant.

"You intend to fight the Blaidd?" asked Fane, aghast.

Blodeuyn did not so much as look at Fane. Her gaze was fastened to a man striding toward one of the fighting rings. The crowds parted before him, shuffling aside so quickly that some were stepped on and a few were shoved to the floor. The crier was continuing to shout about the Blaidd's impressive achievements: his victories in battle, the strength of his fists and arms, how he'd once wrestled an afanc and lived—

That last one was such an obvious untruth that Fane almost snorted through his crooked nose. But nothing about this situation was amusing.

"Are you mad?" he said quietly to Blodeuyn. "Do you know who that man is? Why they call him the Wolf?"

"Yes," she said simply. "I know who he is. Why do you think I came here?"

Fane had made a mistake; he'd never considered that Blodeuyn had come here for reasons other than coin. The way she fought—all short bursts of ferocity—was born of some deep-seated anger. He should have seen that in her before now.

"Blodeuyn," he said. "Please—I don't know why you think this is important, but—"

Blodeuyn rounded on him. "There was a little girl. One without parents. She'd been taken in by a miller, you see. Given food and clothes and shelter. But the Blaidd of Hafn Glawog arrived not a month later. He and his mercenaries required a place to stay—so they took the mill for the night. When the miller protested, the Blaidd set fire to the mill. His ward was inside."

A bitter taste filled Fane's mouth.

"The miller went to the lord of the cantref," said Blodeuyn. "He asked for justice. But the Blaidd was too good a soldier, too useful on the front. Nothing would ever be done, no matter how many homes were burned, how many bones left in his wake. The miller is my cousin—and now he has no home, no livelihood. And he weeps every day for that girl."

"So this is how you're going to avenge his adopted daughter?" Fane said. "You're going to challenge the Blaidd to a fight?"

"No one else is going to stop him," said Blodeuyn. "No one else will. I could not attack him while he's surrounded by his friends. But here, in the ring—I can fight him. And I cannot stand by and watch this brute hurt other people." She pushed her way through the crowd, stepping into the fighting ring.

The Blaidd of Hafn Glawog looked more workhorse than man. He stood a full head taller than Fane and his shoulders and chest were thick with muscle. His features were disarmingly friendly—a smile that stretched across his face and shining blue eyes.

"What is this?" the Blaidd asked. When he laughed, the sound was rich and deep. "Lass, go back home. You don't belong here."

Blodeuyn merely walked up to the bookmaker—a young woman with a quill and a well-worn piece of parchment. Blodeuyn set down a bag of coins. The bookmaker pulled it open and blanched.

Excitement bloomed across the crier's face. "Looks like we have a fight on our hands," he shouted.

Blodeuyn turned to face the Blaidd. She could fight well enough—Fane had experienced that for himself only a few minutes ago. But the Blaidd's weather-beaten face was full of amusement as he strode into the ring.

Fane watched, a gnawing dread taking hold in his belly. He'd seen many a person fight in this building, even watched one man bleed out when another snuck a wholly unsanctioned knife into the match. But he'd never watched someone he considered a friend face an opponent three times her size.

This was folly—but that didn't matter to Blodeuyn. She would fight because this was her only chance to stop him. It was a kind of terrible bravery, and Fane both admired and resented her for it.

He knew a little too well what a person could do with such bravery.

The crier raised a hand, then let it fall.

The crowds screamed as the match began. It started with Blodeuyn; she did not wait for the Blaidd to attack first. She went low, kicking at one of his knees. It wasn't a bad strategy—knees were fragile if hit at the right angle, and such injuries were painful and slow to heal.

The Blaidd wasn't just a large man but a swift one, too. He stepped aside, so that Blodeuyn's kick hit him squarely in the meat of his thigh. Fane watched as Blodeuyn's jaw clenched tight, and then she was punching at the Blaidd's lower belly, aiming for his ribs, for the soft flesh of his stomach. Several of the blows connected, and the Blaidd had to use his forearm to block.

Blodeuyn caught his arm and held him in place, using it like an anchor as she whirled, putting all her weight into a knee strike. There was an ugly *crack* when it connected, slamming into the Blaidd's side. Fane winced at the sound; she had broken at least two of the Blaidd's ribs.

Fury kindled in the Blaidd's eyes. People reacted to pain in different ways—it could drive them to their knees or make them weep or steal the breath from their lungs. But pain only seemed to anger the Blaidd. All the restraint slid out of his posture, and his bared teeth gleamed in the torchlight. People did not call him the Wolf for nothing.

Blodeuyn tried to twist the Blaidd's arm behind his back, to force him to his knees. But the Blaidd shook her off, the full force of his weight and bulk coming to bear.

The Blaidd struck her across the face.

Fane winced. The Blaidd had used his fist, and Blodeuyn looked as bloody and woebegone as Fane himself had during his own fight. Her nose would be broken, and perhaps her cheekbone, as well. But her eyes were full of fire.

It wouldn't change things.

She'd been trained to fight. But the Blaidd liked to kill.

He got her feet out from under her with one savage kick. The sound echoed even above the din of the shouting, jeering, encouraging spectators. The Blaidd followed her down, landing punch after punch. Fane's stomach roiled.

The Blaidd was going to kill her.

No one was going to step in.

Blodeuyn threw a lucky jab, striking the Blaidd at the corner of his eye. He jerked back and she used his distraction to roll aside. She coughed hard into the packed earth, pushing herself onto her elbows. She kept one arm around her chest, her face taut with agony. Fane knew the pain of broken ribs, how they set fire to a person's insides. It was a wonder she didn't simply stay down. Her face was colorless, save for the smudge of dirt and blood across her cheek. But she gazed at the Blaidd with a determination and strength that would have marked her as a hero in one of the old stories.

If this were an old story, she would beat him. She would find a clever crack in his defenses and bring down the murderer, prove that goodness and decency mattered.

But this was not an old folktale; there were no heroes.

The Blaidd moved so fast that Fane barely caught a glimpse of the blow. Blodeuyn hit the ground again, gasping with pain. This time, she did not rise.

There was a quiet in the crowd, the tense moment of a held breath. Everyone was waiting for the inevitable, for the final blow to fall.

And it would have—if Fane had not pushed one of the men aside and strode into the ring. He stood in front of Blodeuyn, his arms loose at his sides and gaze hard.

The Blaidd gave Fane a once-over. "Move, lad. This isn't your fight."

"You're right," replied Fane, his voice quiet but firm. "But I'm not going to let you kill her."

The Blaidd's forehead creased as he took in the sight of Fane. Fane did not often glance into mirrors; vanity was a thing he'd given up years ago. His eyes and hair were both dark, and while he tried to keep himself clean-shaven, stubble traced the line of his jaw. His nose was crooked from several breaks, and a scar forked through his upper lip.

Fane was all rough, unfinished edges—a sculpture abandoned by its artist.

"You sweet on the lass?" asked the Blaidd, amused. He shrugged. "Who am I to deny a man a chance to fight?"

Fane licked his lip again, and the taste of fresh copper filled his mouth. "Leave the ring now," he said. "Let this end here."

The Blaidd let out a bellow of a laugh. "This *will* end here." He reached for Fane's shirt, trying to seize hold of him.

There was no choice.

There were no heroes.

There was only Fane.

For the first time since entering the fights, Fane threw a blow and let it land.

His knuckles barely grazed the Blaidd's cheek—a whisper of scratchy beard across his skin—but it was enough for the magic to take hold.

It was like cracking a joint: There was the sensation of pressure being released, almost a relief, and then the world seemed to fall away. There was no fighting ring, no crowds, no bets, no shouting, no hum of iron against his skin. There was only muscle and bone, blood and sinew.

The Blaidd tried to hit him again, but Fane ducked beneath the strike easily, seized hold of the other man's arm, and yanked him closer. It had the twofold effect of knocking the Blaidd off balance and getting close enough to drive three blows into the man's injured ribs. He felt the bones give way, and there was a bellow of pain so loud it made Fane's ears ring.

The pain made the Blaidd angry, made him reckless. He hunched around his injured side, preparing to fight back.

This was the difference between them all.

Blodeuyn liked to fight. The Blaidd liked to kill.

But Fane was death itself.

And the power had hold of him now.

Fane gave himself over to it. He was little more than a puppet on strings, his body an instrument for a will not his own. He felt the blows land—but he felt them from a distance, from some place that was not himself. For a few moments, he closed his eyes. He did not have to observe the breaking of bones nor the taste of sweat across his lips nor the slickness against his fingers. He tried to ignore the sensations, tried to summon up other memories: the scent of damp oak leaves and the pleasant smoke of a wood fire, the taste of forest berries and the touch of smooth fingers pushing his dirty hair away from his forehead. And the whispered bargain that had forever changed him.

Seven years of service for seven human lives.

He had taken two lives—this would be his third.

When Fane opened his eyes, the match was done.

And so was the Blaidd.

The big man lay in a heap on the ground—and he drew no breath.

Fane's whole body ached. His nose was bleeding, although he couldn't remember the Blaidd hitting him. Fane's knuckles were split and his lungs overfull. He exhaled hard, trying to steady himself. This was the part he hated most. He hated returning to himself after the curse had taken hold. It was like returning to a town that had been ransacked: He had to take stock of the damage, of how much of himself was taken and what could be repaired.

Fane rose to his full height and realized for the first time that the building was utterly quiet. There was no shouting, no jeering, no cries of encouragement, and no clink of coin. Fane walked to the bookmaker. She cringed away from him, as far as she could go on her stool. Her eyes were downcast and she wouldn't look at him as he reached down and picked up both Blodeuyn's and the Blaidd's wagers. It added up to a fair amount. Fane took it all, strode back to Blodeuyn, and dropped his winnings beside her. "For your miller cousin," he said quietly.

Blodeuyn looked up at him. She held herself rigid—from pain, and likely, fear. She feared him. That hurt more than Fane expected, but he couldn't hold it against her.

The crowds parted before him like fields before a strong breeze. Fane walked through them, eyes ahead and shoulders straight.

"Other-touched," someone whispered.

"Not right," came another soft voice.

"Not human."

"Killed the Blaidd like it was nothing—"

"—not right—"

The whispers built and built, a crescendo rising through the building. Fane quickened his step. It wouldn't do for any of the Blaidd's friends to realize how exhausted he was, how vulnerable. His magic would not protect him against a knife in the back.

He stepped out into the night.

At this late hour, the streets were quiet. Fog caught and held the moonlight, casting the city into hues of silver. There were a few people leaving and arriving at the fights—mostly those with unsteady gaits and hoods drawn up to hide their faces. Three people sat across the street on fallen ale barrels, sharing a pipe.

A soft shuffling sound made Fane look down sharply. There was someone waiting for him. Well, perhaps *someone* was too strong a word. The dog had four short legs and when he was standing, the tips of his pointed ears barely brushed Fane's knee. He'd been sleeping in the shadow of an empty rain barrel, his chin tucked against his paws.

Upon seeing Fane, the corgi stood and began wagging his tail in glee. "You better not have stolen anyone's boots while I wasn't around to stop you," Fane murmured, leaning down to rub the dog's ears. Trefor merely licked his hand in answer.

One of the smoking men glanced at the dog and gave Fane a dark look. "What are you playing at?" he snapped. "You want to bring the wrath of the otherfolk down on our heads? Why'd you bring one of their spies into town?"

Trefor looked at the man and wagged his tail in greeting. The man looked thoroughly spooked, even more so when Trefor took two steps closer and uttered the softest of woofs.

The man nearly fell off his barrel. Gaze darting between Fane and the dog, the man hastily stowed his still-smoking pipe into his pocket and trudged away. The others followed.

Fane glanced down at Trefor. "You did that on purpose, didn't you?"

Trefor wagged his whole lower body in reply, tongue lolling.

"Yes," said Fane. "You're clearly a threat to us all."

Trefor made a soft whining sound.

"Beggar," said Fane, but he said it fondly. "Come on. We'll find a bite to eat before bed."

The city wasn't a large one, but it had a few eating houses that would still be serving at this late hour. Fane turned to go when he realized that he'd been followed. Two figures had slipped out of the fights—and they were clearly after him.

The first was a young woman. She had her hood raised, but the hair that fell across her left cheek was a honeyed brown. An older man stood in her shadow. They both wore dark cloaks, and both had the same wary look to them. There was a whisper of iron at the woman's wrists and boots—knives, most likely. There was another bit of metal tucked into her belt that felt less sharp. Maybe a wrench of some kind.

The man had too many blades to count. Merely standing a few strides away was like being beside a beehive. Fane kept his arms and hands in plain sight. "May I help you?"

It was the man who spoke. "You might have, if you'd left the Blaidd alive."

"Pity about that," murmured the young woman, in the voice of one who felt no pity at all.

"Sorry about your friend," said Fane.

The man snorted. "Hardly a friend. We needed to hire a mercenary." The man tilted his head speculatively. "How did you kill him?"

Of all the things Fane might have expected, that question wasn't among them. "What do you mean?"

The man's mouth curved into a smile—but it was the kind of smile that reminded Fane of knives and fishhooks. "You managed to kill a famed mercenary as easily as I'd have slain a snared rabbit."

Fane touched the blood beneath his nose. "Not unless the rabbits of your village can land a good punch."

The woman was startled into a laugh. She touched her mouth, as if trying to hide her mirth.

"It looked like an impossibility," said the man, ignoring her.

"You should visit the mountains," said Fane. "You'll find many such impossibilities there."

Fane was still unused to the way city folk treated magic. For them, it was a distant thing. An impossibility. In the shadow of the Annwvyn mountains, everyone marked their front doors with iron, counted the number of crows that roosted in nearby trees, gave baskets of fresh apples and bread to the forest in exchange for decent weather, and told their children never to make bargains with any folk they came across in the woods.

The man's eyes gleamed with something like avarice. "Then you *are* other-touched."

"I said no such thing," said Fane. He tipped his head in a polite farewell and began to turn.

"We wish to hire you," said the man. "We have a job—it would pay you handsomely."

"I'm not the Blaidd," said Fane. "And I doubt I'd enjoy any job you wished to hire him for." He let out a breath; his mouth still tasted of blood, and he yearned for clean water. But before he could make a show of leaving a second time, Trefor walked away from him.

The corgi trotted over to the young woman, snuffling at her ankles. The woman looked down at Trefor unflinchingly. "Well," said the woman quietly. "Aren't you a lovely one?" She knelt, holding out a hand for Trefor to sniff.

Trefor licked her fingers. And then he sneezed.

Fane felt the bottom of his stomach drop out.

Trefor bounced happily around the woman. His tail wagged and he sneezed a second time.

Magic.

Trefor only ever sneezed when he scented magic upon the air.

"What?" asked the woman, seeing Fane's hard look. She kept her chin angled down, her hair falling across her left eye. She appeared uncomfortable with Fane's scrutiny. "Should I not have touched him? Is he yours?" Her hands fell away from Trefor's ears. The dog sat back on his haunches, disappointed.

"No, you can pet him. He belongs to himself," said Fane. "But he enjoys cheese enough that he's deigned to follow me around the countryside."

"He's a handsome boy," said the young woman, smiling down at Trefor.

Trefor licked at her hands again, trying to coax forth more pets.

Fane regarded the two strangers. "Who are you?"

"My name is Renfrew," said the man. "This is Mererid." He gestured to the young woman.

Mererid was absentmindedly stroking Trefor's cheek. The dog sneezed so hard he fell over. He shook his head, ears flapping.

There was no mistaking it. She had magic, and judging by the strength of Trefor's sneezes, it was not the trifling charms that could be bought from hedgewitches or even the borrowed power that dwelled within Fane's body. She had true power.

"I suppose we can't interest you in a spot of supper?" asked Renfrew. He seemed encouraged by Fane's hesitation. "We could discuss that job I was going to hire the Blaidd for. It isn't killing—I mean, if all goes well, there will be no killing."

"How reassuring," said Fane. "And what makes you think I won't just go to the guards and explain how you tried to hire me for some illegal venture?"

"You were in the fighting rings," said Renfrew. "Law-abiding folk don't fight in illegal rings for coin and glory. And they certainly don't beat infamous mercenaries to death for the joy of it."

Fane wanted to protest that last sentence, but he wasn't sure what part to object to. "I did what had to be done," he finally said. "I'm sorry if you object."

Renfrew shook his head. "Never apologize, dear lad."

Fane began to reply, but he heard the sound of a door crashing open. It came from the direction of the fighting rings. There was a rumble of furious voices, low and intent.

Those would be the Blaidd's friends. It had taken them long enough—they'd likely fortified themselves with a strong drink before venturing out to find Fane. Which meant it was time to leave.

"What kind of supper did you have in mind?" Fane asked.

CHAPTER 4

THE CITY WAS large enough to have a few places with rooms to rent. But Renfrew turned away from the eateries and taverns, from the sounds of other travelers and the warmth of hearth fires. He kept to the shadows, and Mer followed half a step behind. She let him lead.

Some instincts never left a person. And neither did some fears.

Mer listened. She kept her eyes on the ground, focusing on the soft scuffle of her own boots and the sound of the young man behind her. The dog panted as he trotted along. And as always, Renfrew was utterly silent. Once Mer had those sounds fixed in her mind, she turned her senses outward—listening for any disturbances: the thud of pursuing footsteps or the cries of angry followers. The Blaidd's companions would be hunting his killer.

Mer kept her hands out of her cloak, her knives at the ready. But she never needed to use them.

Renfrew led them to the fringes of the city, to where several homes stood empty.

Mer half expected their guest to protest such accommodations, but Fane remained silent. The corgi sniffed at the damp wood of the doorway. Fane stepped inside, seemingly unafraid of being led to an empty building by two people he did not know. That either made him incredibly brave or rather foolish.

Or, Mer reflected, he was just that sure of his own ability to defend himself.

And considering what she'd seen him do to the Blaidd, perhaps he'd earned that confidence.

The empty house smelled of rotted wood. Moss filled in the cracks and the windows were hollow gaps in the walls covered by worn cloth. Renfrew went to look through one of the windows, but Mer caught him by the arm. Her fingers were gloved, but she knew he could feel her nails digging through the cloth. "This wasn't the plan," she said quietly. "We were supposed to hire the Blaidd."

"Come, Mer." Renfrew kept his voice soft, so the words would not carry. "You know how these things go. We make plans and then they collapse around us."

"I'd hoped maybe a few years away from the prince and his games might have changed that," she replied.

Renfrew gave her a soft, almost sad smile. "The game never changes. Nor does our need to improvise." Without so much as blinking, he broke Mer's grip and took hold of *her* arm. It was a gentle reminder that for all he looked like any other man, he was not to be trifled with. "We need a fighter. And that one—he's more than what he seems. I've watched men kill each other for decades, but I've never seen a talent like his. He's coming with us."

Mer glanced to the corner of the room. Fane knelt beside his dog, scratching the creature's ears. "And if he refuses?" she said softly.

Renfrew did not answer, but Mer knew his reply. No one could hear of this venture and not come with them. They'd be too much of a liability.

She pressed a hand to her aching eyes. They'd traveled for nearly a week without rest to get here and exhaustion made her magic sluggish. "I'm tired," she said. "If you want him silenced, do it yourself."

Renfrew's face remained untouched by anger or irritation. "I hope you're not too tired to get a fire going. I'll see if anyone followed us."

She threw him a disgruntled look over her shoulder, then knelt beside the fireplace. Renfrew's footsteps rang out behind her, and then she was alone with Fane.

Exhaling hard, Mer looked down at the fireplace. She reached into her pack and withdrew firesteel. In a few minutes, there was a well-sized fire licking at the dry logs. The corgi waddled closer and plopped down next to her. In the flickering light, his dark eyes glittered with something like intelligence. Or perhaps that was her own imaginings. There were tales of corgis—of how they were servants and messengers of the tylwyth teg. Mer had never given those stories much weight. Surely if the otherfolk were going to have spies, they'd be far less...slobbery.

"Where did you get him?" Mer asked, holding out her hand for the dog to sniff. He snuffled around her fingers, then gave one enormous sneeze before licking at her hand.

Fane reached down to ruffle the dog's ears. "Trefor? He was wandering a forest when I happened through. I gave him some cheese and he seemed to decide I was worth following."

"He's a handsome boy, isn't he?" Mer's voice softened without her meaning to. She let out a breath and glanced up at Fane. He hadn't sat beside the fire; rather, he stood with his arms relaxed at his sides.

He had hard features, as though a carver had coaxed his face forth from some ill-tempered oak. His skin bore years of sunlight, his forearms tanned. It only made his scars all the more obvious. His hands had taken the worst of it—knuckles split and healed, nails broken, and his right ring finger was slightly crooked, as if it had been broken and never set properly. Dark hair, dark eyes, and bruises shaded across one of those eyes. There was strength in his forearms and shoulders, sinewy muscles visible where his shirtsleeves were rolled up.

But all the strength in the world could not save him if Mer turned her power against him. That dampness in the air would make lovely ice, and once he couldn't move, she could either drown him or freeze the very water in his blood and lungs.

It wasn't very kind of her to consider how best to kill most people she met. But Mer had been undone by kindness before.

Renfrew strode into the room, shaking the mist from his cloak. "All right," he said. "I believe it's rather rude of me to discuss business on an empty stomach, but I'd like to finish this before I go out and locate our supper."

"You mean 'buy'?" asked Fane, with a slight raise of his brows.

"He means 'steal,'" said Mer. She could feel Renfrew throw a disapproving glance her way, but she ignored him. He'd drawn her into this mess; she would needle him if she liked.

Renfrew let out a gusty breath, as if she were an unruly child. "You are in need of coin, are you not?"

Fane tilted his head. The glow of the fire cast odd shadows across his crooked nose. "Why would you think that?"

"No one fights in the rings unless they're in need of coin or they've something to prove," replied Renfrew. "You clearly have little to prove, considering how long you spent trying to talk the Blaidd out of your fight."

Fane leaned against the wall; to Mer's relief, the half-rotted wood didn't collapse under his weight. She would have suggested a chair, but whoever had looted this place took all the furniture. "What kind of job is this?" asked Fane.

Mer felt Renfrew's eyes upon her again, and this time, she returned the look. She did not know how much of their plan he intended to share, so she would remain silent for now.

"Garanhir," said Renfrew. "What do you know of him?"

The corgi stood up from his place beside the fire and went to sit by Fane's leg. The young man reached down to absentmindedly scratch at the dog's ears. "Prince of Gwaelod. Rules from his fortress at the city of Caer Wyddno. Known for sending raiding parties into Gwynedd."

It was a rather polite way of putting it. No mentions of the dead bodies or the burned farmlands or the poisoned wells.

"He's a tyrant," said Renfrew simply, "who came into his power too young and had too few people tell him no. He is ill content with his own lands and ill capable of ruling even those. But he does possess one great power." He crossed his arms, leaning forward as if to whisper a secret. Even Mer, who knew all of Renfrew's techniques, was half tempted to lean in closer. There was a power to quiet confidences that shouting could never match. "There is a well in which he has hidden magical treasures. Many have looked for it, but none have succeeded. We intend to take those treasures."

There was a moment of silence.

"You're common thieves," Fane said.

"We're uncommon thieves," said Mer. "Trust me, you'll not find our like again."

Fane glanced between Mer and Renfrew, as if searching for something. "And you think I'll agree? Just like that?"

"Well, we came here expecting to find a mercenary for whom the words 'magical treasure' would be enough," said Mer. "If you were more greedy, this would have been a great deal simpler."

"I apologize for my lack of greed," said Fane gravely. "It must be very trying."

Renfrew held up his hands, palms out. "I saw how you fight, lad. You could have used those skills in the armies of any kingdom, and they'd be glad to have you. That you haven't hired on as a mercenary tells me that you're either running from something or you wish to remain unseen." He gazed at Fane. "Where is your home?"

"East of here," said Fane. "Near the borders of Annwvyn. A small village—you would not have heard of it."

"Family?" asked Renfrew.

"Dead," said Fane simply. "Killed by mercenaries."

No wonder he hadn't minded killing the Blaidd.

"And after that?" asked Renfrew. "Did you join the armies?"

"I had no place to go," said Fane. "So I wandered into the mountains and found employment working for those who dwell there."

For a few moments, Mer was not sure she had heard him right. There were no people in the mountains. There were only—

"The tylwyth teg," said Renfrew, and his stance shifted. It was subtle to anyone who did not know him, but Mer saw the slight flex of his fingers and the way his shoulders straightened. There were blades at both wrists. "You worked for the otherfolk?"

Fane said matter-of-factly, "Contrary to the tales, the otherfolk don't kidnap people for their own ends. Not always," he admitted, after a moment's thought. "But more often, they will employ humans to do work they cannot. It is honest trade, and I only ever dealt with those in the forest—never the nobles. I've never seen the Otherking nor spoken with one of his court." His shoulders rose in a shrug before a wince of pain crossed his face. He must have been aching from that fight. It was a wonder he was still standing, Mer thought.

"And what did you do for the otherfolk?" she asked. "Were you some kind of fighter?" She knew little of the tylwyth teg—only that they were supposed to be beautiful beyond reason and they kept monsters as pets. There were stories of revelries lasting centuries, of wars fought with magic and honeyed words, of enchantment and danger in equal measure.

Fane met her gaze. And while his mouth was a straight line, she thought she saw amusement in his eyes. "I was an ironfetch."

Mer blinked. "A what?"

"It's what it sounds like," he said. "The otherfolk cannot abide the touch of cold iron. Its presence can poison their land, weaken their magic. And yes, that does include the iron in us, too." He tapped a finger against his chest. "There are always humans trying to find their way into Annwvyn. Sometimes they perish. Sometimes they never find their way back. Those bodies have to be removed, lest they poison the magic. So the otherfolk will enchant a few humans to sense iron and send them out into the forest."

Mer and Renfrew exchanged a look. She said, "You dealt with corpse removal."

"And the occasional iron chain, lock, keys, armor…" Fane trailed off. "But mostly bodies, yes."

Of course this was the kind of mercenary they would find, Mer thought, with no small amount of amusement. A former errand boy for the otherfolk, one who fought like death sat upon his shoulder and disposed of corpses for a living.

Renfrew was eyeing Fane like he regretted asking the young man to join them, and somehow, that made Mer like Fane a little more. Perhaps it was sheer contrariness.

"I wasn't the only one," said Fane, as if the silence needed to be filled. "There were quite a few of us. Mortals who needed a roof and warm food, and were willing to do work that the tylwyth teg cannot. I enjoyed the simplicity of it."

"And what precisely," said Renfrew, "did they pay you with? Gold? Spells?"

Fane's fingers twitched, his bloodied knuckles flashing in the firelight. "Death," he said.

If anyone else had said it, Mer would have scoffed. But Fane's voice was uninflected, lacking in pride. He spoke like a merchant naming a price. And perhaps she still wouldn't have believed it—but the blood of the man he'd just killed stained his fingernails.

"You have magic," said Mer. "That's how you managed to kill the Blaidd."

Fane's gaze flicked to hers. "Some are born with it. Some of us traded for it."

Mer swallowed her surprise. He spoke to her like a peer, like he knew what she was—but he couldn't know. Not unless part of his gift was to sense the magic of others. "Why did you leave the other-folk, if you enjoyed working for them so much?"

Fane looked past her shoulder. East, she realized. Toward Annwvyn.

"They had no more need of me in the mountains," he said simply. "I made my way across the countryside. I met Trefor." He petted the dog fondly. "I found the fighting rings."

"You should know that the Blaidd's mercenary band is rather vengeful," said Renfrew. "He earned them a fair bit of coin ransacking villages on the edges of Gwaelod. There were rumors that even Garanhir had paid him to wreak havoc on the other cantrefs."

"And yet you sought to hire him?" said Fane. "Despite knowing of his loyalty to the prince?"

Renfrew shrugged. "Not to state the obvious, but mercenaries can be bought. You clearly had little love for the Blaidd. Mercenaries like him will continue to spill blood along the borders as long as those like Garanhir pay them well. But if we were to weaken Garanhir's power, then he would be forced to call back his forces. Perhaps even begin peace negotiations with his neighbors."

Comprehension sharpened Fane's features. "Ah. Then that is your aim. Not a simple act of thievery—but to strike a blow against a prince."

"We can do both," said Renfrew. "You would be aiding those like that girl you saved, and you would walk away a wealthy man. Surely you would see the nobility in this task."

This was Renfrew's gift. Give him a little knowledge and he'd weave it into a net to entrap enemy and ally alike.

"And I am given to assume that this task isn't some fool's errand," said Fane. "If such a treasure trove exists, I can't believe others have not tried."

Renfrew's eyes gleamed. "They have. But as I said before, the cache is hidden in a well. And we have an asset that no one else did." He put his hand on Mer's shoulder. It did not feel so much like an affectionate touch—more like a breeder putting out a horse for show. Mer half expected him to pull back her lips to show off her nice teeth.

"You can find a well?" asked Fane.

Mer met his gaze squarely. "I would be a sorry excuse for a dowser if I could not."

Fane's brows drew together. She felt his gaze like a challenge and she met it evenly. If he were to join them, then he needed to know of her power. And if he did not…well, then he wouldn't be leaving this abandoned house alive. Renfrew wouldn't let him. She wondered if Fane knew that—perhaps it was why he hadn't joined Mer beside the fire.

The quiet was broken only by the crackle of the dry wood and sparks drifting into the air. Mer shifted where she sat when the silence became uncomfortable.

"All right," said Fane. "I will join you."

Renfrew's smile was sharp and satisfied. He held out his hand to Fane, who began to take it. But Mer rose to her feet.

"And how are we to know that you will keep your word?" asked Mer. Someone had to—she knew that. And as Renfrew was playing the part of the kindly employer, the role of the distruster fell to her.

Fane's voice remained level. "Because when I give my word, I do not break it. And if I swear myself to an employer, I would sooner die than betray them."

Mer considered herself a rather good judge of liars; after all, she'd been raised by a spymaster. And Fane was not lying. He spoke like a man who was laying heavy stones, building the very foundation on which he lived his life.

"All right, then," said Renfrew. "Do you have any other questions?"

Fane seemed to consider. Then he said, "Would I have my pick of the treasures?"

"I believe," said Renfrew, "that could be arranged."

CHAPTER 5

THE FOOTHILLS OF the Annwvyn forest had always been rife with strangeness.

The trees were old, with twisted roots and branches that blocked out sunlight. The undergrowth was a tangle of leaves and wildflowers and berries—and only the bravest dared venture into the edges of the woods to forage. There were tales of people who went looking for game and returned ten years older, having only been gone a single night. And others vanished altogether.

When Fane was a child, his mam slipped a piece of iron onto a leather cord and told him to wear it around his neck or wrist. There were other protections: pockets of stale bread, gorse, and gifts given to the forest. But as the son of a locksmith, Fane wore iron. He liked the metal—his da promised to teach him how to shape it, how to craft the locks and keys that fascinated him.

It had been a promise that would go unfulfilled.

Because when Fane was eleven, his father was visited by a man. He offered no name, no greeting other than a thin-lipped smile. He had an interest in unlocking a certain door—a door that most certainly didn't belong to him.

Fane had been in the room when his da refused. And when the man's gaze had slid to the child in the corner, Da had picked up a heavy poker, its tip still glowing red from resting in the embers.

The man retreated, palms open and smile gone tight.

When Fane remembered that man, it was the smile that came back to him. It had been a silent promise, one that Fane hadn't recognized at the time.

"Who was that?" Fane asked when the door was closed.

"Just a man," said Da, his jaw still clenched, "with more greed than sense." Fane had let the matter fall away, because he was too young to understand.

But a week later, when Fane was across town to buy eggs, he saw the billow of smoke.

He dropped the eggs and ran home—or rather, to what was left of it. The house had caved in upon itself, leaving smoldering embers and the terrible stench of burning meat.

And there was the man—the man who had visited Da a week earlier, striding away from the burning house. Fane cried out, wondering why no one had stopped him, why—

And then he saw the other men. There were six of them, mounted on horses and all of them bristling with weapons. The first man swung onto his horse, murmured a word to the others, and they began to trot away.

Without knowing what he was going to do, Fane started to run after them.

It had been a neighbor who had dragged him back. "They're gone, lad," she whispered in his ear. "I'm sorry, but your mam and da—your brother, they're gone. Come with me now, come—"

The words stung more than the smoke. The men who'd killed his family were escaping and there was nothing he could do. Nothing at all. And so he allowed himself to be tugged away.

Fane was taken in by that kind neighbor—he was bathed and clucked over, kindly hands running through his hair and putting him to bed. He could not sleep; he could barely close his eyes. Finally, when he could bear it no longer, Fane rose from his bed and went to the woman. She sat in a rocking chair by the fireplace, mending a shirt. When she saw him, that concerned half smile flitted across her face. "Can't sleep, lad?"

Fane shook his head.

"Why?" he said. "My family—why?"

The woman's lips pursed and she put aside her sewing. "I don't know. Bad things—they happen sometimes. To good people."

The way she said it made anger roil in Fane's belly. "It didn't just *happen*," he said. "Those men, they did it. Why?"

She sighed, reaching out a hand. He stepped closer, allowed her to touch his shoulder. She had a gentle hand, but it wasn't familiar. She wasn't his mam. "I know those men," she said. "They are swords for hire—and thieves, more often than not. I suspect they wanted your da's help, mayhap breaking into a place they should not be.

And when your da refused them…they had to ensure others would not do the same."

"Who's going to stop them?" asked Fane. "Someone must. We— we could go to the barwn. Surely he would do something." The noble that owned most of the nearby farmland had always been a distant figure to Fane but he seized upon the idea. "These are his lands—he can't stand by and have people murdered on them."

She stroked the hair back from his face. "Dear boy. Those men…" Her gaze drifted to the fire. "They work for the barwn."

The words struck him like a blow. He turned toward his nook of a bedroom, and the woman let him go.

But he did not return to bed. Instead, he slipped from the house and away from the village. He could not stay—not in a land where its ruler employed murderers, where his family would never be avenged, where he was powerless to save them.

The Annwvyn mountains loomed in the distance, the forest only half a day's walk away. Fane turned toward the shadow and began to run. He was barefoot, his toes smeared with mud, his cloak worn thin with age. But none of that mattered. A fury as he had never known bore him on. He ran until his lungs were raw, until all he could taste was the mist of the night air and the greenery of the forest.

He knew the tales. He'd heard mention of changeling children, of monsters, of creatures immortal and terrible. But he also had heard tales in which bowls of milk and trinkets were traded for favors. Of heroes who had gone to the otherfolk and been given magical swords. So he went—because there was nothing else he could do.

Fane wandered for two days before they found him.

He fell to his knees, stomach hollow with hunger and feet bleeding. Later, he would understand it had been the blood that drew the otherfolk to him. Iron sapped magic—and the folk could sense its poisonous presence.

The ones he met were the tylwyth teg of the forest. They wore crowns of white bryony, necklaces of rowanberries, and clothing spun from moss.

If Fane had been afraid, things would have gone differently. He might have been hunted or caged within the roots of a tree. But the otherfolk seemed charmed by his recklessness.

One of them stepped forward. She wore bracelets of juniper branches and her face was lovely, but her eyes were wrong. They were dark where the whites should have been. They were the eyes of a deer—of something wild and inhuman.

Fane gaped at her, too startled to be afraid. "Please," he rasped. "Please."

The lady of the folk knelt before him, offering a smile. She reached out and pushed some of the dirty hair from his eyes. It might have been a comforting touch, if not for the coolness of her fingers. "Why have you come here, mortal child?"

Fane's breaths were ragged. "Seven men," he said. "They killed my family. I want—I want to kill them." It had been a reckless bravery that bid him to say the words, those damning words.

The lady nodded, her strange dark eyes glittering. "And what do you have to offer?"

Only the lost or the desperate went to the forest empty-handed.

Fane had nothing to give the otherfolk, not bowls of milk nor trinkets of gold; however, he had heard of humans being taken into service.

"Myself," said Fane. "Whatever you need of me—I'll do it. Please."

He should have bargained; he should have measured his words the way merchants measured silver. But he had been a child, his feet stinging and belly empty, and every time he closed his eyes, he saw the smoking remnants of his home.

Fane could not let his family go unavenged.

The lady nodded. "Seven years of service for seven human lives." She held out a hand—long-fingered and graceful. Fane touched it.

And the magic had kindled within him.

The morning after he fought the Blaidd, Fane woke to aching ribs and a corgi across his chest.

Trefor panted happily in his face. "Good morning to you, too," Fane murmured sleepily, fingers tangling in the corgi's fur. The dog groaned and lolled to one side, his weight enough to push some of the breath from Fane's lungs. "You're half the size of a pony. Get off."

The dog rolled off, tail wagging ceaselessly. At least one of them always woke in a good mood.

They had all slept in the abandoned home rather than risk one of the inns. The Blaidd's company would be looking for Fane, their ire stoked by the late hour and drink. And Fane had no desire to fight more of them. Which was how he had gone from fighter to hired thief in a matter of hours. Fane had been many things: a son, a brother, a young apprentice locksmith, an ironfetch, a fighter. And now—now he was a killer whose only true companion liked to steal boots and lick his own unmentionables.

Loss had a way of eroding one's sense of self.

The only thing Fane had left was his word, and he'd never broken that. He wouldn't start now. Which meant he would accompany two criminals on their journey to steal from a prince.

The sound of a door being forced open made Fane look up. He reached out with his senses, trying to focus on the iron. There wasn't much metal in the room—a few scattered nails and the bits from a door hinge. The house had been ransacked for valuables, and those included metals that could be sold to a blacksmith.

But just beyond the door, fresh iron sang its sharp song. This metal was edged—knives, then. And a small slip that might have been a wrench. He relaxed just as Mererid stepped into the house. Her hood was drawn so that her face was mostly jaw and a tumble of honey-dark hair.

"Mererid, right?" he said.

She gave him a tolerant look. "Mer is fine." She picked her way across the room. "Renfrew is out, but he rose early and brought back these." She crouched beside him. Wrapped in a cloth were three tarts. He sniffed, catching the scents of goat cheese and leeks.

"Thanks," he said, and took one. Trefor whined and Fane broke the tart in two, giving the corgi half.

Mer eyed him over her own tart. "You're rather softhearted, for a killer," she said.

The crust was dry in Fane's mouth. It took a few swallows for him to gather enough saliva so his voice wouldn't break. "Where is Renfrew?"

"Renfrew is out finding us a way to Caer Wyddno," said Mer. She squatted beside the fireplace, her free hand hovering over what was left of the coals. She kept her face angled away from him. "Word of your fight has gotten out. We'll leave as soon as we can, lest we draw even more attention. We're lucky the Blaidd's friends were too soused last night to search for you properly." She flicked a few crumbs from her fingers. In the same movement, her hood fell back. As she finished eating her tart, he took a few moments to look at her properly. Her hair was that darkened honey and her eyes a warm brown.

"Finished staring?" asked Mer. She pulled a small paring knife from her belt and began gently prying something out from beneath her thumbnail.

"I could stare longer, if that pleases you," said Fane.

Mer continued working the knife. "You never say what I think you will."

"It comes of living in the woods," he said. "Human manners become a little rusty."

"You say that like you aren't human." She grimaced and set the knife down. Her eyes were intent on him. "Renfrew thinks we need you, but I'm not so certain."

Fane did the only thing he could think of: He rose to his feet and walked closer. She didn't move; rather, her body went still. It was the way a cat might freeze when it saw something larger than itself—muscles taut and body poised to attack or flee. Fane reached down, keeping every movement slow and easy, and gestured for her knife. "May I see that for a moment?"

She hesitated. Fane did not blame her; she had watched him kill a man only a few scant hours ago.

With an expert little flick, she turned the knife so she held the blade by two fingers, extending the hilt toward him.

He took it. "Thank you." He straightened, running one finger across the flat of the blade. He heard the iron like the hum of a plucked harp string. *The iron of your magicked blood*, one of the folk had tried to explain, *trying to call out to the iron in the world*. Some of the fetches saw the metal as a glow, while others felt it like cold against their skin. Fane always heard music. This knife's song was crisp and unwavering.

"High quality. Likely mined from the south. And if I were one of the otherfolk, the touch of this iron would burn me." He offered it back to Mer and she took it, tucking the knife into a leather sheath at her wrist. "I'm as human as you are."

"Are you a metal expert?" she asked.

"I could sense it from across the room," he said simply.

Unease flickered behind her eyes. "You're a diviner? Of metal?"

"Not truly," he said. "The otherfolk magic their fetches to sense iron. It's a temporary thing—the spell has to be woven every year at the solstice. And I cannot affect iron, not the way a true diviner could. I just needed to be able to find it, to do my work." He smiled with the corners of his mouth. "Which is how I know you have four other blades on you, as well as a wire tucked into your boot and possibly a wrench at your belt."

She hid her surprise well, he'd give her that.

"You don't need me," he said. "But you might be glad of my presence before this is over." He picked up his pack and walked toward the open door. Trefor followed at his heels, trotting along as Fane stepped outside.

Dawn was making itself known to the east, brightening beyond the mountains. Fane took stock of his surroundings—the abandoned homes and distant rumble of the ocean. At this hour, those who'd been at the fighting ring would be asleep or so bleary-eyed they likely wouldn't recognize Fane. Trefor woofed softly and Fane looked up, gaze snagging on a man striding toward them.

Renfrew walked through the dawn light, his fingers twined around the leather bridle of a horse. The horse plodded alongside him.

"I see you've been busy," said Mer. She leaned against the door frame, arms crossed. "Making friends?"

Renfrew's mouth quirked. "I borrowed the mare from a passing soldier. He won't notice for some hours yet—he was sleeping rather heavily."

"I'm sure he was," replied Mer. "After your hand slipped over his drink."

It was moments like these that made Fane certain these two were more than criminals drawn together for one job. There was a past—shared experiences, memories, and perhaps a home. They were family, even if there was no shared blood.

Renfrew said, "I also found this in the soldier's pocket." He held out a slip of stained and creased parchment. Mer took it, her eyes flicking over the handwritten note. All the color leeched out of her face. Fane leaned forward so that he could just make out the words on the page.

By order of the prince: reward in gold for the water witch.
Poisoner and killer.

Beneath the words was a sketch of a woman. Her hair was long, a few strands obscuring one eye and cheek. A straight nose and high cheekbones. She was lovely as a briar patch in bloom—the kind of beauty best admired at a distance.

It was not a perfect likeness, but it was close enough.

Mer crumpled the parchment. "I hate it when they call me a witch," she said.

Renfrew let out a small breath. "There is a price on your head, dear child. I dare not stay with you. If the prince has any sense, he will have told his soldiers to be looking for a middle-aged man and a young woman. But the two of you should have more luck in slipping into the city unseen."

"You never did tell me how you planned to sneak us into Caer Wyddno," said Mer.

"I assumed you would not need my help," said Renfrew serenely. "After all, you have managed quite well on your own for the last four years." He took a step back, his fingers tightening on the mare's bridle. "Go to a house on Spicer's Row. The second one from the corner, with a red door and periwinkles in the garden." He patted the horse's shoulder. "I have another person to collect. I'll meet you there in two days' time."

Mer frowned. "Another mercenary?"

"Something of the like." Renfrew pulled himself astride the horse, settling easily into the saddle. He smiled thinly, then nudged the horse into a trot.

Mer watched Renfrew's back as he rode away. "Second house from the corner on Spicer's Row," she murmured. "Red door. All right. All right." She straightened, then pulled her hood back into place. "This is your last chance to escape this venture," she said, turning toward Fane. Her mouth pulled to one side in a mocking smile. "There's only little old me to stop you."

Fane inclined his head. "If what that bounty said was true, then you'd have no trouble stopping me."

Water witch, the notice had called her.

True diviners were rare. They were supposed to be the other-touched, the ones with innate magic. Some of them went to the otherfolk for answers and training, trading years of service so as to better understand their power. In his time in the Annwvyn forest, Fane had met two. There was an old man who'd warded away storms with a whistling song and a child who'd been found at the heart of a fire utterly unburned.

Fane regarded her.

Mer was a woman born with magic. And he was a man who'd traded seven years of his life for it.

Perhaps between the two of them, they could do the impossible.

CHAPTER 6

A STOLEN BOAT cut through the ocean waves.

It moved swiftly, unhindered by tides or wind. Mer sat with one hand trailing through the water, her fingers catching in sea-foam.

Ocean waters were not so easily manipulated as fresh ones. It was the salt, she'd come to understand. Salt did not negate magic as iron did, but it made the power sluggish. She reached out with her magic, letting it trickle into the ocean. The waves pushed back; the ocean was not fond of meddling. It was like trying to shove a mountain, throwing herself bodily against solid rock. A headache began to throb in her jaw, around her nose and eyes. But Mer didn't release the power.

She was the last living water diviner.

It was time to remind the ocean of that.

They approached Caer Wyddno by sea. It was the only way— the walls of Gwaelod were impenetrable and guarded by the prince's men. But no one could guard an entire shoreline.

It was late afternoon by the time their boat reached the shores of Gwaelod. Much of the coast was jagged, a rough beauty as greenery gave way to cliffs and mossy rocks. Mer guided the boat onto a pebbled beach. Trefor leapt from the boat, barking wildly at the gulls.

Gwaelod was an expanse of lowland country. From the city of Caer Wyddno, the kingdom looked like a green tapestry threaded by woods. There were isles that could only be reached at low tide, the ocean stealing those paths twice a day. It was not a lush country— the winds coming off the oceans twisted the trees, scoured the rocks, and made the wildflowers sweep back and forth. Anything that grew along the shore had strong roots.

It was beautiful.

Mer breathed in the scents of sweet wildflowers and the tang of sea salt. It was a smell she hadn't found on any other part of the isles, and despite herself, a tight knot unwound within her.

Home. The thought was a siren song, even as she tried to quash it. This was the place she'd been taken to after being dragged from her father's farm. It was not her home—and yet it *was* her home.

She hated it.

And she loved it.

Most of all, she hated that she still loved it.

They walked in silence for a good while. There was a scattering of homes on the rugged shore, lines of clothing blowing in the wind and smoke drifting from chimneys. It was evening when Mer knew they would have to find somewhere to spend the night. The misty winds and sea salt cut through her warm clothing and her belly grumbled like an angry cat.

There was another house up ahead and Mer could see figures through a lone window. The interior was bright and cozy, and Mer smelled roasted onions and potatoes. "How about this," she said. "You knock at the door to ask how far it is to the nearest village. I can slip in through that window."

Fane raised both brows. "And steal our dinner?"

"It's not stealing if I leave coin," she said.

"I think it probably is."

She glowered at him. "Well, unless you're secretly hiding a wheel of cheese under your cloak, we're going to need food."

Fane said, "Wait here." Then, before she could protest, he walked through the yard and right up to the front door. A knock, and then a young woman appeared in the doorway. Her stomach was rounded and her hair held in a loose knot.

Mer couldn't hear the words exchanged, not at this distance, but in a few heartbeats, the woman's expression softened. She looked at Fane, then past him toward Mer. Mer lowered her gaze, reaching to be sure her hair was in place. The last thing she needed was for someone to catch sight of the brand.

Once he finished speaking with the woman, Fane returned to Mer.

"We can sleep in their shed," he said. "And they'll give us something to eat."

Mer gaped at him. "Did you threaten them?"

"No."

"Bribe them?"

"No," he said, seemingly torn between amusement and incredulity.

"Then how did we end up with a shed to sleep in?" she said.

He shrugged. "I asked."

Mer squinted at Fane, trying to see him like a stranger might. "Oh. She must have thought you were one of the war refugees, with your face and all."

He touched one of the bruises. "Your rather bedraggled appearance might have also had something to do with it."

Mer considered a retort, then decided against it. It had been several days since she'd last bathed or combed her hair.

The young woman appeared again in the doorway, a shawl drawn across her shoulders. She gave Mer a gentle smile. "'Twon't be the first time our shed's been used for such a purpose," she said. "My cousin was driven out of his home, too. Relied on the kindness of others until he could reach us."

"Thank you," said Mer, perhaps a little bit too stiffly. The woman glanced at her, but rather than suspicious, her eyes seemed sad.

"Were you both soldiers?" she asked.

Fane shook his head. "No, why?"

The young woman's gaze was sharp. "You've got the look," she said to Fane. "Hair shorn short, built like my man after he was taken for the armies. And she stands like a soldier."

Unease tightened Mer's stomach. She had slipped into her old stance without realizing it—left arm behind her back, fingers near the knives at her belt. She forced her arm to fall, her fingertips brushing her thigh.

The young woman led them to the shed, unlocking the door and apologizing for the chill. The shed was for the family's fishing gear; Mer glimpsed nets hung on hooks, blades along the wall, and a rack of knives meant for cleaning fish. Her fingers twitched, part of her longing to pick them up and examine the blades, but she forced herself to turn and thank their host.

"You do that often?" asked Mer, once she and Fane were sitting in the shed, bowls of cawl in their laps. The meat was a little gristly, but Mer was so hungry she didn't care. "Charm ladies into giving you shelter and supper?"

Fane tilted his head. "After I left Annwvyn, I had little coin. When I'd come upon a village, I'd find someone. I'd offer to chop firewood or do other small chores in exchange for a place to sleep."

Mer frowned. She could not imagine sleeping near strangers. Even now, she was acutely aware of Fane's nearness. It was one thing to sleep in the same house when Renfrew was there—for all of the tangled affection and resentment between herself and her old teacher, there was still a sense of safety. Renfrew was all deft hands and keen eyes, his every word a double meaning and vials of deadly herbs at his belt. But he would never have allowed harm to come to Mer.

But now she was alone with this young man with bruises on his knuckles and death following in his wake. He had been polite, but in her experience, the best monsters were the kind that could walk openly in daylight.

She sat in the corner of the shed, her back to the wall and her eyes on Fane. He ate half his cawl, then gave the other half to Trefor. The dog swallowed it in three gulps, licked the bowl clean, then gazed at Fane as if *surely* there had to be more food. The corners of Fane's mouth curled into a fond smile. He let his hand fall between the dog's ears, rubbing back and forth while he murmured something inaudible.

There were very few things Mer trusted in the world. Among them were her instincts, the strength of the water running beneath the ground, the capacity for human cruelty—and that a person could be judged by how they treated the powerless. She'd seen seemingly kind men kick at beggars and seemingly unkind ones stop to offer a coin and a gentle word. After all, masks were only useful when it mattered who was watching. And the powerless did not merit the facade.

Fane treated his dog with unwavering gentleness. That made her trust him far more than anything he could have said.

"Good night," she said, and tucked her cloak in around herself.

"Good night," Fane replied. He patted Trefor again. "I'll try to keep him over here. Elsewise he might try to snuggle up to you."

Trefor gave a soft woof. It sounded like admonishment.

Mer shrugged. "So long as he doesn't snore."

"He doesn't, but I might." Fane smiled, and the corners of his eyes crinkled and softened.

"I'm sure I've slept through worse," she said, then bit her lip. He did not need to know she'd slept on a cold dungeon floor, dozing in fitful bursts because the rats would come for her. That she'd been feverish most of that time, the brand upon her cheek throbbing and unhealed.

She'd never known fear as a child; she'd run rampant through her father's fields, her bare toes scrabbling at branches when she climbed trees. It was only when she grew older, when she learned the cruelties that people could inflict upon one another, that fear began to follow her like a shadow. It was why she hadn't stayed in one place for too long. She thought perhaps she could outrun that fear, hide away from it. But now she knew that as long as Garanhir hunted her, she'd never manage to escape.

She hated that she was afraid; she resented the fear that had made its home within her. She reached down to her belt, pulled free a small knife. Her fingers curled around the worn hilt.

She could not slay her own fears.

But as for the men who'd made her afraid—they could bleed.

A city could be judged by three things: its food, its sewers, and its thieving guild.

And by all those measures, Caer Wyddno was not to be trifled with. The castell had been carved into the ocean cliffs. The fortress rose high above the city, a remarkable feat of stone masonry that had stood for the better part of three centuries. There were stories that said Caer Wyddno had been created when a sorcerer had been tricked into the service of a prince. He'd bet on a coin toss, the prince boasting that if he won, the sorcerer would craft a fortress like none other. Little did the sorcerer know that the coin itself was a trick—both sides the same.

The sorcerer had kept his end of the bargain, building the castell from rock and stone. But he'd uttered a curse to the prince, saying that while magic had created the fortress, it would also one day unmake it.

Mer had been ten the last time she'd heard the washerwomen telling that tale. They'd liked to bring Mer into their ranks when Renfrew didn't have time for her; they'd feed her treats from the kitchen and ask her to make the water hot without building fires to boil it. She'd sat among them, listening to the gossip and the old stories. Now Mer thought the sorcerer in the tale had probably been a stone diviner pressed into service. It made more sense than a coin toss and a curse.

Mer and Fane arrived at Caer Wyddno around noon. The streets in and out of the city were bustling—merchants with their wagons, guards taking up their positions and eyeing newcomers with predictable wariness, beggars with broken nails and outstretched hands, and the others who could not afford to live in the city. There were always hastily assembled shacks near the edges of cities, little communities sprung up out of desperation and necessity. The guards would try to drive them off every so often, but the houses would be rebuilt.

"Put your arm around me," said Mer quietly as they walked through the outskirts.

She sensed more than saw Fane's surprised look.

"Do it," said Mer. "If any guards are looking for me, they'll be on watch for a lone woman, not a young couple and their hound."

"Ah," said Fane. He put his arm around Mer's waist. His hand was large against her hip, surprisingly warm through her layers of clothing. She immediately yearned to shake the strange weight off, but she gritted her teeth and bore it.

It was the right decision; as they neared one of the streets leading into Caer Wyddno, a guard's gaze slid over Mer and Fane. Mer knew what they looked like: a young couple, their clothing worn but not shoddy, a well-fed dog trotting at their heels. They did not have the look of the poor or the dangerous, and Mer knew those were the kinds of people the guards would try to turn away. Predictably, the guard nodded a silent greeting and then glanced beyond them.

Once they were in the city, Fane's hand dropped and Mer breathed a little easier. Together, they stepped into the bustle of Caer Wyddno.

She felt like some old spirit, returned to haunt the home it had once loved. The city had not changed in her absence. There were the winding, circular streets; the shouts of children trying to lure customers to their employers' stalls; the pickpockets drifting through crowds with as much grace as eels; the scents of damp stone, salt, and brine; and the sight of freshly caught cockles and mussels. She could remember every step and path of this city like she could trace the veins on the inside of her arms.

"Come," she said, and began walking.

With her hood up and head bowed, she was just another person trying to keep the misty ocean air from her face. When a pickpocket sidled up to her, she caught his wrist before it slipped into her pocket. Not that she carried anything of value where it could be easily pilfered, but she liked the flash of surprise across the lad's face. "Go nick some coin from a fatter purse," she told him.

The boy—he couldn't have been more than eleven—nodded in respect. Then he broke her grip, gave her a grin, and vanished into the crowds.

Fane watched him go. "You could've done more than give him a warning."

She couldn't tell if he was admiring or disapproving; again, his voice had that implacable neutrality. "Wasn't about to call the guards on him, was I?" she said, keeping her voice low. "We're supposed to stay hidden."

"You might have broken his wrist," he said. "I've seen others do that to thieves."

She snorted. "For trying what he was trained to do? It's not like anyone wakes up saying, 'My, I think I'll become a thief today. Sounds mighty thrilling.'"

"He chose to steal," said Fane mildly.

"People don't choose any such thing," said Mer, her voice sharpening. "They steal because when you're hungry enough, risking a broken wrist seems a decent trade for a warm meal." Her own memories of hunger were never too far away. It was why she always kept a few coins sewn into the hem of her undershirt or slipped into a boot.

"You sound as though you have experience with that."

"Everything I've done," she said, and her voice was even quieter than before. She wasn't sure he could hear her; part of her didn't care. "Everything—it was to survive. And I won't apologize for that."

Fane wisely did not rise to that bait. "Do you know where we're going?" he said instead. He stepped out of the path of several ladies, chattering among themselves with baskets of laundry balanced atop their shoulders.

"Spicer's Row." Mer turned down a smaller alley, out of the bustling merchant district. They passed through a square brimming with carts and wagons, with shouts and clamor. "I know it. Renfrew said the right house would have periwinkles in the garden."

"Periwinkles," said Fane. "It's an odd choice for a flower."

"Do you prefer daffodils?"

He shook his head. "Periwinkles grow on grave mounds in the north. There are tales that say if you pick them, you'll be haunted for the trespass."

"Well, then I hope no one's buried in the garden," said Mer. "I suppose you think us city folk foolish for giving up old customs." Someone was playing the crwth, and several passersby were clustered to watch. Mer squeezed through the crowd, angling herself to slip between a family.

"Not so much foolish," said Fane, "as different. Cities like these, with all the people and the iron—both in their blood and all around them—it pushes back the old ways. Makes me wonder how things will fare in the future."

"What do you mean?"

"I mean," Fane said, "that humanity has a tendency to push into every corner of a place. And with their iron and their armies, it may be only a matter of time until someone like Garanhir turns his attention on Annwvyn."

That made Mer's steps falter for a moment. "It would be a foolish endeavor. Garanhir would have to invade both Gwynedd and Powys."

"Aren't those the very boundaries that your prince has been testing?" asked Fane.

Mer turned away, quickening her step. "He is not my prince," she said, with such finality that Fane did not speak again.

The journey took them half an hour. Mer doubled back twice, looping through alleys and around buildings until she was sure that any tails would have been lost. Then, her eyes lit upon the right house. It looked to be a nobleman's home: expensive, vulnerable, and far too good to be true.

Mer walked right on past it, half dragging Fane by his arm. He threw a startled look at her. "I think that's—"

"Oh, it is," she said, keeping her eyes ahead. "Don't look at it. Stop gaping."

He jerked his head around. It took only three steps for him to catch on. "You don't trust it."

"Of course, I don't," she said. "This is Garanhir's city. Should he have captured any of Renfrew's people or intercepted a message, this is where he would set the trap." She took a breath. "We're going to find our own entrance."

"And if there isn't one?"

"We'll make one," she said.

She walked to the end of the street, then ducked between two shops. Behind the houses was a narrow alleyway. Very narrow, likely used by stray cats and the occasional slender thief. She angled herself to slip inside, her cloak brushing against the old stone. Fane grunted but managed to follow.

Finally, they came around to the back of the noble house. Mer pushed through a carefully pruned hedgerow, grimacing as thorns scraped her bare skin. She stepped out into a small courtyard. "House like this," Mer murmured, walking closer, "it has to have..." She knelt amid the bushes and pushed one aside, revealing a wooden door set into the ground. "A wine cellar, if I'm not mistaken."

"Ah," said Fane. "So that's our entrance." He knelt and traced the edge of the lock with his calloused thumb. His nails were short, broken. And his knuckles were stained with bruises.

"It's old iron," said Fane. "Not from around here."

Mer blinked, a little impressed despite herself. "Do you make a note of every iron scrap we pass?"

"If I did that, I'd have little thought for anything else," said Fane. "Most of it fades away, like chatter that you can't quite hear."

Mer pulled a small leather wallet from inside of her tunic. This had been an early lesson and one of the most valuable. "Ah, so you do have a wrench," said Fane, seeing the slip of metal and its blunt-edged teeth.

She snorted and slipped the pick into the lock.

"I feel like this is wrong," whispered Fane.

"If you cannot sneak into a house, you're going to have a hard time with a heist," said Mer quietly. She grinned when it came free. Fane reached down and heaved the cellar door open. The cool, damp smell of old oak and wine wafted upward.

For a moment, they both peered into the darkness.

Without waiting to see if he would follow, Mer put one foot on the first step. It was old wood, groaning under her weight as she descended into the dark cellar.

The air was close and still. The tang of wine tickled her nose, and she pressed a hand to it to keep from sneezing. As her eyes adjusted, she could make out the shape of racks of bottles and barrels. Rounds of cheese and jars of preserves were on shelves, and Mer's fingers itched to grab at them, to shove the provisions under her cloak and make off with them. But if this was indeed Renfrew's contact, then stealing from her host probably wouldn't be the best first impression.

There came a creak overhead; someone was walking across the floor. Then the squeal of a door being pulled open.

Mer went utterly still. She held her breath and waited. "—no one's servant," someone was saying. A man's voice, with the accent of the southern port cities. He thudded down the stairs, calling something over his shoulder.

Then the man caught sight of Mer and Fane. He froze on the stairs.

For a long moment, no one moved.

The man snatched up a bottle of wine and flung it at Fane's head.

CHAPTER 7

IT HAD TAKEN Fane five years to understand the bargain he'd made.

He had been sixteen. His days were spent patrolling the Annwvyn forest, using his magicked senses to slip between the enchantments meant to snare other humans. If Fane wandered near a piece of iron, he would hear its song. Sometimes it was a scrap, sometimes it was a lone traveler. No matter the source, Fane would haul it from the forest.

As part of their service, the fetches were given food and shelter. At night, Fane would sit beside a warm hearth with the other human fetches, eating bowls of hare broth flavored with nettles and wild mushrooms.

And he thought about his revenge.

Seven years of service for seven human lives.

He would kill them—all of them—one by one. Those murderers

who'd burned his family. Fane had taken care to remember their faces, to recall everything he could.

The otherfolk had given him magic, that much he knew. Not just the iron-sense, but magic that would help him fight. He'd never tested it; there was no one to test it on besides the foxes and the squirrels. There were the other fetches, but Fane liked them. They were friends, smiling at him in the evenings and making quiet conversation.

All the ironfetches were given a few days off every year. They were given leave to visit nearby villages, to purchase clothing and new boots before returning to the forest. Fane saved those days until he was sixteen. By then, he was tall as a man and strong enough to fight. So he took his leave of the forest, traveled by foot along paths he knew only by faintest memory.

He returned to his village.

Fane wandered through the streets. The constant hum of iron set his teeth on edge. He understood why the folk would never come here. To the otherfolk, iron's rust could poison rivers and leech into the soil to sicken them. It was why he scoffed to hear mothers' rhymes about the folk taking children from cities. No immortal being would have set foot in a human city.

He strode down the dirt-packed streets until he came upon the right house.

It had never been rebuilt. It had been left to rust and molder, to sink into the ground. Fane picked his way through the fallen stones and rotted wood, to the hearth and home he'd grown up in. He knelt, his bare fingers sliding through the ash and dirt until he found what he sought.

A shard of metal. Traces of iron—and blood. It had broken off a sword. A sword carried by one of the people who had killed his family.

Fane curled his hand around that small bit of metal and closed his eyes. The folk had imbued their fetches with the ability to find iron, to trace its source. He knew at once in which part of the isles this sword had been forged. But more importantly, he sensed from whom the blood came. He had only to follow the faint song.

The journey took him two days.

He traversed fields and forest, crossed small streams and muddied roads. He slept in his cloak, eating dried meats and old berries, never stopping for more than a few hours. And then he found the man.

Fane strode into a village not unlike his own. He followed his iron-sense to the right house, crept through the hedges and across a patch of well-tended garden, then peered through an open window. He would find one of the men who had slain his family. He would use his newfound magic to finally avenge them. But as Fane looked into the house, his stomach lurched in surprise.

The man wasn't alone. A babe bounced on his knee, chubby arms waving in the air. A second child, a daughter perhaps five years old, was playing with a wooden horse on the floor. And a woman was working on a square of embroidery in a rocking chair.

The man was singing. A quiet, crooning lullaby—and Fane recognized it. His mam had sung it to all her children when they had nightmares.

The killer had a family. Of all the possibilities Fane had imagined, this one never entered his mind. He had thought of ambushing the mercenary on the road, demanding to know if he remembered Fane's family. Fane had thought to use the magic he'd been gifted—that glorious, untested magic—to fight like a hero from the old tales.

Fane gazed through the window, his gut squirming with hot fury and something like—

Longing.

It was longing and shame. He remembered his mother telling him to fight when there was more than pride at stake—and there were no stakes here. No battles, nothing to be won but Fane's own satisfaction. Hurting that man would not change his past, wouldn't bring back those lost. All it would do was create more orphans.

Fane took several steps back, stumbling through weeds and over a neighbor's chicken. A few people gave him odd glances, but Fane ignored them.

Grief blurred his sight; his breaths hurt, lungs aching and throat too full. He'd spent years planning how he would avenge his family—and it had all been for naught. Rain began to fall and Fane knew he should have found shelter, but he couldn't bring himself to care. He needed to be away from this place, back in the quiet safety of the forest.

He'd barely made it out of the village when the robbers appeared. Half-dazed by rain and shock, he did not see them until he nearly walked into one.

It was a man. With a grizzled face and blade-scarred hands. He held a dagger, and there was a woman at his side. "Now, now," said the older man, voice soft, as though he were talking to a spooked horse. "Give us your coin. Hand it over and we'll leave you be."

Fane looked at the two thieves, barely comprehending. "What?"

"You daft?" asked the woman. She was a few years younger than the man, with silver eyes and shining golden hair. "Hand over your purse or my friend here'll open up your neck. Don't think he won't."

Fane gazed at them blankly. He felt utterly removed from this encounter, as though he were watching it happen to someone else. "I don't have coin."

The man laughed. "Don't have coin? Hear that often enough. Keep bleatin', friend, but we'll—"

It was the woman who struck first: a fist thrown at Fane's stomach. He brought up his arm, trying to protect himself. The movement drove his knuckles into the woman's shoulder.

And the magic took hold of him for the first time.

At first, it was exhilarating. He felt lighter and faster, and there was no pain. Not even when a wound opened up above his left eye or when the man slammed his knee into Fane's gut. Fane caught the man's arm, twisted it on instinct and felt something snap. He would break the man's arm, then escape. Just escape and—

But Fane couldn't stop.

Not even when he tried.

And he did try. Every muscle in his right arm clenched, trying to hold himself back, but the magic was too strong. He drove the man to the dirt and struck, splitting his knuckles.

He kept raining down blow after blow. And when that man was unmoving, he whirled on the woman. Her face was bloodless, terrified, and he wanted to stop. He didn't want to hurt her. But his body was not his own. Fane choked back a cry, closed his eyes, and tried to separate himself from the nightmare.

He was on his knees when he returned to himself. His knuckles bled, his ears rang, and there were two bodies around him. The thieves were horribly, unmistakably dead.

Staggering upright, he barely managed to take three steps before he retched into the grass. His stomach clenched, the taste of sick hot on his breath.

When he listened to stories of knights and heroes, Fane had never considered what slaying a man might entail. He had only ever thought of shining swords and good intentions.

But Fane was no knight and this was no tale.

There was only iron.

Iron sang all around him. Smeared across his hands, spattered across his face, in his hair—

He retched a second time.

When he was finished, Fane found refuge beneath an old oak tree, trying to take stock of himself. His whole body ached; he felt as though he'd awoken from some terrible night's sleep. But it wasn't a dream. Those people were dead. Did they have families? Hungry children waiting for them at home? Or were they merely bad people?

Fane did not know. And he never would.

As he sat there, his panic gave way to a numb despair.

Seven years of service for seven human lives.

He had taken two lives. And he could not imagine wanting to take more.

He looked at his hands. Death lurked in the shadowy spaces between his fingers.

Sitting beneath the oak tree, Fane whispered a promise. He would never use that power for himself.

A wine bottle flew at Fane's head.

He ducked, falling to one knee and rolling out of the way. The damp cellar floor was hard against his knees. He kept his arms tucked in close, afraid he might accidentally strike someone in his scramble to escape.

A knife flicked into Mer's fingers. Silver spun through the air, then thunked into the wooden door frame a finger's width from the man's nose. He jerked back, snarling in surprise—then stumbled and began falling down the stairs.

Mer spat out a curse and grabbed for Fane's arm. He half expected her to try and throw him like she'd tossed that knife, but she yanked him back, hands fumbling at his belt. He wasn't armed; of course, he wasn't armed. He opened his mouth to tell her as much, but then her fingers found the water flask at his belt and she yanked it free, uncorked it, and tossed the contents across the floor. "Back through the cellar," she said tightly. "Go, now—I'll deal with him."

Before his eyes, the water shimmered and hardened.

The man's foot hit the bottom step. He tried to right himself, staggering toward Mer, but he fell over sideways. He skidded, sliding like he was on—

Ice, Fane realized. She'd frozen the floor.

The man tried to stand but his feet went out from under him again. Mer retreated, never turning her back to the man, one arm thrown out to push Fane back like he was some unruly sheep that needed herding.

And perhaps they might have made it out of that cellar, if a certain corgi hadn't rushed at their attacker.

Trefor had been bouncing around Fane's ankles, making excited little yipping sounds. At the sight of the fallen man, the corgi rushed forward, tail whipping in glee as he fastened his teeth to the man's boot and gave a jerk of his head.

The man bellowed—more in outrage than in pain. Trefor growled and lowered his front legs, settling into his stubborn stance. Fane usually saw it when Trefor played with a piece of frayed rope or spotted a hound much larger than himself. "Come on," said Fane, his voice rising in alarm. "Trefor!"

The corgi gave another yank. Mayhap the dog thought he was helping or perhaps he just really, really wanted to taste fine leather.

The man raised a hand to strike at Trefor and Fane lunged forward, pushing Mer's arm aside.

Fane took the punch intended for the dog on his left shoulder. Pain jolted down his arm like a lightning strike. Jaw clenched, Fane hunched over Trefor, trying to scoop up the dog and get him to safety.

The boot came free. Trefor growled in triumph while the man let out an even louder bellow. He tried to stand again, but he was hopping on one booted foot and the floor still shone with that thin layer of ice. The man stumbled, grabbing for something at his belt. It was a hunting knife. "You wretch, give that back—"

Time seemed to slow. Fane knew that if he was going to fight back, this was the moment. He would have to knock that arm aside, strike so that the knife would fall. But to let that blow land would be to trigger the magic within him. He wouldn't be able to stop, not once that first punch landed.

Could he do it? Kill this stranger?

The answer came to him in a heartbeat—and it was almost a relief.

No. No, he could not. He would not. It didn't matter what orders he'd been given, who he served. This power was his alone and if it were up to him, he would never let it have hold of him again.

He saw the knife come down and Fane swallowed, bracing himself for that flash of agony.

But the man's arm never fell. Rather, his expression did.

All the fury left the nobleman's face; his arm was poised in the air, held there. The man's shoulders rolled, as if he were trying to free himself from invisible bonds. Then, his face went utterly bloodless.

The knife clattered to the ground but Fane wasn't looking for it. He was watching the man, whose face had gone from pale to red in a matter of heartbeats. Fear, true terror, flickered through his eyes.

Then Fane heard the slight inhalation behind him.

Mer.

Her hand was outstretched, her teeth sunk so deep into her lower lip that it looked painful. But that wasn't what drew Fane's attention.

For the first time since he'd met her, her hair wasn't hanging across her left cheek. It must have been pushed back in the scuffle. Her chin was raised high, her warm eyes blazing with an inner fire. And upon her left cheek, near the corner of her eye, was a deep red scar.

No, not a scar. It was a brand. It took a few moments for his eyes to follow the curving shapes and see them for what they were: lines laced into a knot. It marked her as a prisoner, as property, and Fane felt a flare of anger. He knew something of being bound. But even the otherfolk, for all that they did not understand human mercy, had never marked him. His own bonds had been through word and obligation, but with the knowledge that his freedom would be earned and given. He could not imagine a human being branding another.

A strangled gurgle made Fane's gaze jerk back around to the man. He was tugging at his collar, trying to loosen it, and Fane realized what she was doing. She was using her power just as she said she would: for survival. Her eyes were hard, her teeth sinking even deeper into her lip.

She was killing that man. And Fane couldn't stand by and let that happen, either.

Fane was caught between them—unable to strike either, unable to move. So he did the only thing he could think of. He ducked down, snatched the boot away from Trefor, and then he tossed it at Mer.

That broke her concentration. She reached up to grab the boot out of the air. It had a few teeth marks and a dribble of dog drool.

The man slumped to the ground, gasping in great shaky heaves.

He coughed, turning toward the stairs. "Good," he wheezed. "About time—"

Fane heard it a moment later—footsteps above them. Fresh fire coursed through his veins, rekindling his heart into a gallop. They had to leave now, before this man's allies arrived and called for the guard. Fane whistled for Trefor, who'd been eyeing the man's other boot with a kind of calculating avarice. The corgi threw Fane a disappointed look.

But before any of them could make it to the cellar door, a new figure appeared on the stairs.

In the sharp lantern light, Fane almost didn't make out his features. Then he saw the prominent ears and pale hair.

Renfrew stood on the stairs, his arms crossed and brows raised. He regarded the situation like a man who'd found rats in his cellar. That the three of them appeared to be grappling for their lives did not seem to occur to him—or if it did, it didn't seem to matter. Renfrew ambled down the stairs, picked his way across the icy floor, then reached for the wine rack. "I told you to retrieve the red," he said to the coughing man. "And as for you"—he turned his gaze on Mer and Fane—"would you mind not attacking the other allies in our little venture?"

Mer's chest rose and fell, her breathing ragged and cheeks a little pink. The boot dropped from her fingers. "Renfrew?"

"I told you to use the front door," said Renfrew.

"I had to make sure it wasn't a trap," said Mer.

The man stumbled upright, red-faced and furious. "Would anyone care to tell me what's going on?"

"Emrick," said Renfrew. "I told you they were coming."

"You didn't tell me they were going to sneak in through the wine cellar," replied Emrick. "I thought they'd knock at the front door. She—she almost killed me."

"I froze your tongue to your teeth," said Mer. "Not pleasant, but it wouldn't have killed you. If I wanted you dead, you'd be fodder for the rats by now."

Emrick took half a step forward, his face shining with fury. "Insolent wretch—"

Renfrew *tsk*ed lightly. "Ah, I see we have a need for introductions. I shall handle that once we're all dry and perhaps more well fed. Emrick, tell the servants to prepare the other rooms. And perhaps to retrieve some chopped meat for the dog." The bottle still in hand, Renfrew turned and climbed back up the stairs.

The three of them were left to gaze at one another, breaths uneven and tension still thick through the air. Then the man, Emrick, held out his hand and said, "Boot."

No one moved.

"My *boot*, if you'd be so kind," said Emrick.

Fane knelt and picked up the boot—toothmarks and all—and handed it over.

Emrick gazed at the boot with disgust, then pulled it on. "My thanks," he said coolly. He turned and strode up the stairs. His left boot squished audibly.

Fane and Mer stood there for a few moments. Trefor leaned against his ankle. The corgi gave a slight whine, as if in question.

"Do all his jobs go like this?" asked Fane.

Mer's chin fell and her hair tumbled forward—covering her brand. "You mean Renfrew keeping everyone in the dark? Yes. Normally there aren't so many wine bottles involved, though." She turned to look at him. "Your shoulder all right?"

"Fine," he said. He wondered if he should thank her for defending both him and Trefor. Instead he said, "You froze his tongue to the roof of his mouth?"

"It always causes a panic. Some people think they cannot breathe, even if it does nothing to obscure the airway." She gave the smallest jerk of her shoulders. "Panic makes a person vulnerable, less able to defend themselves." She exhaled hard. "Come on. Might as well see what we've walked into."

She strode past him, up the stairs. Her shoulders were straight and her steps even, but he did not have to use that iron-sense of his to know she had a knife tucked against her palm.

CHAPTER 8

The Finery of the bedroom made Mer's skin itch.

The curtains were the first things she noticed—they were thick, embroidered with delicate thread, and a glorious red. They cost more than her room at the Scythe and Boot. As for the rest of the room, it was just the same: a sturdy bed frame, a mattress stuffed with feathers rather than straw, a desk, and a wooden floor softened with rugs. The bedroom was awash with comforts that Mer had long ago given up on.

But this was where Renfrew had chosen for a hideout, so she would go along with it.

Once she'd bathed and changed clothes, the first thing Mer did was take stock of her escape routes. There was a way out through the kitchens, the cellar, and the front door, of course. But there was also a window on the second floor with a wide ledge, and Mer decided that if the worst happened, she could leave that way. She turned and walked down the stairs, following the sound of voices to the dining room.

There were four men sitting at the long table. The first was Renfrew, and across from him sat Fane. Trefor was curled up at Fane's ankle, gnawing on a bone.

Mer walked to the far end of the table and sat down. The cook, a kindly looking woman of middle age, poured a cup of tea and offered her a fresh slice of bara brith. Mer thanked her, then turned her attention to the other two men.

The first was the man from the cellar—Emrick. Now that she was no longer trying to fend him off, Mer could get a proper look at him. He had the ashen look of a man who spent his days indoors; he was slender, but she could tell from the unblemished skin and good teeth, he'd never been hungry. He might have been considered handsome, if Mer were attracted to young men who looked as though they'd spent their whole lives buried in books and ledgers. But Mer had always liked men and women who spent more time outdoors.

"Ah, now that we're all here," said Renfrew, "I believe proper introductions can be made." His voice was quiet and level as a frozen lake—with as much warmth. He sat with his left hand atop the table, his missing index finger on display for all to see. The room fell quiet at once.

"This," said Renfrew, gesturing idly at the nobleman, "is Emrick. Cousin to Lord Something-or-Other, in whose home we are currently residing."

Renfrew might play at ignorance, but it was just that—a play. He would not only know the name of the lord, but also the names of his spouse, his children, and every servant in their employ. One did not survive as a spymaster without a good memory and keen attention to detail.

Mer nodded to Emrick. "I don't feel so guilty about your boot, then. At least I know you can afford plenty more."

Emrick raised a cup of tea to his lips. "I rather doubt you feel much guilt about anything." Mer took note of everything from his accent to the stitching on his sleeves. Emrick was not from Gwaelod. One of the southern cantrefs, perhaps from a family who had dealings with Garanhir. Some nobles did keep summer homes in this city, paying taxes to the prince in exchange for a safe place to enjoy the sea air during those warm months.

"And this is Gryf," continued Renfrew, with a wave at the other man.

The second man had the broad shoulders that accompanied years of hard labor. He couldn't have been much older than Mer, and his gaze rested on her in a manner that could have been interpreted as flirting. His full mouth was soft and welcoming, even with a scar dimpling one corner. He picked up his bread with scarred hands. A soldier, then.

"Pleasure to meet you," Gryf said. "Pay no mind to our host. I heard the servants say he's a right terror until he's had at least three cups of tea."

Emrick made a sour noise, but Gryf merely refilled the noble's cup.

Renfrew ignored the exchange. "I've dealt with some of you

before"—a nod at Emrick and a glance at Mer—"and others I've chosen for their reputation or because I've seen a glimmer of potential." A look at Fane and Gryf. "For those who don't know, I was once Garanhir's spymaster." Out of the corner of her eye, Mer saw Fane look up sharply. "However, our parting left much to be desired." He spread his hands, his half-severed finger visible. "I bear no love for my former employer. And I will not weep to see him weakened. Nor would any of you, I think."

Mer made a show of looking around the table. "So this is our crew?" she asked. "A ring fighter, a lordling's cousin, a soldier, a spy, and a poisoner?"

"Which one of you is the poisoner?" asked Gryf, his tone as light as if he were inquiring who had cooked their meal.

"That depends on which of us you ask," replied Mer.

"I'm not a lordling," said Emrick, affronted.

"I said you were a lordling's *cousin*," said Mer. "Much, much less important."

"To be fair, I'm not a soldier," said Gryf, his manner still relaxed and easy. "But it's a common mistake."

She frowned at him. "What are you, then?"

"That depends on which of us you ask," he said, his smile widening.

"Hired sword," she said.

Gryf shook his head. "Wrong again."

"Personal guard."

"No."

Mer narrowed her eyes at him. "You're lying."

"I never lie," said Gryf easily.

"I see you two are going to get along well," murmured Renfrew, stirring milk into his tea.

"I'm not here just because I'm someone's *cousin*," said Emrick. "I am the foremost expert on—"

"You forgot the dog," put in Gryf, ignoring Emrick. "Which role does he play?"

Emrick began to turn an interesting shade of red.

Trefor was sitting under Fane's chair, content with his bone. "Boot thief," said Fane.

"And a handsome one," said Gryf. "May I?" He held out his hand and Fane inclined his head in assent. Trefor snuffled Gryf's proffered fingers and gave them a lick, his tail thumping against the floor.

Emrick's cup clattered against its saucer. "Their kind are spies for the tylwyth teg. We should not even have him in the room."

"I'm surprised at you," said Gryf. "A learned fellow such as yourself telling fairy stories."

"They're not stories," said Emrick indignantly. "And even if they were, most stories do have a basis in fact. Which you would know if any of you bothered to ask why I'm here."

There was a moment of quiet. Renfrew poured himself another cup of tea.

Mer kept silent out of sheer contrariness, enjoying every second of it. Emrick's face reddened further.

"All right, all right," said Gryf, with the air of one placating a child. "I'll put an end to your suffering. Why are you here?"

Emrick sat straighter. "I am the foremost expert on the tylwyth teg, with a particular interest in ancient artifacts. Particularly, old magical traps."

The silence around the table grew heavier.

"Ah," said Emrick loftily. "That got your attention, did it not? None of you besides Renfrew has given any thought to what might be awaiting us. The tylwyth teg—or the otherfolk, if you want to be common about it—were the original owners of the Well. And they did not leave their magical cache unguarded, if old texts are to be believed. While tales of the Well are rare, they aren't wholly unheard of. People have attempted to retrieve those treasures before and failed in the attempt."

Renfrew nodded. "Emrick is right." He steepled his fingers, and his blue eyes lingered on every person at the table for a fraction of a moment. "There are several small islands off the coast of this city. The Well is on one such island only accessible by land at low tide, when a narrow shoal connects it to the mainland. Royal guards ensure that no one can cross by land. If we try to cross that shoal, we'll be riddled with arrows."

"Then we approach by boat," said Gryf.

Mer made a derisive sound in her throat. "Not possible. This coastline is all rocks and cliffs. Fane and I took a boat from the south, but we had to make land a day's walk from Caer Wyddno."

"Then how are we to approach?" asked Gryf.

Renfrew said, "I have spoken to those who make their living traversing impossible borders."

"Fancy way of saying, 'I bribed a smuggler,'" murmured Mer.

Renfrew spread his hands, palms up. "There are sea caves. Which will flood at high tide, of course. But we have someone here who has navigated them before." With the air of a showman unveiling a wonder, he gestured with one hand toward Mer. Which would have been more impressive if she hadn't just bitten into a large slice of bara brith. She swallowed the sticky bread, knowing that her teeth were probably pockmarked with dried fruit, and smiled broadly. Emrick grimaced, hiding his disgust behind his teacup.

"She's a water diviner," said Renfrew to the others. "The *last* living water diviner."

Both Gryf and Emrick turned to look at her.

"Truly," said Gryf, with that flirtatious smile. "I've heard talk of diviners, 'course, but I've never had the pleasure." He touched something at his collar—a heavy iron coin strung on a leather cord. It was an old-fashioned protection against enchantment.

"Were you born near Annwvyn?" asked Emrick. His gaze slid over her, evaluating. "Were there portents at your birth?"

"No, and no," said Mer. "If any of the tylwyth teg blessed my mam, she never told anyone."

"Did you go to the otherfolk to understand your gift?" asked Emrick. His long-fingered hands twitched, as if he longed for a quill and parchment.

"No," she said. "Until a week ago, I was serving drinks in a tavern."

"They can walk unnoticed among us," said Emrick quietly, as if to himself. "Less so with all the iron in the cities—but still." He glanced sharply at Trefor. "They have eyes everywhere."

"The particular sea cave we need is through the sewers, behind a locked gate," said Renfrew, gently pushing the conversation back on course. "I have a contact who deals in stolen items—and he promised me a set of guards' keys." Another nod toward Mer. "Mer will go to the contact and buy the key. Emrick will be reading up on the old legends concerning what traps the otherfolk might have left within the sea caves. Gryf has his own instructions."

"What am I to do?" asked Fane quietly.

Renfrew turned his attention to Fane. "Your part will come later. For now…" He seemed to cast about for an answer, then said, "Go with Mer. You look the part of a hired sword, so you might as well play one." He leaned back in his chair, his hands vanishing into his lap. "The moon will be full the day after tomorrow. We shall leave the day after that."

"A spring tide," Mer murmured, understanding.

Renfrew nodded. "When the tides are at their highest—and their lowest. We shall use that low tide to traverse the caves."

All the pieces were falling into place. Mer could see the shape of the plan, the way she'd used to watch the prince sketch out troop movements. But one thing still nagged at her.

"It is too easy," she said. "The sea caves are treacherous, yes. Knowledge of the Well was kept secret. And if there are magical traps, then I could see why this is dangerous. But 'dangerous' doesn't mean 'impossible.' As you said—there have been others who attempted this." She fixed Renfrew with a hard look. "What aren't you telling us?"

An uncomfortable silence fell across the table. Mer could sense

Emrick shifting in his seat; Gryf looked more interested than wary; Fane merely reached down to stroke Trefor's back.

"Ysgithyrwyn," said Renfrew.

For a moment, a shocked quiet fell across the table. Then everyone started talking at once.

"—Ysgithyrwyn," said Emrick, aghast. "The boar from the legends? Surely not—"

Gryf frowned. "I get legends confused. Is Ysgithyrwyn that boar who is actually a cursed man and someone has to get the comb out of his hair?"

"I thought it was a pair of scissors," said Fane. "Or a razor."

"It was all three," said Emrick, with a lofty irritation. "Clearly none of you have educated yourselves on the legends. And that's not even the right boar. You're thinking of Twrch Trwyth." He took a breath. "Ysgithyrwyn is known as White Tusk, the chief of all boars."

"That sounds unpleasant," said Mer.

Emrick continued, "Ysgithyrwyn is a giant magical boar who has *eaten* every knight sent to defeat him. No combs involved."

"Very unpleasant," said Mer. She threw a look at Renfrew. "So this is your plan? And why in the name of all the fallen kings should we even have a hope of success?"

"Because," said Renfrew, "we have the foremost expert on magical traps." A nod at Emrick. "We have an expert in his field." Another nod to Gryf. "We have the last water diviner." Mer huffed when all eyes fell to her. "And a young man magicked with the ability to kill opponents far beyond his ability. He will deal with the boar."

"I will?" said Fane with mild surprise.

"The boar is magic," said Renfrew. "You are magic."

"I *have* magic," said Fane. "There's a difference."

"Is that how you made coin as a fighter?" asked Gryf, interested.

Fane let out a heavy breath. "It was supposed to be, until these two found me."

"And how are we to return once we're done?" asked Mer. "Are we going back through the caves?"

Renfrew gave her an opaque smile. "Don't I always have two ways out?"

"Treacherous sea caves," she said. "Potential magical traps. And the chief of all boars guarding the Well." She folded her hands beneath her chin, leaning on them indolently. "And here I thought this might prove difficult."

CHAPTER 9

THE FIRST TIME Mer saw Prince Garanhir execute a traitor, she had been only ten.

After two years living at the castell, she knew how to move through it unseen and unnoticed. She was even better at it than Renfrew was—mostly because no one gave a child dressed in servant's livery a second glance. She could go where she wanted, when she wanted. With one exception.

The dungeons were barred to all but the guards and the prince's personal servants. But Renfrew could come and go as he pleased; there was a ring of keys on his belt that would let him walk through any door. Mer thought it rather unfair, as he was training her, that he would keep such keys to himself. After all, if he wanted her to be his student, then surely she should go where he went.

So one day, she stole those keys.

Renfrew had been schooling her on the history of the cantrefs when a fire broke out in the stables. Forehead creasing with irritation, Renfrew went to the window and peered downward. Their lessons were always in the west-facing tower, where Renfrew kept his books and his papers. His desk was always fastidiously neat, save for the letters that the servants dropped off. Those were balanced precariously on the edge, wax seals bright red in the sunlight. As Renfrew walked around the desk, his sleeve caught those letters and a few fluttered to the ground. With a sigh, he knelt to retrieve them.

As Renfrew reached for one letter fallen beneath his desk, something glittered at his belt. Mer's eyes fell on the circle of keys, greedy as a magpie. Her small fingers reached out and unhooked the keys, tucking them inside her shirt while Renfrew wasn't looking.

She half expected Renfrew to see the theft, to gently chide her. But he merely patted her head with one large hand, told her to continue her reading, then strode from the room.

Leaving Mer alone—with all the keys to the castell.

She could go anywhere, do anything, if only for a few hours. She would put the keys back under Renfrew's desk, of course. Hopefully he would think he had merely dropped them.

The door that led down to the dungeons was on the western edge of the fortress. It took a few minutes to find the right key—she kept listening for anyone happening by, and her heart was a hammer inside her chest. Finally, the latch turned and she heaved the door open.

The descent made her dizzy; the stairs were circular, winding down and down into the depths of the fortress. Finally, she came around the last bend in the stairs and found herself in a shadowy corridor. A single torch flickered along the wall. Mer remained still, ears straining. She'd heard tales of the criminals brought to the dungeons. Children often delighted in stories that would make the adults shudder and tell them to hush. Part of Mer wanted to see if they were true.

She heard the voices while creeping around a corner. They echoed, hollow and watery, off the damp walls. Fingers knotted in her own shirt, Mer walked on the balls of her feet like Renfrew had shown her—quiet, ready to run if needed.

"—cannot tell me."

That was the prince. She had only ever spoken to Garanhir a handful of times, but of course she knew his voice. He would say a few words at feasts, at holidays, and talk with Renfrew in the corridors. He had a voice better meant for bards than royalty—it was soft, almost musical in its intonations. She had always wondered why he didn't shout commands like princes in tales—but now, listening to the melodic cadence of his words, she felt rooted in place.

"I have told you!" A second man's voice. This one Mer also knew, if only in passing. He was Renfrew's spy, sent to the eastern border wars. He was one of the few people who'd always greet Mer instead of ignoring the child lurking in Renfrew's shadow. A few times, he had brought her a sweet or a flower. "Gwynedd will not go to war with Annwvyn. The royal family won't risk it—not for any alliance."

There was a dull sound, like flesh hitting flesh. It took Mer a moment to understand that the prince must have struck the spy. She edged forward, her body pressed against the wall, until she peered around the corner.

The spy was strung up by his wrists, spattered with sweat and—blood? *Yes*, Mer thought. It was indeed blood. Her first time seeing so much of it.

Prince Garanhir had dark, sleek hair and broad shoulders. From the back, the little she could see of his face looked pale and cold. "That is why I told you to take other measures," he said quietly.

The spy spat on the floor. "No. I'll not do that, not for you, not for Gwaelod—"

Garanhir moved so quickly that Mer almost didn't catch the strike. One moment, the prince stood before his prisoner—and then he lunged forward and buried a knife to the hilt through the spy's left eye.

Mer jerked back, as though she had been the one struck. Shaking, she retreated. Fear flooded her mouth—she was suddenly all too aware of how she should not be in this place.

She turned to leave.

And she ran headfirst into the man standing behind her. She opened her mouth to yelp in surprise, but a hand descended and clamped down the words. She was dragged away from that dungeon, toward the stairs. When the torchlight fell across the man, she realized it was Renfrew. He released her and she stepped back, wiping at her mouth. She expected him to scold her or worse.

His eyes were blue and calm as a frozen lake. "Come, dear child," he said, hand on her shoulder. His grip was firm, unrelenting. "We should return to your lessons."

She had been so shaken that she did not protest; she was only grateful that he did not tell the prince she'd been spying on him.

It was years later that Mer realized those keys had been all too easy to lift. Renfrew had let her take them. He had wanted her to see. To watch what happened to those who betrayed their oaths to the prince. That was the lesson he had intended her to learn.

To this day, she was unsure whether it had been a warning—or his subtle way of insinuating she should have escaped earlier.

When Mer ventured out of Emrick's house, she did not look like the young spy who once dwelled within the prince's castell.

It had been a painstaking effort on her part—face paint, to hide the brand beside her left eye. It took an hour of careful brushing, of matching her skin tone just so, but she was satisfied with the result. Her lips were darkened, her hair twisted into an elaborate braid. And she wore a fine red gown with knives hidden up her sleeves.

Fane stood by the front door, dressed in the simple, clean lines of a servant. With his scarred hands and broken nose, Renfrew must have decided against disguising him like a nobleman.

"Trefor not coming?" she asked. While the dog would no doubt draw unwanted attention, she would have liked his companionship.

Fane gave a small shake of his head. "He was asleep."

"I hope you asked one of the servants to take him out if he needs to go outside."

"No need," said Fane. "He's rather good at escaping locked doors."

Mer threw him a look, unsure if he was jesting or not. For all this talk about corgis being servants of the otherfolk, she still didn't know if the rumors held any weight. She'd heard ravens and black dogs could be heralds of magic, but corgis were just so…cute. And smiling. And rather memorable. It seemed the worst combination for a spy.

"What do *you* think he is?" she asked.

A faint smile touched Fane's lips. "Hungry."

With that, they stepped out into the city.

There were fisherman yelling about fresh cockles and oysters, bakers with stalls brimming with barley and rye, children with baskets of fresh flowers and herbs, and even a young man calling out that he could tell people's fortunes for a few copper coins. Mer slipped through the crowds like a fish through familiar currents. No one gave her a second glance; half of going unseen was to be comfortable with one's surroundings. Folk had a good sense for fear, just like animals. They could sense nerves or unease, and would pick those people out of a crowd. Even the pickpockets seemed to take note of Mer's relaxed stride and watchful eyes—or perhaps they simply did not want to risk the wrath of the hulking man at her shoulder.

Caer Wyddno was a circular city, with the castell at the top of the ocean cliff and the lower city curving beneath it. The farther one got from the castell, the more dangerous the city became; the houses grew more dilapidated, the roads pockmarked with holes. Many of those who passed by bore a simple iron broach.

"The mark of the thieves' guild," Mer murmured, answering Fane's question before he spoke it. "Those who travel through seedier parts of the city wear them to show they've paid their protection fees."

Fane grunted an acknowledgment.

The shop they needed sat between an old tannery and an abandoned home.

It was a shop with no particular specialty—bundles of dried herbs hung from the ceiling rafters, heavy iron keys with no locks were knotted together with twine, jars of pickled seeds and berries stood on dusty shelves, and an old saddle moldered across the back of a wooden chair. The man behind the counter eyed them warily. Clothes hung from his thin frame like billowing sheets around a half-dead tree. His hands had an unsteadiness about them—as if he were suffering from exhaustion or coming off a bad night of drink.

"Hello," Mer said, with a polite inclination of her head. At least with the face paint, she didn't have to worry about the brand being so visible.

"Huh," said the man.

"I've been sent to pick up a package," said Mer, recalling the code Renfrew had repeated to her. "Gooseberry jelly for the widow living across from the apothecary."

Understanding flickered in the man's eyes. "Ah, I see. You've payment?"

Mer reached into her cloak and withdrew a pouch of coins. The man twitched the pouch open, thumb moving across the gold inside. It was a small fortune.

The man began to pull the pouch toward him, but Mer snatched at his wrist. He jerked back as if she had burned him. "Not until we have the jelly," she said. She tried to speak as Renfrew did when he was displeased—quiet and cold.

Something dark flashed across the man's face, but before he replied, his gaze settled on Fane. Fane had not said a word nor made any movement, but he still made quite the figure. Mer was almost glad to have him along, if only because he looked far more intimidating than she did.

The man said, "All righ'. Hold on, hold on." With one last look over his shoulder, he ducked behind a musty curtain and into the back of the shop.

Mer watched him go, unease knotting at the base of her spine. She rolled her shoulders, resisting the urge to pace the length of the small room. She contented herself with studying some of the shop's wares.

"What is this place?" asked Fane quietly. "And why would that man have the key we need to enter the sewers?"

Mer touched the old saddle. The leather was buttery soft with age, but it needed a good cleaning. "This shop is a front. The man here—he sells stolen goods for a price. Does deals between the guild and other criminals. If you have need of a certain illegal tool or forged papers or even information, you would come here or someplace like it."

Fane shifted on his feet. She sensed more than saw his disapproval.

"For someone who fought in illegal fighting rings," she said, "you're skittish about crime."

"For someone who was serving drinks in a tavern a week ago," he replied, "you're not."

She allowed herself the smallest of smiles—his comment had

earned that much. "It's rather like riding a horse, as it turns out. You remember how."

Fane opened his mouth, then tilted his head. Like a dog hearing a distant whistle.

"What?" said Mer.

Fane's eyes closed for the briefest moment, then they flashed open. "Iron," he said. "In the door. Some mechanism just moved."

Mer went to the door, reached for the handle, and tugged at it. It was immovable as stone. Mer gave it a good yank, but to no avail. "Fallen kings," she snarled. "You try."

Fane did. His forearms were corded with lean muscle, and his scarred hands pulled at the door with more force than she'd managed. "It's locked, somehow," he said, grimacing. He touched a hand to the wooden panel. "Reinforced with metal."

"There must be a way to lock it from outside," said Mer. Her heartbeat was rising in her chest, but she wasn't afraid—not yet. "It's a trap. He must've figured the guard could pay him more than we could. Or—or the guild. It's a toss-up which one might want me dead more."

Fane threw her an exasperated look. "You just seem to have that effect on people?"

"It's my charm," she said grimly, reaching for her belt. A knife came free easily, resting in her fingers like a familiar friend. "Come on—there's more than one way out of here." She made for the back of the shop, knife held at the ready. If that shopkeeper had a crossbow, this would all be for naught. But she was hoping the man had simply fled once he'd activated that trap. He didn't seem the fighting sort.

Pushing aside the cloth curtain, she found herself in a small storage room. The shelves were laden with broken bits of metal and wood, half-rotted cabinets with hinges rusting and a few tools meant for breaking locks. There was no sign of the man. Mer saw a door that must have led outside. She pulled on the latch, but it didn't budge.

A loud thump made her jump. There was someone pounding on the front door.

Her heartbeat quickened. "You need a weapon?"

Fane shook his head. "No."

"If they're guards, they'll be armed," said Mer.

Fane's gaze was steady on hers, his face implacable. "I won't fight them."

For a moment, she was sure she hadn't heard him. "What?"

"I won't fight them," said Fane.

"What kind of hired muscle are you?" said Mer.

"The kind hired to fight a boar, not people with families and lives," he said, his voice sharper than she'd ever heard it.

There was another loud crash. It sounded like someone was kicking at the door. Mer whirled on the spot, trying to find another way out. There were no windows, no places to hide. Just junk, waiting to be sold, and a moldy old rug. The man must have tripped over it in his haste to leave, because one of its edges was rolled up.

Or maybe...

Mer pushed back the rug, revealing a small trapdoor.

"He must have gotten out this way." She pulled the door open.

Damp, cold air wafted upward; it smelled of wet stone and something foul. Mer wrinkled her nose. She turned, angling herself down into the opening. There was a ladder that looked like it should hold her weight, but she couldn't see where it went.

"Do you know where that goes?" asked Fane.

"Away," said Mer, and began descending into the damp dark. She'd never been all that fond of ladders or heights, but she didn't hesitate. She'd much rather deal with a dank tunnel than the city guards. Overhead, she heard Fane exhale, then he was above her, pulling the trapdoor shut.

They plunged into darkness.

Mer just breathed for a moment, trying to get her bearings, then continued her descent. She counted thirty rungs before her foot hit something solid. She stumbled, then stepped back. There was a thump as Fane followed.

The darkness was absolute. Mer heard something skitter to her left, but she didn't flinch away. Instead, she delved into one of her pockets and came up with a small candle. Her firesteel was in another pocket, and it took a few tries to set the candle alight. The wick caught, and the tiny flame flickered. Mer cupped her fingers around it, glancing at their surroundings.

"I should have known," she murmured. "A criminal fence would have a trapdoor to the sewers."

The tunnel was carved into a perfect circle. Mer took a moment to orient herself, then began walking to her left. Fane followed. "Why would a criminal want access to the sewers?" he asked quietly. His voice echoed from the stone walls.

"The sewers are one of the highlights of Caer Wyddno," she said. She could almost feel his frown. "You're jesting."

"I'm not," she said, grinning despite herself. It was the warm glow of escape, the flush of victory still high on her cheeks. "When the city was built, diviners were brought in. They carved these sewers out of the cliffs, so that people wouldn't just throw muck and worse out into the streets. It all flows out into the ocean." She took a small breath through her mouth, trying not to smell the stuff clinging to her boots. "It's a...less than ideal way to travel. But criminals will use it, if they have need. Just don't look at what's flowing around your boots."

For a few moments, they walked in silence. Mer kept going left until she found what she was looking for: a mark carved into one of the stone walls. The guild had gone to great lengths to map the sewers and etched the corresponding street names below. She could find the way out from here—and now that she knew she had her escape, she could turn her mind to other things.

"Why didn't you want to fight?" she said.

"Because I would have killed them all," Fane replied.

She squinted at him through the flickering candlelight. "What?"

"I told you. My magic—it's death." His gaze was distant, as if these memories were so old they could not touch him. "I was young, caught up in fantasies of avenging my family. I didn't understand what I was asking for. The otherfolk used their magic to give me what I wanted—to kill the seven men who slew my family." He continued ahead, water sloshing around his ankles. "Now—now I cannot throw a single punch without the magic waking up. And once it does, the fight will not end until my opponent is dead—or I am. It also makes me quite a good fighter, so no one has bested me yet."

Mer frowned. "That doesn't sound so bad." Her magic was strong but could be turned aside with the smallest scrap of iron. And while Renfrew had taught her to fight, it was mostly evasion and quick strikes meant to disable an enemy before they noticed her. She had learned how to be a deadly shadow, but Fane had the power to walk where he liked without fear. She didn't understand why he sounded so haunted.

Fane laughed but it came out hollow. "Then I haven't explained well." He extended a hand, hovering over Mer's shoulder. Then he pulled it back, clearly measuring the distance between them. "I have to be aware of my every movement," he said. "Were I to accidentally strike you with my elbow, it might summon the magic."

Mer sucked in a breath. "You mean—you don't choose when to use it?"

"No," said Fane. "The magic takes control. I am merely a vessel for death—seven deaths, to be precise."

While she'd never chosen to be a diviner, Mer's magic had always been the one thing she had power over. She chose when to call on it, not the other way around. And while there were always people who tried to control her, the magic itself was blameless. She had never resented it. But Fane didn't have that kind of choice. Suddenly it all made more sense—why he stood apart from the others, why he had never touched her without prompting. He couldn't trust his own body.

That sounded *nightmarish*.

Fane said, "Do you understand why I couldn't fight? Because I wouldn't be able to stop. And I won't be responsible for a death that I didn't choose."

She did understand. Perhaps far too well. All of the envy she'd felt for his power dried up in a matter of moments.

"And this is why Renfrew hired me," he said, a vein of bitterness in his voice. "Because I am a killer. Because he wishes me to kill—and even if it is just a boar, it's yet another life. I am sick to death of killing, of only ever being a weapon in another's hand. But I shall do so, because we all have our parts to play."

"Do you think your magic will work on the boar?" she asked.

He waggled one hand around in an uncertain gesture. "I don't know. The boar is supposed to be magic—as is my gift." He gave the last word a bitter little twist. "Maybe I can slay the monster. Or maybe I'll be eaten alive. It's not quite the future I envisioned for myself as a child, but these things happen."

A flicker of shame went through her. She had thought of him as a vessel for his abilities, rather than as a person. It made her no different than the people who'd used her, and the revelation made her feel a little ill. An apology was warranted, but she did not know how to phrase it without making herself all the more guilty.

Perhaps a trade.

A truth for a truth.

"I suppose you wonder how Renfrew and I know each other," she said.

He cast a look at her. "I had considered that, yes."

She inhaled, trying to ignore the stench of the sewer. "We both served Garanhir."

He turned, the line of his shoulders mirroring hers. "You worked for the prince?"

"Royals take diviners," she said. "As servants. As soldiers. As spies. That is why so many of us often try to go unnoticed. I was taken to Garanhir as a child, educated by Renfrew and trained to be a loyal spy. And I was, for a time. I went into the borderlands between Gwaelod and Gwynedd, where Garanhir wished to invade. He told me I would be using my power to find wells and other water sources for his soldiers. So I did." She let out a bitter little laugh. Even now, the words tasted like bile. "And then he poisoned every single one of them. Countless innocent people died, drinking from those wells. It was a form of warfare—to take a land by destroying its people."

In the years since then, Mer had tried to harden herself against those memories. She told herself the past could not be changed, that she had to move on, and all that mattered was the here and now. But she had never felt at ease within herself, caged within the body of a person she'd come to despise.

She hated Garanhir, yes.

But she'd always hated herself more.

"You didn't know," said Fane quietly. It was partly a question.

"No," she said. "And when I found out…" She swallowed. "He tried to make it impossible for me to leave his service." Her hand rose involuntarily toward her brand but she caught herself in time.

"And that's why you took this job," said Fane. "Because you wish to avenge yourself upon the prince."

"Partly," she said, because she wouldn't lie about that. "But mostly—mostly I cannot earn enough coin by legal means, not if

I want to disappear." She exhaled hard, blowing out a frustrated breath. "I was arrested just after Renfrew found me. The only reason I'm not imprisoned is because he broke me out—and it made me realize I'll never be free, not unless I have enough coin to escape the prince. This venture may be desperate, but it's my best chance."

To her relief, there was no judgment in Fane's face. "I understand. People like us—we rarely have the luxury of choices."

They walked for a time, ankle-deep in foul water and trying to ignore the rats. Mer reached out with her magic, followed the current of the water.

"So how are we to get down into the sea caves?" asked Fane. "We didn't retrieve the key."

Mer had been trying to avoid that question—but now it had been stated outright, she found herself turning it over from every angle. "We could try to pick the lock," she said. "But many of the gates near the castell are magicked against that sort of thing."

"Could we destroy it altogether?" asked Fane. "If we were to get hold of black powder..."

Now *that* was a good question. "I know little of explosions," admitted Mer. "I've never spent any time near mines. But it seems... I mean, I wouldn't try it unless I was sure the sewer wouldn't just collapse in on us. And the noise would surely draw attention."

"True."

Perhaps it was standing in this sewer, so close to the memories of old jobs, escaping the guards, every step laced with a reckless remembrance. She recalled slipping through the streets of Caer

Wyddno like a wraith, cold fingers twined with her own. The sound of a familiar laugh, the taste of stolen sweets.

Mer knew how to get that key.

But it would mean talking to *her*.

"I think I know a way," she said.

"How?"

"I know the heir to the thieves' guild," she said.

Fane frowned. "A thieves' guild is hereditary?"

"Not always." Mer stepped over a pile of something that looked suspiciously squishy. "Nearly every kingdom has one. Sometimes they are run by families. Some even have blood ties to the nobility. The guild of Caer Wyddno—it is run by a pair of married women who are supposedly third cousins to some nobles."

"And the prince allows this?"

"The nobles support him with their coin," said Mer with a shrug. "So royals don't really mind who thieves steal from, as long as it isn't them. Merchants who wish to keep their shipments safe will pay the guild fees, and any pickpockets or criminals working in the city must pay taxes—or face the wrath of the guild. It means that mostly outsiders get robbed, which everyone seems happy with."

"And who is this heir?"

Mer's shoulders slumped. "She's a thief. A very good thief."

"But if this guild respects the nobility," said Fane, "why would they help us go after the prince?"

"The guild will not," said Mer. "But its heir just might." She straightened, as if forcing herself to face a cold wind. "She owes me."

He studied her. "There's a problem, isn't there?"

"There are three problems," Mer said.

Fane raised his brows in silent question.

"First," she said, "the thief in question…well. Let's just say we have a past." Her cheeks reddened and he seemed to understand.

"You courted?" asked Fane.

That color deepened. "'Courted' seems too dignified a word for it. We were young and foolish and utterly smitten with each other. It was unwise, as she was the leader of our thieving crew."

"And the second problem?" he asked.

"She betrayed me the last time we worked together," said Mer. "That abruptly put an end to the aforementioned courtship."

Fane's forehead scrunched. "And yet you wish to work with her again?"

"It's less about want and more about running out of options," replied Mer grimly.

"And what is the third problem?"

Mer let out a breath. "I did some asking. She's in prison."

The Thief

THE MANOR OF *the noble house of ap Madyn remained locked at all times.*

There was a twofold reason for this—first, it was to ensure that uninvited guests could not approach without stealing a key or bribing a guard. And if an enemy managed such a theft, then they would often find themselves in the employ of the ap Madyn family. As for the bribery, that helped weed out untrustworthy guards.

The second reason was only ever uttered in whispers, in shadowed corners and under one's breath.

The manor was the court for a guild of thieves.

The house overlooked a sheer drop into the sea and on stormy days, the windows were flecked with salt and ocean spray. Someone had cut—or magicked—stone steps that led down the cliff, toward the froth and foam of the water. There were rumors that some boats risked the approach, rowing toward the manorhouse laden with ill-gotten treasures.

One such boat sailed toward the house.

But it did not bear gold nor silver. Rather, a fourteen-year-old girl lay with a cloth around her head and wrists bound with iron. The thieves bore her weight, half carried and half dragged her up the stone steps. She was taken through the house, her stolen clothes dripping seawater onto the fine wooden floors.

When the bag was yanked from her head, she found herself in a sitting room.

"We caught her running from the guards," said one of her captors. He was a middle-aged man with cold hands. She knew that because he pressed one of those hands to the nape of her bare neck and shoved her down before two women.

They did not sit on a throne. The girl had seen a throne before and it was nothing like the comfortable settee that these women lounged upon. One of them was rather short, with golden hair bound into braids around her head, and the other tall, with crimson hair that tumbled in waves down her shoulders. Both regarded the girl with less-than-pleased stares.

There were others in the room—two armed guards, a servant pouring tea, and another girl—this one with dark hair and fingers that moved ceaselessly, trailing the embroidery in her chair.

"Good evening," the first woman said. "I understand you found something of value for us."

"Show them your face," the man said, and gave a yank on the girl's hair. She had no choice but to lift her chin, her hair falling back to reveal the fresh brand at the corner of her eye.

It shone red, the wound still raw and healing. It burned like a small sun had kissed her flesh. The girl hadn't managed more than a few hours' worth of sleep without the pain rousing her.

The taller woman drew a sharp breath through her teeth. "That's the prince's mark."

"Aye," said the man. "He'd likely pay a pretty bounty to have her back." He retreated a step, bowing as he did so. The girl realized what she was: tribute, paid to these two women.

And abruptly, she knew who they were.

These were the noblewomen of ap Madyn—the two ladies who ran the thieves' guild. The spymaster had taught her a little of the guild, outlined how they worked and how they paid enough into the royal coffers that the prince allowed them to operate within the city's walls.

The two women regarded her with mingled curiosity and doubt. "Branding children now," murmured the second woman. She touched a finger to her painted mouth. "To whom do you belong, child?"

The girl swallowed. Her throat was dry; her tongue clicked against her teeth when she spoke. "No one."

The second woman let out a soft breath. "Answer the question. It won't be asked again."

The girl shifted in her crouch, the iron creaking against her wrists. It was so cold it hurt—everything hurt, ached, or burned. The girl bit her lip and did not answer.

"Put her in the cellar," the first woman said. "We'll decide what to do with her in the morning. Mayhap the prince will let us only send half of this month's taxes if she's valuable."

A flutter of fear beat within the girl's chest. She staggered up to one knee before the man slammed his hand upon her shoulder and shoved her back down.

The girl tore herself from the man's grip and lunged forward. Every person in the room jerked in surprise; guards pulled knives from belts and the first woman went very still. But the girl merely clutched at the woman's gown, like a much younger child pleading for a sweet.

"Please," said the girl. "Don't send me back."

The second woman seized the girl and threw her to the floor. She flicked her fingers at the man. "The cellar."

It was useless to protest so the girl did not try. She allowed herself to be yanked to her feet and marched out of the sitting room. The girl's head tipped forward, hair falling across the healing brand and her tear-stained cheeks.

And so no one noticed when silver flashed between her fingers—a stolen hairpin. The sound of metal working against metal was covered up by the tromping of booted feet against wooden floors.

A door opened—and then they were descending stairs. Damp cellar air brushed the girl's wet cheeks. She had learned how to cry when needed because tears often made people uncomfortable or sympathetic. The tears had no effect on this man, save for making her seem even weaker in his eyes.

Which was his mistake.

The pin caught and turned—and the chains came free. The girl did not release the iron, not yet. Instead, she tightened her grip on it, whirled around, and slammed the chain as hard as she could into the man's face. It caught him just above the brow, and he cried out in startled pain. Blood poured forth from his forehead and he swiped at his eyes. The girl kicked him in the back of the knee. He fell hard, barely catching himself on the heel of one hand. He reached for her, but the girl was gone.

She rushed back up the stairs, her heart a hammer in her chest.

She had not survived the kiss of a brand only to be returned to the man who had placed the iron into the coals. She sprinted through the house, trying to find her way back to those stairs. If only she could descend to the ocean, perhaps she might have a chance. She could take a boat and sail far from Caer Wyddno, find a new home—

A servant appeared in a doorway, carrying a tray of drinks. The girl smashed her fist into the tray, upending the wine.

Magic sang through her, familiar and welcome, and the crimson wine froze the servant's feet to the floor. Then the girl pushed on.

She couldn't stop. She had to run, to keep going.

There was the door.

All she had to do was step through it and she would be free.

Her fingers landed upon the door and she yanked. It didn't budge. She pressed her hand up against the frame, called to her magic a second time. There would be water in the wood, perhaps enough water to—

But her magic faltered.

With a snarl, the girl jammed the stolen hairpin into the lock. Her fingers were unsteady but she took a breath, trying to calm herself.

"There's iron in the frame," said a voice from behind her.

The girl whirled, back pressed to the door, pin held out like some kind of weapon.

Someone stood a few strides away. It was the other girl, the one from the sitting room—with the smiling mouth and twitchy fingers. A thief—she must have been, to live in this guild.

"Who are you?" asked the thief. She tilted her head to one side, dark hair slipping from an untidy braid.

For some reason, the question made the girl go still. Perhaps because the thief was the first person to utter it. No one had asked her such a thing in a very long time—those in the prince's employ knew of her and everyone else merely wished to know what they could get from her.

The girl's breaths were uneven. "Mer," she said. "My name is Mer."

The thief took a step closer.

But Mer raised her hand, fingers extended. "Don't—no closer."

The thief's smile widened. "You're magic, aren't you?" Another step. "I saw what you did to the servant."

"Yes," said Mer. "And if you've any wits at all, you'll open this door and release me."

One last step, and the thief was close enough to touch. Mer's fingers brushed up against the thief's shoulder, settling there. The thief wore no iron; she would be easy to harm. All it would take was a sharp twist of magic.

But the thief did not flinch. Instead, her own hand came up. Her touch was so gentle that Mer barely felt it—the thief carefully brushed Mer's hair behind her ear, revealing the ugly brand. Mer expected her to grimace and look away. But the thief did no such thing.

"You survived him," she said. "The prince, I mean. And you escaped one of our hirelings, too." Her dark eyes roamed across Mer's face. "You stole that pin from my mother. My mother—the queen of thieves."

Mer swallowed thickly. So that's who this girl was: not merely a thief, but a princess of thieves.

"You," said the thief, "are going to be fun, I think."

There was a clatter of booted feet and Mer looked up. Several guards were running toward them; she flinched and drew back. But the thief's gaze never left her face.

"Stop," said the thief, raising a hand. The guards stopped. "Tell my mothers she is joining my crew."

One of the guards spluttered. "Lady Ifanna—you cannot—"

"Oh, I can," said the thief. "My mothers wish for me to take on more responsibility? Then I will. I want this girl on my crew. I've never had someone who could use magic before."

The guards drew back, looking both dubious and wary. But they did not dare argue, Mer realized. If her mother was the queen of thieves, then this girl was her own kind of royalty.

"And if I don't want to join you?" said Mer. "What's stopping me from escaping the moment I have the chance?"

The thief threw back her head and laughed. "Then," she said, "I'll just have to make things interesting enough that you won't want to escape. Come. I'll have some supper sent up to my rooms. I'll want to hear your whole story."

"I'm not a thief," said Mer. She wasn't sure what she was, not anymore. She wasn't the prince's diviner; she wasn't the spymaster's apprentice. There was only one thing she was sure of—Mer was going to be hunted. By the prince's soldiers, by the city guards, and by Gwynedd. Too many people had drunk from those poisoned waters.

Perhaps her best chance was to remain in a guild of thieves, among those who knew how to thwart such hunters.

Mer gave the thief a narrow-eyed look. "And I'm not a prisoner? I won't belong to you?"

The thief's hand dropped to her side and in doing so, her fingers brushed Mer's. The touch sent a spark of sensation through her.

The thief's smile sharpened to a wicked point. "That is entirely up to you."

CHAPTER 10

IFANNA VERCH ALDYTH AP MADYN did not commit the crime she'd been imprisoned for.

She stood accused of kidnapping a nobleman's son. And while it was true that she had found herself in possession of a lanky young man, she hadn't *kidnapped* him. He'd been soused after a night of carousing with other young nobles, stumbled into a cart that wasn't his, and passed out. Ifanna hadn't known he was back there when she'd stolen that wagon; she only discovered him after they were out of the city limits, when he sat up and blearily inquired about breakfast. If she had known, she wouldn't have gone near that wagon. The stolen silver was not worth the smell of sick.

For some reason, this argument did not impress the guards.

Which was how she found herself locked up for a month, pending a journey to the cantref court. She sat in her cell, wearing the rags she'd been given and quietly cursing that nobleman's son.

"Morning, your ladyship," said Llygad. He was one of those guards that resented his posting; he'd probably joined the service of the prince hoping to become a dashing soldier. Instead, he patrolled a prison. It wasn't even the prince's dungeon—no, Llygad did not have the honor of guarding traitors or murderers. This prison was for those who could not pay their taxes or passed forged papers. It must have been desperately boring.

Ifanna would have felt sorry for Llygad, if he weren't such an arse.

"Thank you kindly," she said, in a clipped imitation of the fine accent Ifanna's mothers had tried to drill into her.

"Don't know why you aren't with the others," he said, making no attempt to hide his own bitterness. "Why you get special meals and treatment."

Ifanna sat up a little straighter; her back was to the cell wall, her wrists encased in iron.

"Well, I picked the lock of the first cell they threw me into," said Ifanna. "Your kind should search your prisoners more thoroughly. One might sneak a bit of metal in, knotted into her hair."

Llygad scoffed. "There are other places to keep you."

"You mean," said Ifanna, "the prince's dungeon? I wouldn't fit in."

The thieves' guild had grown like an old tree in Caer Wyddno—its roots were driven deep beneath the streets and couldn't be ripped out without disturbing the city's foundations. The ap Madyn household had its own crest and noble history—and while there were whispers of forgeries, nothing was ever proven. More importantly, the guild paid its share into the royal coffers. There was an unspoken alliance between the guild and the royal family; one did not touch the other.

"You're all criminals," said Llygad sullenly.

Ifanna rolled her shoulders, trying to work out some of the knotted muscles. "My dear prison guard, there are different types of criminals."

Llygad's lips curled back in disgust. "You thinkin' to lecture me about crime?"

"Well, I mean, I do have more experience."

"I'm a guard," he said.

"Precisely," she said.

Llygad glowered at her. It was probably unwise to taunt him, but there was no other entertainment; Ifanna had to take her joy where she could find it. "You're a ploughin' robber. Stop trying to pretty it up."

She leaned forward, so that her elbows rested on her knees. "I can spill a coin purse without spilling a single drop of blood. That takes skill. That takes artistry."

"Don't matter how pretty your crimes are," said Llygad. "You're still never going to see anything but the inside of a cell or a quarry—not as long as I'm still breathin'."

Llygad was lucky that Ifanna was not one of those criminals he'd so unfairly compared her to—because if she had been, that last statement might have seemed a challenge.

But for all of Ifanna's flaws, she had never been inclined toward violence. She could use it if she had to, but it was the way healers used herbs to induce vomiting—it was an ugly last resort. And Ifanna was nowhere near that desperate yet. Her cell was dry and solitary, and while the food wasn't good, it was edible.

"Enjoy my company that much?" she asked.

Llygad made an irritated sound, stepping forward as if to strike her.

A soft shuffle made him go still. A girl with mud-brown hair and a dirty tunic stood in the hallway. There was a tray in her hands and her head was tilted forward in deference. When Llygad's scowl fell on her, the girl dropped in a wobbly, nervous curtsy. "Pardon me, sir. I have the prisoner's evening meal." She scurried toward the cell, dropping the tray to the space between bars and floor. Ifanna eyed the fare. It looked to be a bowl of runny porridge, a crust of stale maslin bread, and a cup of watery red wine.

"Wait," said Llygad, and the girl froze with her fingers still around the tray. Llygad held Ifanna's eyes as he took the bread. "Good night, ladyship." He turned and sauntered down the hall.

"Pay him no mind," said Ifanna, nodding to the kitchen girl. "He's a right arse when he's tired but he's not that bad. You don't need to cower like—"

The girl looked up and Ifanna's words froze on her lips.

It was no kitchen girl kneeling an arm's length away.

Mer had grown leaner since the last time they had met; there was a hardness around her mouth, a mouth that once whispered quiet, sweet promises.

"You came all this way to visit me?" asked Ifanna. She kept her voice light, her mouth crooked into a smile. She was always smiling, no matter her mood. Smiling seemed to unnerve people, to make them think she had the upper hand. She would go to her death smiling, if only to spite whoever managed to slide in the knife.

Mer tilted her head so that some of her hair slid back, revealing the brand at the corner of her eye. It was a deliberate little gesture, a reminder of the scars that lay between them.

Ifanna swallowed but she did not stop smiling.

"I thought you might want a drink," said Mer, with all the warmth and reassurance of a rusty nail. She pushed the tray beneath the bars.

Ifanna's eyes fell upon the cup. "Poison?"

"It's dwale." Mer reached down, placing a finger into the wine. She placed a single drop on her tongue, her eyes on Ifanna all the while. "Hemlock, white poppy, and henbane."

"You could have simply said yes," said Ifanna.

"It won't kill you," said Mer, "but it should render you senseless for a good few hours. Long enough for me to call for the guards, to claim you choked on your food, and for you to be carried out with the corpses."

"*Should* render me senseless?" Ifanna rocked. "Is this an attempt on my life or a rescue?"

Mer did not smile, but the corners of her eyes quirked upward. "I suppose that depends on whether I managed the right dose."

Ifanna exhaled in a long, slow gust. "After you left, I kept expecting you to return."

She knew better than to tell Mer that after they'd parted ways, she spent months avoiding puddles and streams, that even taking a bath had felt like tempting fate. Mer had been spymaster-raised and guild-trained, and if she had wanted to kill Ifanna for her betrayal, she could have done it.

But she hadn't. And after half a year had passed, Ifanna realized—with a twinge of disappointment—that Mer wasn't coming back. Not for revenge and not for Ifanna.

"After I *left*?" Mer's words sharpened, twisted like a knife. She gripped the bars of the cell like she wanted to rend them apart. "I didn't *leave*. I was chased away by royal soldiers. The ones you set on me."

"And you escaped your pursuers," said Ifanna. "I knew you would."

"Did that thought soothe the sting of your betrayal?" said Mer.

Ifanna's smile became a little rueful. "A bit."

Perhaps it was an unwise truth to utter aloud, but Mer's anger seemed to falter. She dropped her gaze to the floor, fingers loosening around the bars.

And Ifanna waited for the inevitable question. For the question that Ifanna had been composing answers for ever since that last job. Ifanna had only ever broken one promise in her life—and even now, she felt that broken promise like shards of glass beneath her skin.

Why? Why did you betray me?

Ifanna saw the shape of the question on Mer's lips but she never uttered it.

So Ifanna did. "Why? Why did you return?"

"Not for you," said Mer. Her eyes flashed, catching the torchlight. While some people became ugly with fury, Mer's temper had always rendered her more beautiful in Ifanna's eyes. Her cheeks would flush, and her jaw became more pronounced. Or perhaps it was just that Ifanna had a fondness for all things lovely and perilous—and Mer had always been both. "I am here for him. For the man who carved himself into my skin, who made me into the sword that fell upon whole villages, for the one who still hunts me."

Ifanna looked at Mer and understood. "And to do so, you need a thief."

"I need a thief," agreed Mer. "And honestly, I'd rather have found someone else, but you're the best. Don't preen—you know it. If you agree to work for me—"

"*With* you," put in Ifanna.

"—then drink that wine," said Mer. "You'll fall asleep in that cell and awaken elsewhere. And then we'll steal a prince's fortune."

Mer had never been prone to boasting. While some in the guild would spin intricate tales out of an easy job, Mer had been content to sit in the back, to sip a warmed drink and listen. Which meant she spoke the truth.

A prince's fortune. Ifanna's heart quickened at the thought.

It was one thing for Ifanna to escape prison; her mothers expected her to. But to escape and return with a fortune...that would earn back the respect she'd lost on a cartful of stolen silver.

"I get half," said Ifanna.

Mer shook her head. "One-sixth."

A six-person crew. It couldn't be Mer leading it—Mer had been many things, but never a leader. She hadn't cared for the responsibility, nor did she have the patience needed to deal with others. And there was only one person who could command Mer.

"Your spymaster will agree to that deal?" Ifanna said.

Irritation flashed across Mer's face, but she didn't deny it. "He will, once he realizes there's no other choice."

So not only was Mer speaking to Ifanna of her own volition, she had done so without the spymaster's knowledge. Ifanna tucked that information away for later.

"So you want me to drink poison," said Ifanna, "trust my senseless body to a person who would happily dump me in a river, join a six-person crew run by a former spymaster, and steal from the very prince that rules this city?"

"Yes," said Mer. "And you will."

Ifanna snorted. "That so?"

Mer edged closer to the bars. Her brown eyes burned like caught tinder. "Because no one's ever managed it before."

The words were like a fishhook, bright and dangling, a *lure*. Ifanna knew that. She knew she could have turned away, but she had always been infatuated with possibility. She loved danger and risk, loved the fear-laced joy that came with every challenge. The way her mothers told it, Ifanna had been born with her fist in the pocket of a midwife, trying to reach for something that wasn't hers.

Ifanna was not just a thief.

She was the lady of thieves. It was her blood, her birthright.

Ifanna picked up the cup, raised it to Mer in a silent toast, and then drained the poison dry.

CHAPTER 11

HAVING WORKED FOR seven years as an ironfetch, Fane was practiced at carrying bodies. Although those bodies had always been *dead*.

The thief's breath was hot against his bare neck. He had her slung across his shoulders, his cloak drawn over her so it looked as though he were merely carrying a heavy pack. Mer had emerged from the prison with an empty cup and a grim, satisfied look. They'd only had to wait for an hour before the guards brought the body out, hefting it onto a cart. Likely the morning shift would take any corpses for burial or burning.

"So this is your thief," said Fane. "She snores."

Mer let out a soft breath. "Yes, that would be her." She had taken the lead and Fane was glad to let her. The crowds of people, the thrum of conversation, and the constant presence of iron made him uneasy. There were too many people he might bump into; he couldn't let his guard drop for a moment.

"Where are we taking her?" asked Fane. "Back to the house?"

"Not precisely," said Mer. "Come on, I know a place."

Of all the things Fane expected to happen in this criminal venture, having Mer toss a towel at him and say, "They won't let you in clothed," was not among them.

The bathhouse was all shadow and steam, and every breath was heavy with the scents of meadowsweet and rose. After Mer had knocked on a door and given a murmured word, they'd been led down stone steps, deep into the depths of a bathhouse. The air was warm and close. Ifanna had been laid out in a changing room; she'd begun to rouse as they approached the bathhouse. Mer had placed a bucket beside the young woman, told an attendant to keep an eye on the thief in case she was sick, and then strode into the adjacent changing room.

"Why are we here?" asked Fane.

Mer touched a mud-stained strand of her hair. "Ifanna smells like prison. I'm carrying half a sewer in my boots. And you don't smell like flowers, either. I don't think Emrick would let any of us into his home at the moment." She shrugged. "This bathhouse is not owned by the nobles nor the thieves' guild. It's neutral territory. It's also got a few well-armed enforcers at the doors, in case anyone tries to make trouble. I thought Ifanna's first true talk with us should be in a place where no one is armed."

Fane raised both brows. "Except for you."

Mer threw him a startled look that melted into a half smile. "You catch on quick."

"I try," he said. He turned and began unbuttoning his cloak. "Does she know?"

There came a huff of breath behind him, followed by a rustle of fabric. "Oh, yes. Ifanna knows all that I can do. The guild wouldn't have shielded me otherwise—I was too valuable. I could soften harsh tides, let smugglers approach the coast cloaked in mists, guide thieves through the sea caves without fear of drowning."

Fane pulled his shirt off, placing it into a woven basket. His boots and trousers were next. They would be laundered. Finally, he wrapped a towel around his waist. "And yet you said they betrayed you to the prince," he said.

"Yes," said Mer, her voice taut. "*She* did."

There was a tap on his bare shoulder and he turned. Mer stood behind him, her own towel wrapped around her torso. Her hair was bound up, save for a few strategically arranged tendrils that fell across her left eye and cheek. "Come along. There's a tub in the farthest corner I wish to claim before anyone else. No one will overhear us there."

"You've been here before," said Fane.

Mer nodded. "Ifanna's always had a fondness for this place. Or rather, the diod sinsir they serve. Come along."

The smooth stone was warm against Fane's bare feet. There were several tubs carved deep into the floor, likely fed by a hot spring. Golden candlelight struggled to illuminate through the billows of steam. It looked like a comfortable, warm cave—if a giant had polished it smooth, carved elegant pictures into the walls, and added a few bouquets of flowers.

Ifanna floated alone in a pool that looked like it might have held five or six people, provided they didn't mind brushing elbows. She sat with the water up to her chin, her eyes closed and face relaxed. "If I'd known this was where you were planning to take me, I'd have drunk the poison faster," she said.

Now that she was properly awake, Fane took her in. Ifanna was a little taller than Mer, with broad shoulders and a narrow face. Her hair was a chestnut brown and her skin lightly tanned. But it was her fingers that drew his attention—they skimmed the surface of the water like restless fish.

Fane kept his towel firmly in place as he sank beneath the water. Ifanna opened one eye, then winked at him before closing it again. She was utterly at ease, loose-limbed and content, not at all fearful that she was sitting in a tub of water with a diviner.

Mer sat rigidly. "Well," she said. "Aren't you going to say anything?"

Ifanna kept her eyes closed. "Just enjoying the water. You have no idea what it's like to be imprisoned in a place like that."

The water in the tub *rippled*.

"Actually," said Mer, baring her teeth, "I do."

The water grew noticeably colder and Fane's heartbeat quickened. He hadn't felt fear for many years—no, that was untrue. He had not feared for *himself* in many years. He feared for those around him, feared that he might harm them through accident or inattention.

In that moment, surrounded by bathwater and steam, he realized something. If he were to fight Mer, he wasn't sure he would win. She could freeze him in place and cut his throat. And she was just ruthless enough to do it.

Fane found himself smiling.

Because for the first time in many years, there was someone he could not kill. And that thought relaxed him far more than the bath.

"Make no mistake," said Mer, and her voice was very quiet. "You are here because I need you. I had few other choices." In the low light, her brand looked like a shadow inked upon her skin. A swirling knot—like an adornment rather than a punishment. "If you think what you endured in that prison was terrible, let me remind you that I know the smell of my own skin searing under hot metal." The water suddenly felt hotter. "And I will make this brand look like a mere bruise should you betray me a second time."

Ifanna sat up straighter, her fingers vanishing deeper into the water as she braced herself on the stone bench. "I never do the same job twice." Her smile was knife sharp and viper swift. "Tell me what you're going to steal."

And to Fane's surprise, Mer did. When she was finished, Ifanna tipped her head back and laughed.

"Let me see if I have this right," said Ifanna. "You're going to rob the prince. By finding a magical well. Across a heavily guarded shoal. And then he'll fight a legendary monstrous boar." She threw a skeptical look at Fane. "You think he can slay an immortal beast?"

Fane shrugged. "Things are only immortal until you kill them."

"Your hired muscle should have been a philosopher." Ifanna stretched, her shoulders cracking. "All right. When do you need this key?"

"As soon as possible," said Mer. "Look for the house on Spicer's Row. Periwinkles in the garden. No bodies, as of yet."

Fane looked down to hide his smile.

Ifanna merely cocked an eyebrow. "Well, that's reassuring." She rose from the tub, wrapping a clean towel around herself. "I'll be by in a day's time." With another wink, she walked away from the tub. Fane watched her go.

"You think she'll betray us?" he asked.

Mer shook her head. "I wouldn't have told her that much if I did."

"She betrayed you once already."

"Yes," said Mer. "Which is why she won't do it again. Ifanna is half in love with her own reputation—and the lure of this job is one she can't resist. She yearns to make a name for herself outside of her family."

"You're betting on her nature," said Fane.

"I'm betting on her ego," said Mer. A few strands of steam-dampened hair fell across her cheek. "I'll not trust her again, not with any part of myself. But with business...yes. That I know she'll not betray."

Fane looked down at the dark water; candlelight glittered across the surface. It seemed a dangerous bargain to trust this thief with the knowledge of their heist. But then again, he could not judge another's bargains.

CHAPTER 12

$\mathcal{M}$ER HAD BEEN with the thieves' guild for two years before Ifanna betrayed her.

It had been a simple job—the kind that made Ifanna turn up her nose and squint at her mothers as if they'd asked her to eat a live frog. "Taxes? You want me to go collecting taxes?"

The guild's tax was something Mer had come to understand over the years. It was a payment given to the guild by the wealthier traders and merchants of the city, and so long as they paid, their wagons and shipments were safe. And more than that, no other thieves would dare rob them. Should a rogue try, they would find the full force of the guild hunting them—and Mer had seen what happened to such people.

Ifanna's mothers were in one of the manor's sitting rooms. Aldyth had thick golden hair and eyes that seemed to miss nothing. Melangell was slender, with dark reddish hair and the same long-fingered hands as Ifanna. They were both in their mid-forties, beautiful and aloof as a winter's morning. And Mer had never managed to endear herself to either of them. But she was a useful tool, earning her weight in gold over the years. She had aided smugglers by boat, guided the guild's people through sewers and sea caves, and perhaps most importantly, she was Ifanna's second-in-command. The other thieves and pickpockets had learned to trust her, to accept her orders, to expect the diviner by their leader's side. It helped that she was kind to them, knew their names, and used her magic to warm drinks on cold nights.

In those days, she didn't hide her brand—not from the guild. The young thieves saw the scar as a badge of pride.

Yes, I belonged to the prince, Mer would say, *but he couldn't keep me.*

With the implication, of course, that Ifanna could.

It wasn't quite a lie; Mer simply prettied up the truths she liked. She *had* escaped the prince. She just never told them that she still had nightmares of cold fingers against her chin, of the smell of burning flesh and the blinding flash of agony when hot metal pressed to her cheek.

She had escaped. That was the only thing that mattered.

And she had found a place to belong. A person to whom she wanted to belong.

"Yes, dear," said Aldyth, pouring a cup of tea. Ifanna sat in one of the high-backed wooden chairs—as befitted her station. And Mer stood behind that chair, as befitted hers. "The cartwrights are late with this month's payment."

"Then send an enforcer," said Ifanna. "What am I supposed to do? Steal the coin?"

Melangell's long fingers curled around her own cup of tea. "No enforcers necessary. The cartwrights have always been prompt; likely, something has gone awry—a fire or an illness. You will go because the guild needs diplomacy, not swords. And if you are going to rule this guild someday, then they need to know your face. To associate you with leadership, not"—she flicked her fingers, as if brushing away a gnat—"petty crimes."

Ifanna bristled. "My crimes aren't petty."

"Then I suppose those rotten butcher scraps threw themselves into the eastern guard barracks," murmured Aldyth.

Mer kept her mouth still. That had been her idea. A bit of revenge after a few swigs of stolen wine. They'd thrown the entrails through a window from a nearby roof, laughing quietly to themselves as they escaped in a heavy fog. Ifanna had kissed her, fingers tangled up in Mer's hair, and she had felt the thief's smile.

"Go to the cartwrights," said Melangell. "Find out what has gone awry with their payment."

Ifanna picked up her tea, drank it in a gulp that made Aldyth wince, then rose from her chair. "All right."

She and Mer left the sitting room. Once the door had closed behind them, Ifanna slowed her step so that Mer walked beside her. In private, they stood on equal ground. Ifanna relied on her as much as Mer relied on Ifanna.

"Taxes," said Ifanna, her smile wrinkling at the corners. "That's what they have me doing. Tax collection."

"They're not entirely wrong about you needing to be seen," said Mer. "The guild knows you'll be their next leader, but those outside of it need to know, too. It's better to establish that authority bit by bit than try to seize it, should something happen to your mothers."

Ifanna snorted. "Now you sound like them." But even as she spoke, she reached down and wove their fingers together. "Come along. At least we'll have a nice morning walk."

The two of them wore hooded cloaks and kept to the shadowed alleys, but Ifanna stopped by a merchant's stall and bought a handful of fresh raspberries to be eaten along the way.

The cartwrights worked their craft on the southernmost edge of the city, where the buildings gave way to coastal fields. Mer stood by a wooden fence, as was her duty, while Ifanna walked inside the workshop. Carts were decent for smuggling and the thieves' guild had an arrangement with these builders: The cost of protection was lowered, so long as the cartwrights crafted secret compartments into the wagons sold to the guild. It was an old alliance and Mer had no doubt that the cartwrights had simply forgotten to send payment or something equally innocent.

But when Ifanna emerged from the workshop, Mer knew something was wrong.

Ifanna was always smiling—it was both armor and weapon, a sly dagger used to pry away her enemies' defenses and a mask to hide her fears. There were lines at the corners of Ifanna's mouth, carved from years of smirks and grins.

But as Ifanna stepped into the sunlight, there was no smile.

"What's wrong?" Mer asked.

Ifanna spoke slowly, gaze somewhere on the horizon. "There's... a shipment. Gone awry. I have to look into it." Every word came out slowly. Then she shook her arms, as if she were brushing away cobwebs. "I need to do this myself. Can you meet me in the courtyard behind the chapel? The one near Miller's Lane?"

Mer took her by the hand, squeezing lightly. "I'll come with you, if you want."

The faint ghost of a smile touched Ifanna's mouth. "I know. But not this time. You're right, that people outside the guild need to know my face. And they don't need to know yours."

She cupped one hand around the back of Mer's neck, fingers touching the small scar behind her ear. The touch sent a shiver of pleasure through Mer. The kiss was light and tasted like berries. "I'll see you after the job," said Ifanna. Her hand fell away and the last Mer saw of Ifanna was a flash of dark hair in the sunlight, vanishing beneath a hooded cloak.

Mer took her time walking to the chapel courtyard, meandering through familiar streets and sucking at the raspberry seeds stuck between her teeth.

The courtyard was a lovely one—pruned roses and hedges, kept carefully tended by mindful gardeners. There was a high wall and one entrance so she could keep an eye out for Ifanna's approach. Mer lingered on a stone bench, waiting for an hour, then two, until her nerves were sharp and tight. Perhaps something had gone awry. Ifanna could need her.

She rose from her seat and began to stride from the courtyard when the clang of metal armor froze her in place.

She knew that sound. She still cringed from it when the guards patrolled nearby streets. She had tried to steel herself against the memories, to turn them into a glorious tale of escape. And while she could lie to everyone else, she'd never managed that trick with herself.

Three soldiers stood in the courtyard's entrance.

There was no mistaking the heraldry that decorated their breastplates. It was the same knot of lines that adorned her cheek.

Mer shrank back, glad for her hooded cloak. She could pretend to be just another woman taking refuge in a chapel garden. She stepped back, head bowed, but then she heard the sound of a sword being unsheathed.

And that was when she knew.

A courtyard with one entrance and high walls. Three armed soldiers. One escape route blocked by swords. This was no coincidence, no mere chance encounter.

I'll see you after the job.

Mer had been the job.

"Let me see if I understand this," said Renfrew. "You vanish for nearly a whole day. And you tell me that you spent that time running from guards, breaking the heir to the thieves' guild out of prison, telling her our plan in its entirety, and then you return here with no key."

Mer sat comfortably on a cushioned chair, her legs tucked up beneath herself. Trefor had come running as soon as they'd returned, first throwing himself at Fane's legs and then greeting Mer with a few enthusiastic licks. He'd sprawled himself across her lap while she idly scratched at his ears. Renfrew stood at the center of the sitting room, his arms crossed, regarding Mer like a baker who'd brought him a burnt loaf of bread.

"That's not all I did," said Mer. "I also took a bath."

Renfrew's disapproval collapsed in on itself; he pressed a hand to his eyes, shoulders shaking with silent, rueful laughter. Mer's mouth twitched, warmth suffusing her at the sight of Renfrew's amusement. To the outside world, he was a polite and very dangerous man. But from a young age, she'd been able to make him laugh. Those rare moments had been the memories she clung to in times of hunger or fear—and it was nice to see she still had the touch.

"Well," he said, recovering himself. "I'm glad you accomplished that, at least." His face smoothed out. "Am I to presume this thief will be aiding us?"

"If anyone in the city can get us that key," Mer replied, "it's her. The guild used to keep a locksmith on retainer at all times when I worked with them." She frowned. "I'm surprised you're not angrier about this."

Renfrew let out a sigh. "It was my fault. I was the one who picked the fence. He must have recognized you, decided that it would be more profitable to sell you to the prince."

A chill ran through Mer. Her fingers stilled upon Trefor's head for a moment; he looked up at her as if to say, *Why did you stop?* She continued petting him and the corgi let out a happy sigh.

"If that is true," said Mer quietly, "then I shall have to remain indoors until we leave. If word has gotten out that I've returned—"

"The prince will scour the city," agreed Renfrew. "Yes, you're right, of course. When will your thief be contacting you?"

Mer considered. "Likely a day or two, at the most. I told her of the tides, when we'd have to leave."

"Was there anything you did not tell her?" asked Renfrew, with mild exasperation.

"I did not tell her why you and I embarked on this mission," she said. "She thinks we're all in it for the coin."

Renfrew nodded. "A wise choice. The guild, for all of its criminal endeavors, is still governed by a noble house. Were they to discover that I wished to destabilize the prince...I doubt even your friend would help us."

Mer looked down at Trefor, at her fingers tangled in the dog's clean fur. She watched the rise and fall of his back; he breathed deeply, contentment evident in his relaxed face. In times of strife, it was always the helpless who suffered more than anyone else. If they did succeed in destabilizing Prince Garanhir's rule, she did not know what would happen. Perhaps he would try to consolidate his power by bringing his armies away from the borderlands. Or maybe Gwynedd would invade.

Mer saw the paths of the future and felt a swell of exhaustion.

"Are you having doubts?" asked Renfrew, breaking into her thoughts.

Mer shook her head. "No. Just considering the cost of things. How much do you trust the others?"

The edges of Renfrew's mouth twitched. "I trust no one, my dear child."

She snorted. "You trust me, for all that you still tell me little." She adjusted her position on the chair, unfolding her legs so that she could rise at a moment's notice. "It's the reason I'm the only one of our crew you let wander the city without you."

"I raised you," he said. "And I did send Fane out, too."

"Yes," she replied. "But only because I could watch him."

"You don't trust him?"

"I trust that he will keep his word," said Mer. "I've got a pretty good sense for lies. He hasn't uttered one yet."

"That would require him to do more than grunt occasionally."

That was true; Fane hadn't spoken much with the others.

She shook her head. "And what about Emrick? Gryf? Where did you find them?"

"Emrick is a scholar, as he mentioned before," said Renfrew. "I found him in a gambling den, a blade to his throat."

"Your blade?" she asked.

"For once, no," Renfrew replied. "His gambling debts are far more severe than he would ever admit. His family won't aid him, not again. I paid his captors enough that they let him go—for now. This job and its wealth are his best hope to keep his head."

"And Gryf?" Mer stroked Trefor's ears. "Not a soldier, or so he said." Her mouth pursed. "Intelligence, then. Don't think I haven't noticed his accent. He's from Gwynedd." She spoke the words quietly, but with certainty. "You've made yourself a traitor twice over, if you've brought Gwynedd's spies into the city."

Renfrew started to pat her shoulder, then his fingers brushed at the strands of hair hanging near her left eye. He pushed them back behind her ear, exposing the brand. That skin was pale, kept hidden from the world. She was not used to others seeing it so readily.

"There is always a cost," he said. His thumb touched the brand lightly. She could only feel the pressure—she'd lost sensation where the hot iron had pressed against her skin.

Then his hand fell away and he stepped back, leaving Mer to her unsettled thoughts.

The rest of the day and night passed in uneasy quiet.

Mer could not leave Emrick's home, but she wasn't idle. After years of working with Renfrew, and then with the guild, she knew what mattered: her knives, first of all. Those she sharpened and cleaned, and tucked into their places at her belt, her wrists, and boots. Then there was a length of slender, sturdy rope, the sort that fishermen used to moor their boats. She made sure she had her lockpicking tools. And lastly, there was a small leather flask. It held fresh water untainted by metals or salt. In her hands, that water would be more a weapon than any knife.

She was not the only person making preparations. More than once, Mer nearly tripped over Emrick. He stalked from room to room, muttering about one tome or another, always with at least one book crammed under his arm. "Nerves getting to you?" she asked.

Emrick glared at her. "Not nerves," he said, voice taut. "Merely a respect for the endeavor to come."

Mer gave him a skeptical look. "Doubt anyone's ever started trembling out of respect before."

"I am not trembling." Emrick's arms pressed more tightly to his sides, as if he could force himself to stillness. "You have not studied magical wards as thoroughly as I have. What could be hidden in those caves—"

"Could probably kill us in horrible and rather inventive ways," Mer said. "Truly. You think to lecture a diviner on magic? You should try warning the dog—he might get a little more out of it."

Then she turned and walked away, leaving Emrick sputtering with anger.

It cheered her greatly.

As for Gryf, he sat in the kitchens and seemed content to taste whatever the cook was preparing. Mer felt his eyes on her whenever she passed by. She ignored him. If he was a spy from Gwynedd, then she would be a fool to return his flirtatious smiles.

The cook was bustling about, setting hot katt pies upon a table. Mer stole two when the cook's back was turned. She found Fane in his bedroom—or rather, he was sitting on the ledge of his window, long legs dangling out onto the roof. At the sound of her footsteps, he glanced over his shoulder. She half expected a grunt of acknowledgment—which was how he greeted everyone else in the house—but he said, "Does Renfrew want to see me?"

"No, not yet." Mer held out one of the small pies. "I thought you might be hungry."

Fane took the pie with a nod of thanks. "Will you stay?" he asked, to her surprise. "Or do you have work to do?"

"I can stay," she said.

Trefor, who had been napping in the corner, lifted his head and sniffed the air. There was a boot tucked firmly between the dog's forelegs. It didn't look like Fane's.

Mer sat down on the floor beside Trefor. She broke off an edge of her small pie and set it before him. The dog gobbled it down in two swallows.

They sat in companionable silence for a few minutes. The pie was lamb, flavored with mint and onions. Trefor watched her eat, a tendril of drool escaping his mouth. It pooled on the boot beneath him. Mer gave in and tossed him another piece of crust.

"Can I ask you something?" she said.

Fane brushed a few crumbs off his shirt, then pulled his legs inside, turning so that he faced her. The sun shone against his back, lighting up a few highlights in his dark hair. "Of course."

"Why do you talk to me?" she said. "You said perhaps two sentences to Ifanna, and that's more than you've uttered to Gryf or Emrick."

He hesitated. "I could tell you a reason, but you won't like it."

She frowned at him. "All right, now I *have* to know."

"I'm comfortable around you," he said simply.

Her frown deepened. "Why wouldn't I like that?"

Some unspoken emotion flitted through his eyes. "My magic—the one that forces me to kill—has rendered me unable to maintain close friendships. I'm aware of how easily I could hurt someone through inattention. I dare not even embrace most people, for fear of bumping against them too hard. But you—you would not hesitate to kill me, if you had to. I find that comforting."

She sputtered out an incredulous laugh. "You think I'd kill you if your magic went awry."

"I think," he said, "you're the only person in this city who could."

Of course. Of course, that was why Fane wanted her close. Because this was all Mer was—a weapon to be sharpened and used. The warmth she'd felt for Fane drained away and he must have seen the change in her expression because he leaned forward, concerned. "I said something wrong, didn't I?" he said. "I apologize—if I gave offense—"

"No," she said. "It's fine. Most people keep me around because of my magic. It makes sense you would, too."

A flicker of regret passed over his features. "Mer," he said, and his voice was as soft as when he spoke to Trefor. It made her want to snap at him, to lash out because no one had offered her that kind of gentleness since she was a child. "If all I wanted was an executioner, I could find that elsewhere. But you're the first person to accept me and all that I am since I left the mountains. I value that far more than your magic."

She swallowed, unsure of what to say. She could have answered that she liked his company, too. Fane was quiet and undemanding. There was too much cruelty in the world, but he never added to it. But to utter any of this felt like prying away some of the armor she'd built up around herself. "I like your dog," she said instead.

That startled him into a laugh. She found herself smiling in answer, but before he could reply, something sailed past Fane's head and landed on the floor.

Fane flinched, whirling around to face the open window. Mer glanced down at the object, heart pounding, half expecting to see a bolt from a crossbow. They'd been found—they must have been found. They would have to run, have to—

It was a pebble.

Just a pebble. Mer picked it up, weighed it in her hand. She stepped up to the window and peered through.

Standing in the small courtyard was Ifanna. She was tossing something from hand to hand—probably another rock.

"About time," she said. "Let me in, I'm starving."

Ifanna sat at the dining room table and devoured a plate of griddle cakes while Mer introduced her to everyone. Mer kept any mention of her and Ifanna's past relationship quiet; she merely introduced Ifanna as a former ally, the heir to the thieves' guild, and the procurer of a key that no one else could lay their hands on. Emrick fumed and glared. Renfrew watched and waited. Gryf took two of the cakes for himself, smiling like he was watching a show and enjoying it greatly. And Fane said nothing at all.

"This cannot stand," blustered Emrick. His spider-thin fingers waved through the air. "If we were allowed to bring in outside contractors, I could have—"

"Brought an army of scholars?" said Gryf. He sat comfortably beside Emrick, brushing crumbs from his fingers with a clean napkin. The beds of his fingernails were stained dark, Mer saw. As if by ink or dye.

Emrick sputtered, but before he could voice another complaint, Renfrew spoke for the first time.

"Where is the key?" he said.

Ifanna slouched in her chair, with all the insolence of a well-fed cat that had stolen its master's supper. "Not here. I'd not risk any of you cutting my throat, taking the key for yourself, and getting all the treasure."

Gryf opened his mouth, considered, then closed it again.

"What?" said Ifanna, eyes on the burly young man.

"I was going to say that we aren't murderers," said Gryf, "then I remembered that I could only speak for myself. And likely Emrick, although I cannot be sure he hasn't bludgeoned anyone with some rare tome in a fit of pique."

Emrick sniffed. "As though I would. Use a book, I mean. It'd be a waste of good parchment."

"Glad to see your priorities are well in order, friend," said Gryf.

"What bargain do you propose?" said Renfrew, ignoring them. His steady gaze never wavered from Ifanna. If she were a contented cat, then he had the sharp eyes of a circling hawk.

"An hour before you need to leave, send Mer to the Crooked Goat," said Ifanna. "I'll have the key, and we can venture down into the sewers."

"What makes you think we won't simply cut your throat down there?" asked Emrick. "Take the key, leave your body in the sewers?"

All eyes turned to him.

"What?" he said defensively. "I can't have been the only one thinking it."

Gryf let out a low laugh. "You're making me regret I never had more schooling. If all scholars are like you, I missed a grand time."

"Because," said Ifanna, "I'll have arranged a letter to be delivered to the guild. If I'm not back in two weeks' time, they'll have your names. I'll sketch your likenesses. The entire guild will know you killed their lady. And it will be as though you stomped on a wasp's nest. You will never know peace again."

Mer was a little impressed, despite herself. By coming here, Ifanna had ensured that she knew everyone's names and, more importantly, their faces. She could make the lives of everyone in the room uncomfortable, if not outright dangerous. Every kingdom had a guild of its own, and if this one decided to put a price on their heads…it might not matter if they destabilized Garanhir's rule. They could still be hunted across the isles.

Silence fell across the room. It had a weighted quality, smothering any flippant comments. Mer held her breath, waiting for Renfrew's answer.

It finally came. "One-sixth," said Renfrew. "I know the guild traditionally claims one-fourth of all crimes in the city, but it will be one-sixth. And you needn't accompany us. I will ensure the guild receives what it deserves."

Ifanna shook her head. "I'm coming with you."

"Because you have to prove yourself," said Mer, with a flash of irritation. "Regain your pride and dignity after being imprisoned. Doesn't matter that if something happens to you—if you get killed by some magical trap and your letter is found by your mothers and the rest of the guild—we'll all be hunted by them."

Ifanna gave her an indulgent look. "Then I suggest you do your best to keep me alive." She rose from her chair, brushing sugar from her trousers and scattering crumbs across the rug. Emrick made a soft sound of protest, but no one paid him any mind. "When you leave, send Mer for me. I'll have the key at hand." Her gaze passed over everyone at the table, lingering for a heartbeat longer on Mer. With one last nod to Renfrew, Ifanna strode from the room. Mer heard the servants as they opened and closed the front door.

Renfrew glanced at Mer. If there was disappointment in his face, he kept it well hidden. "The day after tomorrow," he said. "We leave in the early morning hours." He rose from his chair. "Mer, a moment, if you please."

Feeling a little like a scolded child, Mer followed Renfrew from the dining room.

"I know," said Mer, before he could speak. "It's not what you wanted. It's less treasure—but Ifanna will come through for us."

Renfrew's face was impassive. "If you trust her, then I expect she will. But you should talk her out of coming, if you still care for her," he said. Mer winced. Of course he would know about her and Ifanna's past, even if she never told him.

Renfrew said, "Take nothing you aren't willing to lose."

CHAPTER 13

FANE DID NOT sleep well in the city.

Caer Wyddno felt like a beehive—all swirling streets and constant, humming noise. There was the clatter of rolling carts, the snorts of horses, the baying of hounds, the talk of every passerby, and the distant rumble of ocean waves. And the *iron*. There was so much of it; the metal sang in every house, every street, on every person.

Fane lay in his bed, Trefor snoring softly by his hip. The dog's face twitched in dreams, and Fane found himself smiling, gently stroking Trefor's head. Fane closed his eyes, tried to center his breathing in his belly. Perhaps if he fooled his body into thinking he was resting, his mind would follow.

As he breathed, Fane heard something.

It came slowly, so slowly he didn't recognize it at first. A quiet whisper—like a child with a half-remembered song. Then the sensation sharpened into a quivering painful note, like a chapel bell struck at a wrong angle.

Iron.

Iron freshly wrought into armor and swords. And the song grew louder.

Fane bolted upright. His heart tore into a gallop and he found himself flinging his bedcovers aside, all but tossing them across Trefor. The corgi let out a startled little yip and scurried out from under the blankets, giving Fane a half-reproachful, half-concerned look.

Fane pressed a finger to his lips. He seized his boots and his pack and hastened from his bedroom.

He didn't have much time; he went to the nearest door and tried it. To his relief, it came open easily. Fane poked his head inside and said, without knowing to whom he spoke, "Get dressed—guards are coming."

There was a choked-off snore, then Emrick's voice. "What?"

"Guards," hissed Fane. "Get up now."

A moment of quiet. Then, "What?" Emrick sounded utterly bewildered.

Frustration tore hot through Fane's chest; there wasn't time for this. He strode to the next room, leaving Emrick to fend for himself.

The second door was locked. Fane grimaced and pounded hard on it. There came a soft sound—another note upon the air that only Fane could hear. Someone inside had drawn a blade.

"Yes?" came Mer's voice.

"Guards," said Fane. "They're approaching the house."

Like with Emrick, there was a moment of quiet. Then the door swung open, and Mer stood with her own pack in hand. She was dressed in all but her boots, and the only evidence she had been asleep was her messy hair. "How many?" she asked.

He felt a swell of gratitude that she hadn't doubted him. "At least twenty."

She let out a soft curse, yanking her boots on as she did so. He had to admire her reflexes—most people would have been sleep-muddled, but she reacted as if the attack had arrived at midday.

Another door opened and Renfrew stepped out. "What's wrong?"

"Guards," said Fane. "They're surrounding the house as we speak."

If he were surprised, Renfrew didn't show it. His cold blue eyes flickered toward the stairs. "Change of plans," he said to Mer. "We're leaving now."

Emrick stumbled out of his room, his face blurry with sleep. "How did this happen?" he said, sounding more offended than afraid.

Renfrew did not answer, but Fane saw his gaze settle on Mer's. The two exchanged a wordless glance that seemed to contain an entire conversation.

"If it was her...," said Renfrew.

"I'll slide the knife in myself," said Mer. "But I don't think Ifanna—"

Something crashed downstairs. Fane heard the creak of straining wood, then a snarl from outside. He closed his eyes for a moment, trying to reach out with his other-touched senses. "Battering ram," he murmured. "They're trying to break down the front door."

Emrick sputtered in protest. "That door is over a hundred years old—"

Renfrew ignored him, jerking his chin at Mer. "Go, dear child. We'll meet at the sewer gate."

Fane looked to Renfrew for orders. He said, "Stay with Mer. Keep her alive—we need her, if this venture is to succeed. Get the sewer key from the thief, even if she doesn't wish to give it up."

Fane snapped his fingers; Trefor had been idling into Emrick's room like a child toward a jar of sweets. The corgi looked up, his face all innocence. "Come," said Fane, and followed Mer downstairs.

The house was cast in shadow, the lanterns having been doused for the night. To Fane's surprise, Mer turned toward the front door. She knelt in the hallway, her fingers splayed on the wooden floor.

Swirls of frost spun out from where Mer knelt. The ice was beautiful, glowing like a winter's night. Mer rose, pulled a flask from her belt, and tossed a handful of water to the floor. Holding out her hand a second time, she gave a sharp jerk, like a weaver breaking a thread. Water snapped up from the puddle, freezing into sharp icicles angled at the door.

Whoever came in here would likely slip on the ice, then fall onto the sharp spikes. It was a brutal defense, one devised in a matter of moments.

Something slammed into the door. Mer turned to him. "We're leaving," she said quietly. She breathed hard through her nose. "Two escape routes. Always two."

There came the shatter of breaking glass from the dining room. Fane tensed.

A door opened to their left. Mer whirled, her fingers extended, but it was no soldier. The cook stood there, dressed in her nightclothes and holding a lit candle. "What's going on?" she asked. In the quiet, her voice sounded like a shout.

Fane opened his mouth to warn her, but he never got the chance.

He felt the arrow before he heard it. Iron-tipped. It sliced so close to his shoulder that he heard the whisper of air. A second arrow slammed into the wall behind him. The sharp thud of metal cutting into wood made his breath catch.

The iron of human blood was different from that of a weapon. It was softer, warmer, the song like the steady beat of a drum. He heard the rhythmic pulses—until the heartbeat went quiet.

Fane choked back a cry; he turned toward Mer, half expecting to see her on the floor. But she had her back pressed to the wall, gaze fixed on something behind him.

It was the cook. The first arrow had struck her through the throat.

He hadn't known her—he hadn't even asked her name. And now, seeing her bleeding out felt like a terrible kind of intimacy without that knowledge. He should have asked for her name; he should have shouted a warning. But there was nothing he could do now. He wondered if the cook had any family—and if so, who would tell them about her death.

Mer lowered herself to a crouch and darted down the hallway. Heart racing, Fane followed. Trefor bounded along beside them, his tail tucked hard up against his belly. Mer pressed her ear to the cellar door.

Fane shook his head. "No one down there," he murmured.

She looked at him sharply. "You're sure?"

"No moving iron," he said.

She nodded and eased the door open.

The cellar smelled as it had that first time—all damp wood and the musty tang of wine. Fane drew the door shut behind them, wishing he could lock it. They'd have to hope that none of the intruders would think to search the cellar yet.

With the door closed, there was no light. None at all. The darkness was all-consuming—the kind that seemed to close around a person, to fill their every breath.

He took the stairs one step at a time, moving as silently as he could. Mer was somewhere ahead of him, her breaths soft and quick. Trefor's nails clicked lightly against the wooden steps.

Overhead, a floorboard creaked and a bit of dust fell to the floor.

As Fane stepped down, he bumped into Mer. It was light—just a gentle thud of his shoulder against her back—but it set his heart to racing. He had spent far too many years avoiding physical contact, fearful of hurting another.

"Sorry." Her words were barely a breath. "Trying to remember where the door is."

He nodded, then realized she wouldn't see it. Instead, he closed his eyes.

He could hear the iron song of the nails in the wine barrels, in the hinges of the door, and in the rusted lock outside. The old iron sang of mountains, of breathtakingly cold streams, of fallen snows.

Before he could stop himself, Fane reached out. His fingers clumsily bumped into Mer's side, then skimmed until he found her arm. He traced downward, until he had hold of her sleeve. Just her sleeve—it wasn't her, so it shouldn't be dangerous. "Follow," he whispered.

He half expected her to protest that she could find the door herself. Perhaps it was the taut silence, the painful waiting, the knowledge that there were enemies above—whatever the reason, she did not pull away. He stepped forward, gently tugging on her sleeve to guide her alongside him. Every movement was half memory, half instinct. It was perhaps ten strides to the stairs leading out of the cellar, but it felt like a hundred.

As they walked, her thumb stroked across the soft skin of his inner wrist. He felt the contact run up his arm, like lightning cracking apart a struck tree. A shudder tore through him. It felt too good, a taste of something forbidden and not his to enjoy. Touch was one of those things he had denied himself.

His foot stubbed against the bottom stair and he dropped Mer's sleeve. The sound of his boots and his breath were loud in his ears. His fingers met the cellar door. He waited a few breaths, then he pushed.

The trapdoor came open quietly. Fane breathed in the scents of periwinkles and damp stone, distant horses and the ever-present tang of iron. City smells.

He hastened up and out of the cellar, his eyes roaming over the small courtyard. Mer followed silently, dropping into a crouch. Trefor whined softly behind them.

There was someone moving in the courtyard. Fane sensed the iron a mere moment before he saw the soldier. The figure was armored, a blade unsheathed in their hand. They were peering through a window.

Mer reached down and took Fane's arm. Pale moonlight gave her face an unearthly cast; she could have been one of the otherfolk, if not for her human eyes.

She tilted her head toward the armored figure—and Fane read the silent question.

He shook his own head. He would not attack, not unless there was no other choice.

Her mouth tightened, but she gave him a nod of understanding. Then she reached to the clasp at her throat, unbound her cloak, and crept toward the figure. She couldn't use her magic, Fane realized, because the soldier was clad in iron. But that didn't deter her.

She moved like a cat, keeping low to the ground. A predator stalking prey. Then, when she was two steps away, the guard heard her.

The figure whirled around—and Fane saw a beard and hard jaw. The man gaped at Mer, fumbling for his sword, but the young woman was faster.

Mer threw a jab into his throat, cutting off the cry before it could leave his lips.

She didn't move like the fighters Fane had observed in the rings. There was no grandiose posturing, no smirks or flourishes. Mer fought like she was taking something apart—piece by methodical piece. She dealt with the sword by grabbing the man's arm and slamming the back of his wrist into her knee. Then she seized his armor, dragging him forward, keeping him off balance, before sweeping a leg around the back of his ankle. He stumbled, crashing to the ground.

The man exhaled a startled grunt, but before he could shake her off, Mer fitted her arm around his neck and pulled tight. Fane counted his breaths—one, two, three—and then the man seemed to go limp. Mer held on another moment longer, then released him. The guard slumped to the ground.

It had taken all of half a minute.

And Fane appreciated for the first time that Mer had been raised not as a child, but as a weapon. As something to be sharpened and honed and then turned against the prince's enemies. She was a diviner trained to spy, to kill, to slip behind enemy lines.

She could have brought kingdoms to their knees.

Maybe she would yet.

"Is he alive?" Fane asked quietly.

"Likely," said Mer. "He'll awaken at any moment, though. We can't linger." She inhaled sharply, raised her hand. And then mist swirled around her fingers. Mer's lips were parted, her shoulders heaving as though she were running. This magic was not without cost.

Fog filled the spaces between her fingers. Mer closed her hand into a fist, her arm shaking with the strain, then she flung out her fingers like she was tossing something into the air.

A heavy, impenetrable mist flooded the night. It swept like a wave through the courtyard, across the houses, swirling into tree branches and between homes.

Cover, Fane realized. She had just created a thick fog for cover—to aid the others in escaping the house and to hide their own retreat.

And the three of them—the diviner, the ironfetch, and the corgi—all fled from the house that had been their only sanctuary in an enemy's city.

CHAPTER 14

MER'S KNUCKLES THROBBED with every heartbeat.

Her body was all instinct—weaving through the city like a mouse through old hollowed walls. There was a brothel three streets down, and even at this late hour, its lanterns were lit. Mer used the light to examine her hand; her skin was unbroken, but the deep ache meant she'd be bruised for several days. At least the guard hadn't been wearing a gorget—then she'd have broken her hand when she struck him.

And she was thinking of her hand because otherwise she'd be contemplating other things. Like the cook falling, an arrow through her throat, her eyes wide and unbelieving. She hadn't been involved in any of this, but her ignorance hadn't saved her. Her mere proximity to this job had gotten her killed.

Mer pinched her eyes shut for a few heartbeats. Sometimes it felt as though she were more storm than person, bringing chaos and pain everywhere she went. She knew Renfrew could take care of himself and the others, and for all of them to stay clumped together would mean certain capture. But part of her still twinged with guilt at having left him behind.

Do not apologize. That's the one thing I wish I could have taught you.

Mer lifted her head, checked to be sure her hair covered the brand, then glanced toward Fane. He knelt beside Trefor, looking over the dog's paws. Trefor was panting happily, as if their midnight escape were just a late-night jaunt for his pleasure.

"Are you all right?" said Fane, rising to his feet.

Mer rubbed her sore knuckles against her tunic. "I'll be fine. I've had worse."

"I know, but..." He exhaled. "I'm sorry."

"What are you sorry for?" said Mer, confused. "Unless you were the one who betrayed us, you couldn't have stopped that attack."

"Of course, I didn't," he said. Contrition seemed to weigh heavily on his shoulders. "But I couldn't help fight that guard for you. And I couldn't save the cook."

"I don't need you to fight for me," said Mer. "As for the cook... I couldn't save her, either." She swallowed, trying to push back the memory of blood spilled in a dark hallway.

"Where are we going?" asked Fane.

Mer considered her answer. She knew a few bolt-holes in the city, places she could vanish into like a rabbit darting down a warren. But disappearing wouldn't help anyone. They had to find Ifanna— and Mer knew the place where the thief would be waiting. "The Crooked Goat. It's an eating house in the tradesmen quarter. It's also commonly known to be a front for the guild. It's where Ifanna meant to meet me."

Fane frowned. "How does an eatery survive if everyone knows it is a front?"

"Because they make the best cakes in three cantrefs," she replied. "One time, a few overambitious guards decided to try and raid the place, but there were so many customers they couldn't get through the door."

Fane chuckled. "I suppose that's one way to stay in business." His expression sobered. "Do you think she betrayed us?"

And that was the question. Mer grimaced. "I don't know. Part of me thinks she's too enamored with her own legend, with being the best thief that ever lived—she wouldn't pass up the opportunity to do a job no one else could. But if she told another at the guild..." She shrugged. "Her mothers were never fond of me. They were going to sell me back to the prince before Ifanna took a liking to my magic. She stepped in, took me on as part of her crew. I agreed, because I didn't have anywhere else to go."

"Hiding the prince's diviner in his own city," said Fane. "That seems...risky, even for a guild of criminals."

"Ifanna likes risk," said Mer. "Sharp blades, dangerous people, unbeatable odds—those are as intoxicating as drink."

There came raucous laughter from the brothel. The door swung open and a man stepped out, readjusting his cloak. Mer sidestepped until she stood in Fane's shadow. Without hesitation, she took his arm and slipped it around her waist.

The man barely gave them a glance before striding down the

street. Mer watched him go, but she didn't pull away from Fane. Two lovers out for a stroll would draw less attention.

"Come on," she said. "We shouldn't remain too close to the house."

Mer led them unerringly through the streets. The market stalls were shuttered for the night, but one building was lit from within, candlelight spilling out through cracks in the walls. A wooden goat had been carved into the sign above the door. The sign was notably crooked.

Mer walked around to a side door, raising her hand to knock loudly.

Footsteps rang out, then an older woman opened the door. "Not open," she began to say.

"She's here, isn't she?" said Mer.

The woman brandished a wooden spoon like it was a knife. "Now, lass, I don't know who you're—"

"Ifanna," said Mer, and the name startled the cook. Mer pushed past her, stepping into the light and warmth of the kitchen. Fane gave the cook an apologetic smile before easing past her. Perhaps it was the sheer brazen nerve or that Fane towered over her, but the cook merely sighed, threw an irritated glance toward the ceiling, and went back to her work. A younger girl, mayhap twelve or thirteen, poured batter onto a hot griddle. The air was full of steam and the sweet scent of warmed sugar; Mer's stomach lurched to one side, as if it were trying to get at the hot cakes.

It had been several years since she set foot in the Crooked Goat, but she knew her way through the kitchen, past an empty front room, to a stairway. She took the steps two at a time, and it felt like walking into a memory: stolen moments in between jobs, the taste of sugared berries when Ifanna brought up cakes from the kitchen, the warm glow of satisfaction after smuggling a shipment of stolen artwork into the city, the golden flicker of candles as Ifanna bent over a map, her long fingers sweeping across the lines.

It had been in these rooms that Mer had reclaimed some old scraps of herself—her laugh, the joy that came with work, the feeling of belonging to something and someone.

And then she'd lost it all a second time.

Mer did not bother to knock. She merely pushed open the first door on her left. It opened into a small room with a cot and desk, an unlit candle set on the windowsill.

Sure enough, Ifanna was asleep in the cot. She looked smaller beneath the blankets, her fist curled beneath her cheek. Mer slid her pack from one shoulder and dropped it to the floor with a loud thump.

Ifanna jerked awake. She sat up, blankets falling away. "What's going on?"

"We're leaving," said Mer. "So I hope you have that key."

Ifanna blinked a few times. "Did I lose time? Or are you early?"

"Early," said Mer. "On account of the prince raiding our house."

The last remnants of sleep fell away from Ifanna's face. "What happened?"

"A company of guards," said Fane quietly. He lingered in the doorway.

If Mer hadn't known her so well, she wouldn't have seen the flash of alarm in Ifanna's eyes. The rest of her face was still as she absorbed the news.

"It wasn't me," said Ifanna, after a moment's silence. "I know—Mer, I know you've no reason to believe me because I've done it before, but I told no one. I haven't even returned to the guild, because that would invite questions."

Not everyone could lie well. There were certain indications—a gaze that would slant to the left, fumbling hands, words tripped over, even the word *honestly* was all too often used in untruths.

Ifanna was many things, but she had never been a liar. If someone asked what she was doing, she'd offer up a wink and say, *Illegal ventures*. To Mer's knowledge, Ifanna had only ever lied once.

I'll see you after the job.

And perhaps this was what made Mer the worst judge—she wasn't sure if she wanted to believe Ifanna or not. Regardless, Ifanna couldn't be left behind. Either she was an asset or a traitor—and if she was the former, they would need her; if she was the latter, they couldn't allow her to sell more information to the prince.

"You have the key?" said Mer.

Ifanna swung her bare legs over the side of the cot. She wore only a long shirt and there was an unfamiliar scar along her thigh. Mer glanced away from it before Ifanna could catch her looking. "I'm not the best thief in the city for nothing," said Ifanna. She nodded at the desk. "Second drawer, false back."

Mer retrieved the key while Ifanna pulled on her clothes. The false back sprung open when Mer pressed her fingers to the seam of old wood. Inside were a few folded papers, a scattering of gold coins, and a heavy iron key. It was unornamented and Mer did not need Fane's powers to know the iron matched that found in the sewer grates—it was the same dark gray, flecked with rust.

"How did you get it?" asked Mer.

"I have a man in the guards," said Ifanna, buttoning her shirt. "Paid him off. He took it from inside the castell."

Mer threw her a startled look.

"Not every job has to be stylish and elaborate," said Ifanna, a bit begrudgingly. "And I needed rest."

Mer slipped the key into her pocket, where it sat against her hip like a weight. Ifanna picked up her own pack, tucked her hair beneath a hood, and strode from the room. They descended the stairs, back toward the kitchens. Ifanna spoke a quiet word to one of the cooks, coins exchanged hands, and then Ifanna took a cloth bundle, steam rising from the knotted fabric. And then they were out of the Crooked Goat. Mer found herself gazing at the sign for a moment, her throat a little too tight.

This would likely be the last time she ever looked at that sign. If the job succeeded, she would flee Gwaelod and never return. And if the job failed—

She wouldn't think of that.

Ifanna unknotted the cloth, passing a small cake to Mer and one to Fane. "I doubt either of you ate before fleeing your house," she said.

It was a small kindness. A peace offering.

The cake tasted of currants and honey, crumbling apart between her fingers. Warmth—sweetness. Mer savored the taste. A person had to take what pleasures they could.

"Best to eat them before we walk through a sewer," she said to Fane, who was eyeing his own small cake.

Ifanna swallowed hers in three bites. "There's a guild-controlled sewer entrance on the next street over. We'll go in there."

"I think I've seen more of this city's sewers than the markets," remarked Fane.

"Come back with a full purse in a few weeks," said Ifanna. "I'll take you to the evening markets when the late summer harvests have been brought in. We've a festival that lasts three nights."

"Don't take her up on that," said Mer. "The last time I attended that festival, I could do little more than sip tepid water and nap in a quiet room for a full day."

"I *told* you not to drink the day-old cider," said Ifanna.

"A kind offer," said Fane. "But I believe I'll have had my fill of cities by the time we're through."

Ifanna screwed up her face, as if she could not imagine such a thing.

The entrance to the sewer was through a small grate. Handholds had been carved into the stone, and Ifanna went first. Fane stood over the entrance, eyes scanning the dark streets for observers. Mer glanced at Trefor. He cocked his head back and forth, as if listening. "What are you going to do with him?" asked Mer.

Fane knelt down.

"Come here," he said.

Trefor took a step back.

"Oh, stop being a coward," said Fane, pulling off his cloak and knotting it around his shoulders. It looked as though he had done this before. In a few moments, he had rigged up a makeshift wrap to keep Trefor on his back. Trefor whined but allowed himself to be bundled up. Mer found herself smiling at the dog, reaching out to ruffle his ears. Trefor licked her fingers.

"You go next," said Mer.

Fane's long legs looked a little awkward as he crouched and contorted himself to fit down inside the grate. Mer looked up, her gaze roaming over the city streets.

It was her home and not her home.

And now it was time to leave it.

Mer took a deep breath, then lowered herself into the waiting dark.

CHAPTER 15

WATER CHURNED BENEATH Caer Wyddno.

The sewers had begun as sea caves, tunnels carved out by centuries of tides. The city's builders had repurposed the caves, ensuring that Caer Wyddno would not suffer the diseases and filth that came with people dumping their muck in the streets. Instead, it went out with the waves. The sewers had been reinforced with stonework and magic, and they were tall enough for even Fane to stand comfortably.

The moment Mer's feet touched the water at the base of the sewer, she sensed the webwork of tunnels. They were all connected by water—like veins through a body. Mer could close her eyes and find her way by magic alone. The rest of the world fell away, leaving only the ebb and flow, the tickle of salt in her nose, and the weight of the nearby ocean. She sensed its power, its depthless strength.

Behind her, there came the sound of firesteel being struck. A hiss of flame, then Ifanna straightened. A small glass lantern swung from her fingertips, casting a merry glow across the tunnel. Several small, furry forms skittered away.

A growl emanated from Fane's back.

"Did you just growl?" said Ifanna.

Fane turned and Ifanna saw the dog strapped to his back. "I cannot believe he stands for that."

"He likes it," said Fane fondly. "Or at least, he does when we're walking uphill and his legs get tired. And I'd rather not have him chase rats or go into deep water."

Trefor raised his snout, sniffed the humid air, then gave a small sneeze.

The sewer curved downward, carrying water toward the ocean. Mer took careful steps, mindful of the slickness and the occasional rat. Ifanna's lamp bobbed behind her, casting a steady glow. Mer let herself fall into the old rhythms—her magic guiding her along the paths of water, avoiding those sewers that were blocked or collapsed. She moved soundlessly through the water, keeping her senses attuned to their surroundings. When a particularly large rat swam by, Mer swept out an arm and pushed Ifanna and Fane to the side of the tunnel.

The path to the western gate took about half an hour. The heavy iron grate would allow water and fish to pass through, but nothing larger.

For a moment, Mer saw only darkness—and her heart lurched. Renfrew was a capable fighter and she had aided him as best she could with the mist, but she couldn't be sure he and the others had escaped.

Then the wavering light from Ifanna's lantern fell across three figures.

Renfrew stood with one hand on the iron grate, fingers resting lightly against the lock. Emrick looked like a well-bred cat that had been dunked in a barrel. One of Gryf's hands was bandaged, but he seemed otherwise unharmed. He leaned against the sewer wall comfortably.

"Renfrew," said Mer, with no small amount of relief. "Glad to see you all looking so well."

Renfrew nodded at her. "Your fog helped."

"How did you manage?" she asked.

"We went out through the upstairs window, onto the roof," said Emrick. "Then we jumped onto another rooftop, then another, and finally landed in someone's rosebushes." True to his words, he did have several bleeding scratches.

Renfrew's icy gaze fell to Ifanna. "Was it her?"

"If it had been, do you think I'd still be alive?" said Ifanna. "If I had sold you out, I certainly wouldn't have gone to the aforementioned meeting place where Mer could find and kill me."

Renfrew blinked once. "I suppose that is reasonable."

"Of course it was her," said Emrick. "Who else—"

"It could have been anyone," said Mer. "One of us—or mayhap a chance encounter in the streets. Someone could have recognized myself or Renfrew and offered up that knowledge for a fistful of coins." She infused a bit of steel into her voice. "It does not matter, not now." She turned to Renfrew. "We weren't supposed to leave tonight. If we go now, we'll have less time to traverse the caves."

"We don't have any other choice," said Renfrew quietly. "Can you keep the tides at bay?"

Oceans could not truly be controlled; they were wild, unrestrained. When Mer matched her will against the tides, she always came away parched, nose bleeding and head ringing. It wasn't an experience she was eager to repeat, but she knew her duty. She pulled the heavy key out of her pocket and handed it to Renfrew. "I can try."

He weighed the key between two fingers, eyeing the piece of metal. Something crossed his face—a flicker of emotion she couldn't put a name to.

Mer held her breath as he fitted key to lock. If this key didn't work, all of their preparation would be for naught. They'd have to leave Caer Wyddno—or at least, she would. She didn't dare stay in the city, not with the prince's men hunting her.

The lock gave an audible click. Something thunked, and then Gryf heaved at the gate. It creaked, old rust flaking into the water as it came free. Fane stepped forward, and the two of them managed to open the gate just enough for a grown man to slip through.

The air smelled of muck and rust, but beneath it were notes of seaweed and brine.

"Emrick," said Renfrew. "You and Mer take the lead."

Emrick's face was wan in the lantern light. "But I—"

"Was hired to look for magical traps," said Renfrew evenly. "If any exist, you find them."

Emrick drew himself straight. He nodded, but Mer saw the slight shake of his fingers as he fumbled a second lantern out of his pack.

There was no true threshold to step over, but Mer still felt a slight shiver when she walked through the gate.

And they left the city behind.

The only sounds were those of the ocean and the scrape of boots over jagged rocks.

It took the better part of an hour for the carved sewer to give way to natural caves. The change was a gradual one, but Mer could see the places where someone had called to the stone, smoothed it into the tunnels—and then where they had given up. Whoever had hewn the roots of the city had only reached so far.

Tendrils of dead seaweed were slick against the floor and Mer took care to step over them. Once, she heard Emrick slip on one and utter a soft curse as his bare palm scraped against a rock.

There were small animals in some of the tide pools; Mer caught sight of a darting fish and something long and slender. She would have liked to explore, but there was no time.

Emrick followed closely behind her, placing his boots where she did. Mer tried to ignore his presence; she needed all of her attention on the caves. She was aware of every passing moment—they only had a few hours to make this crossing before the tides would sweep in and drown them all.

She sent small, searching pulses of magic through the water. She could feel the webwork of caves, sense the ebb and flow of the ocean pounding against the rocks overhead. There was a weight, a heaviness to the stone all around them, and while Mer had never been afraid underground, part of her yearned to be free of this place. The salt in the water hindered her magic and she had to work harder to find her way.

The first fork in the tunnel made her pause. She stood still, gazing at the two caverns. The left was a little smaller, narrowing dangerously. And the other seemed to edge upward, but it was wider. Emrick's lantern wavered as his gaze jerked from side to side. "Which way?" he said.

Mer closed her eyes and breathed in. The air had that heavy salt and brine smell, but now there was something a little sweet. Rot and decay. Likely dead fish—or perhaps an animal wandered into the caverns only to drown. Pushing aside that thought, she knelt and dragged her bare fingers through the cold water.

The water trickling through both tunnels was stagnant, waiting for the tides to return it to the sea. But there seemed more of it in the left tunnel, and she sensed the way it seemed to veer west.

"Left," she said, rising from her crouch.

Emrick made an uneasy sound. "Are you certain? It looks—"

She ignored him, striding into the left cavern. She had to turn to one side, angling her body to fit through the narrow space. She heard a huff as Emrick followed, and the others trailed behind. There was a pained grunt; it sounded as if someone had bumped their elbow or knee. "Got to put him down," said Fane, and Mer realized that he probably had to untie Trefor from his back. "Ifanna, can you...?"

"Got it," said Ifanna brightly, and there was a wobbling from her lantern. Mer would have liked to look, but her attention was needed elsewhere. She maintained a steady hold on her magic, using it to guide her feet. The ocean had carved these tunnels, and even while the tide was out, water still clung to every surface. There were tide pools, torn bits of kelp still plump with seawater, and droplets hugging the walls and stone overhead; even the very air was saturated with moisture.

An hour passed in near silence.

Mer's mouth became parched and the throb of a headache started at the base of her neck. She pulled out her flask and drank deeply. The cool fresh water was a balm against her dry, sticky tongue. Behind her, she could hear Trefor's panting and the others' footsteps. Emrick had a book in one hand and his lantern in the other, his gaze darting between the cave and his tome. "You see any traps?" she said quietly, so no one would hear.

One corner of Emrick's mouth pulled tight. "In the other places I've gone," he said, also keeping his tone low, "there was more evidence of the tylwyth teg. Runes carved into old tombs or mounds of earth that gave way to old paths. This place is...just a cave. I've seen no hints at traps. Perhaps they thought the princes of Gwaelod would protect the Well, keep that shoal guarded so that none would attempt to steal its treasures."

"Or perhaps," said Mer, as the lantern light illuminated a jagged edge of rocks, "these caves themselves are the trap. A labyrinth where anyone but a water diviner would be lost."

"A pleasant thought," said Emrick tightly. She had the distinct impression that he did not like to be reminded of the danger. He put his book away and stepped past her, his gaze set rigidly ahead.

Mer let out a dissatisfied sigh and pushed on. They walked for another half hour, pausing only for sips of water and for Mer to take stock of yet another fork in the tunnel. She took the right path, leading the small group into a wider cave. It had a small pool of water along one side, and Mer caught a glimpse of a few tiny fish darting back and forth. Loose rocks lay sprawled across the rest of the cavern. Emrick lifted his lantern, casting light across the uneven floor.

"What is that?" said Gryf, somewhere behind her. "Slate?"

"How should I know?" said Emrick irritably. "It's a cave. It's dank and wet and—" He tripped over something and fell to one hand. He pushed himself upright, then glared at Mer as if it were her fault he'd stumbled. She glared right back. His lantern hadn't gone out, but it had fallen to the rocks and tilted dangerously to one side, wax dribbling onto the glass. She reached down to pick it up.

It was as she bent over, her fingers on the wooden handle of the lantern, that she saw those shapes were not slate. They were not rocks at all.

What she had assumed to be a rock was dark wool—the edge of a cloak. It was sodden and bloated, soaked through by seawater. She touched it, pulling at the fabric. It came apart in her hands and beneath it—

The grim-toothed smile of a skull gleamed up at her.

She fell back, the lantern dropping from her hand. It cracked against the rock. Mer staggered and hit someone—Emrick, by the sound of his startled cry. Then someone was hauling her up, and Ifanna was stepping forward with her own lantern in hand.

"It's a body," said Gryf quietly.

"Well spotted," said Emrick. "And you thought it was slate."

Mer stepped away from whoever had hold of her. A glance and—it was Fane. He had pulled her upright. "Thanks," she whispered, and he nodded in reply.

Ifanna had lifted her lantern and the light fell across—

Mer would have called it a graveyard had all the corpses been buried. There were scattered bones, rotted clothing, and countless boots left to molder. Jewelry gleamed on bony wrists, hair waved gently in tide pools like kelp, and the scent of old bones wafted on a breeze. Mer pressed her sleeve against her nose, trying to ignore her stomach's desire to heave. They were just bodies. Old bodies, at that. It wasn't as if they could hurt anyone.

"I think," said Gryf, "those people tried to find the Well. The tides must have pushed their bones back into this cave."

"Fallen kings," murmured Ifanna, as she bent over one of the bodies. She brushed a golden bracelet with her thumb. "There must be at least a hundred of them." She picked up the bracelet.

"Put that down," said Mer irritably.

Ifanna looked up. "What? It's not like they're using it."

"We're not grave robbers."

"Is it grave robbing if there are no graves?" said Ifanna.

Renfrew stepped around her. "A philosophical question best pondered when we aren't on a rather tight schedule." He walked through the fallen bodies without a second glance.

Trefor trotted up to one of the skeletons, eyeing the bones with the same kind of interest Ifanna had given the gold. Fane snapped his fingers. "Don't even think about it."

The corgi looked crestfallen.

Mer took a shallow breath through her mouth. Gryf and Ifanna followed Renfrew, picking their way through the old bones.

Emrick reached down to retrieve his shattered lantern. He shook it and watched as the broken glass clinked to the rocks. "We only have two of these," he said, with a dour look toward Mer.

"You dropped it first," she said.

"Because I tripped, not because I lost my nerve." He shoved the broken lantern at her and she caught it on reflex. Emrick strode past her, jaw tight. Of course he would blame her. She knew his type—all puffed up and arrogant, like a lady's lapdog trying to bark down a wolf.

"You're bleeding," said Fane.

Mer set the lantern down. Sure enough, the broken glass had cut a thin line along her hand.

"You could sense that?" said Mer. There were times she forgot that he was spelled to sense iron—and she'd never thought he could sense something as small as a few drops of blood.

He nodded.

She sighed through her nose. "When this is all over, I'm going to shove Emrick in a deserted tunnel when no one's looking." She lifted her hand to get a better look at the small wound. As she did so, two droplets of blood slipped down her wrist.

The drops fell, and for a moment they hung in the air like tiny rubies. Then Mer watched as they hit the stone floor, plunking into a shallow puddle of water.

The moment Mer's blood hit the water, she sensed the change.

It was not a sound—not quite. There was a rumble, like the reverberation of a struck bell.

Magic. It was water magic.

And it wasn't hers.

"What is it?" said Fane. "Mer?"

She swallowed, holding up a hand for quiet.

Thud-thud, thud-thud.

The sound. It was rhythmic, a rolling gait that she would never have expected to hear underground.

Thud-thud, thud-thud.

"What is that?" said Emrick, his voice echoing from the cave walls.

Mer looked up at Fane, and the bottom of her stomach dropped out. His face had gone bone white.

Thud-thud, thud-thud, thud-thud. It was coming faster now—a rolling canter giving way to a gallop.

"Renfrew—" Mer began to call.

A creature burst from one of the pools of water.

It had the shape of a horse—one cobbled together of childhood tales and nightmares. Its edges were too sharp, its features too lean. Steam billowed from its nostrils and its eyes were empty.

It pawed the ground, and as it did so, Mer saw that its edges were shifting.

It was a creature not of flesh and bone, but of seawater and magic.

CHAPTER 16

FANE'S FIRST THOUGHT was that he should have known.

He had spent years in the presence of the otherfolk. He knew what drew their attention: the sound of human song, the cries of ravens, a child's laugh, the smell of ripe blackberries, and the rust-cold poison of iron. The folk were faster, stronger than most humans, and many of them were ageless. Their few weaknesses were carefully guarded—and the presence of iron was among the most dangerous.

It made sense that other magical creatures would sense it, too.

Standing in a cavern full of old bones, discarded clothing, rotted maps, and old tools, Fane realized that this was what must have killed them: the presence of iron. Only humans would carry it. And so, iron would be the perfect trigger for a trap meant to kill any mortal trespassers.

Mer breathed, "What is that?"

"Ceffyl Dŵr," he said, voice taut with fear.

The Ceffyl Dŵr were not as well-known as the afanc or hounds of the wild hunt. But there were still tales, mostly sung during the clapping games played by children. They would sit in a circle, striking one another's open palms with every chanted syllable.

Old farmer Ilar
Found a mare
White and winged
And oh so fair
No bridle she'd wear
She took to the air
Then she dragged him
Down to the depths
WHERE HE COULD NOT SWIM

The last words of the rhyme were always shouted, and whoever ended the rhyme started the next. Back then, Fane had never given much thought to that old farmer, that man who'd tried to tame a mare of the mists. One glance at those sharp hooves and Fane thought that anyone who tried to ride a Ceffyl Dŵr rather deserved to be drowned for their foolishness.

The steed was beautiful in that way that all deadly things were—the lantern light shone on the sharp, almost skeletal edges of its form. Those strange eyes had no pupils and were the color of clear water. Its mane and tail were formed of sea mist.

"Move!" Renfrew's voice rang out, sharp and commanding.

They ran. They could do little else—the bones of the fallen were proof enough that fighting was in vain.

The water horse charged them, breath snorting and teeth bared.

It had been a long time since Fane had been frightened of anything besides the power that resided within him. But this was a foe he could not do battle with. An immortal horse, ephemeral as mist and deadly as a storm, was not something he could pummel with his fists.

The cave was long and wide, but it narrowed perhaps fifty paces ahead. If they could get that far, perhaps Mer could use her magic to fend it off. Out here, in the wide expanse of the cavern, Fane knew they had little chance of survival.

Because this was the one thing he did know of horses: They rarely traveled alone.

"Faster!" The word burst from Fane. Renfrew was ahead, darting around the bones. Ifanna moved as nimbly as a doe through woods. Gryf and Emrick were somewhere behind Fane.

Thud-thud, thud-thud, thud-thud.

The sound of galloping hooves became louder, until it was all he could hear. Trefor sneezed as he ran, stumbling for a moment. Fane's heart lurched and he reached down to grab the dog, to carry him.

The pause cost him. Gryf and Emrick rushed by, heedless of Fane and Trefor, and then Fane felt cool mist against his skin. It stung, needle-sharp and cold, and he rolled to the left, dragging Trefor with him. A hoof slammed into the stone, cracking it.

Fane rolled again, pulling Trefor close to his chest. In the dark, he could barely see the water horse. But he felt the impact of its hooves upon the ground, trying to trample him.

His hand hit something hard and cold—and Fane realized that he'd stumbled into one of the fallen. The slickness of rotted cloth and old bones made him want to pull away, but he pushed the instinct back. Instead, he scrabbled about for something, anything.

His fingers found the sharp edge of a knife, and he grasped at it, throwing the blade with all of his strength at the Ceffyl Dŵr.

In the waning light of Ifanna's lantern, he saw the horse rearing up, muscles bunching. The knife flew right through it, as if Fane had tossed a pebble through fog.

There was the terrible scream of a wounded horse—and then the creature broke apart into mist. The water scattered upon the stones.

Cold iron. It broke apart the magic, poisoning the water horse's power.

"Fane!"

That was Mer's voice, only a short distance away. Fane pushed himself upright, Trefor still under one arm, and turned toward the others.

A flicker of movement caught his eye. Something moved behind the others—and he cried out a wordless warning.

Ifanna whirled, her lantern swinging in one hand. The candle-light fell across the form of another horse rising from the still water. There was a whisper of movement in the darkness, and Fane knew it had to be another water horse. And another, and another, and—

It was a herd of them—coming awake all at once. Perhaps it was one of their own being struck by iron that had summoned them. Or perhaps it was the scrape Fane felt running along one knee. He was bleeding.

"Iron!" he bellowed. "It can hurt them!"

Ifanna pulled a small crossbow out from under her cloak, took aim with her free hand, and fired a bolt through the eye of the nearest horse.

The creature screamed and shattered into water droplets.

Ifanna loaded another bolt and fired again. Fane reached Ifanna and Mer, his breath sawing hard in and out of his lungs.

Renfrew and Gryf had not waited; they were halfway to the end of the cavern, toward that narrow passage that might provide cover. Emrick was cursing, trailing after them. His own passage was hindered by the heavy pack swinging from one shoulder. "Leave it," snapped Mer. "It's slowing you down!"

"No," said Emrick, knuckles tight on the strap. "It's all of my books on the otherfolk—"

"Which aren't a great help unless you think you can fend them off by reading to them," said Mer.

Ifanna raised her crossbow a third time, snapping off another shot. This one hissed past Fane's temple, so close he felt it stir his hair. The horse that had been moving up behind him let out a terrible sound and broke apart.

Together, they sprinted for the far cavern wall. Fane was aware of every passing moment; it felt like they were moving through thick mud, every step too slow. Hoofbeats thundered all around them. Ifanna's mouth was tight and smiling as she fired bolt after bolt.

Mer let out a furious snarl. "I can't control them," she said, her voice wavering with panic. "I—they're beyond my power."

"Keep moving," said Fane. "Just—keep moving."

One of the horses appeared from the darkness, lunging for Mer.

A small knife appeared between her fingers and she flicked it hard. It arced through the air, sailing through the horse's throat.

Fane was looking at her—so he didn't see the horse coming up on his left.

There was a terrible, pained cry.

Emrick.

One of the horses seized his cloak with its teeth, yanking him off his feet. He fell backward, fingers fumbling at his cloak, trying to pull it off. His pack full of books fell across his legs and he kicked out, but he was tangled in the pack's strap.

Mer rushed toward him, her face stark white and hand extended. It was Ifanna who caught her around the middle, hauling her back toward the narrow exit of the cavern. "No," Ifanna snarled, loud enough that Fane heard her over the sound of the hooves and Emrick's panicked shouts. "I'm out of bolts."

Fane froze, torn between Emrick and the promise of safety. But before he could choose, the decision was made for him.

The horses descended on Emrick like carrion on a fresh carcass. Hooves slammed into unprotected flesh; teeth snapped; water splattered against the rocks.

And then those rocks turned crimson.

Fane heard the drumbeat of Emrick's heartbeat. And then he heard it stop.

Mer made a choked sound, but Ifanna was still heaving her away, and Fane followed after.

The end of the cavern was ten paces away—then five. Renfrew

and Gryf were waiting, and Renfrew gestured them past, his expression like granite. Ifanna and Mer hastened by, and then Fane. He heard the hooves, the *thud-thud* of a gallop, and he turned to see another wave of water horses charging them.

It was Gryf who stepped forward, holding something in his tight, gloved fist. He flung what looked to be a handful of silver dust at the nearest horses. But Fane sensed the iron the moment it was scattered into the air.

Iron filings. Gryf had brought tiny iron filings with him.

The horses broke apart into mist and fog, swirling into the air.

Trefor barked and Fane realized he was still clutching at the dog. He set Trefor down, and the corgi sprinted, tail firmly tucked between his legs, into the waiting dark. Fane knew how he felt; all he wanted was to be free of the cave. They set off at a quick pace, breaths churning the moist air, the only light from Ifanna's shaky lantern. Gryf took up the rear, and Fane saw him scattering more iron behind them, blocking off the entrance to the tunnel.

And none of the Ceffyl Dŵr followed them.

No one slowed their pace, nor spoke a word until perhaps a quarter of an hour had passed. The cavern twisted and turned, Mer taking the lead as she used her magic to find the right path. They crawled up a steep incline, Fane's bare fingers scrabbling at slick rock, and then around a wider passage half-filled with water.

"Stop for a moment," said Renfrew. His voice was hoarse. He moved to the far edge of the cavern, and Gryf went with him. The two spoke quietly together, but for once, Fane did not speculate on their words. He felt as though he'd left his curiosity back in that last cavern—with the bloodstained stones and sounds of pounding hooves. He leaned on his own knees, trying to draw himself together. He had seen much worse tragedies in his time; losing one scholar— and a rather unpleasant one, at that—should not have fazed him so. But he could not forget the wild fear in Emrick's eyes as he'd been dragged back.

No one deserved to die like that.

Ifanna leaned against the wall. Her damp hair clung to her forehead and her nose ran. She scrubbed a sleeve across her face. "Well," she said. "Is anyone else going to mention how utterly *useless* our arcane expert turned out to be?" Her words were deceptively light, but her hard gaze sat upon Renfrew. He turned away from his conversation with Gryf and his expression was frosty.

"I knew there would be something in these caverns," he said. "I expected traps, puzzles, mazes. I did not think monsters lived beneath the city."

"Only within it," murmured Gryf, as if to himself.

"Well, perhaps you should have hired someone who knew better than to carry half a library with him," said Ifanna.

"Can we not speak ill of the man who was just trampled alive?" said Mer sharply. She had taken refuge on the ground, her back to the cavern wall.

Ifanna scowled at her. "I thought you all knew what was down here."

"And I thought you knew the risks," said Mer. "This isn't a pleasure walk, Ifanna."

Deep-seated anger flickered through Ifanna's eyes. She was afraid, Fane realized. Ifanna's fear was the kind that manifested as fury, because it was something she could control.

"You were the one running toward those creatures," said Ifanna, her voice low and hard. "If I hadn't grabbed you—"

"Don't pretend that was for my benefit," said Mer with a bitter little laugh. "You were protecting your reputation. If I die, then who will find the Well? And if we can't find the Well, then there goes your giant pile of gold and treasures. You'll have to slink back to the guild empty-handed."

"You think I grabbed you because I want gold?" said Ifanna, incredulous.

"It's why you sold me out the first time, isn't it?" Mer spoke the words through a clenched jaw. "Lives mean little to you—I knew that. But to laugh at a man who just perished and to pretend that you need me for anything other than your own gain…don't, Ifanna. Just don't."

Ifanna's lips pulled back in a snarl. "I wasn't laughing at Emrick," she said. "He was a fool and an arse—which is why he never should have been brought on this job. It's a crew leader's responsibility to know who should be out in the field, and who shouldn't be." She nodded in Renfrew's direction. "He should've known that, if he's leading you all." She took a deep breath, but Fane heard a slight shake on the inhale. "And if you think I'm here merely for gold, then you never knew me at all." She strode away and Mer watched her go.

Fane didn't know how to offer comfort to her—so he kept his silence instead. Trefor whined softly and pawed at Fane's leg. He knelt beside the dog and petted him.

Mer blinked several times, and then said, "Is he hungry?" She sounded as though she needed something else to focus on, and Fane could understand that.

"Thirsty, I think," he said. "Mind cupping your hands?"

She nodded, leaning forward and forming both hands into a small bowl. He poured a little water into them and Trefor lapped it up greedily. Fane poured a little more. When the dog had finished, he began licking Mer's wrist and arm.

Mer gave him a wavering smile, patting Trefor's side. "Good boy," she murmured. She lifted her eyes to Fane. "How are you?"

"I feel as though I should be asking you that question," he said.

Her mouth pinched at the corners. "Ask me again in a few days. For now—I don't know."

"If there's anything I can do," he said, and let his offer end there.

She pushed herself to her feet, rubbing at her backside with a small grimace. Those rocks did look rather sharp. "Thank you," she said quietly. She took a breath, and he watched as she seemed to detach herself from the fear and grief—her shoulders squaring, her eyes distant. "But unless you can stop the tides, we should keep moving."

CHAPTER 17

THE OCEAN WAS coming in.

The lantern was beginning to wane and flicker, and Ifanna replaced the candle, striking another to life. She hung back, never quite meeting Mer's eyes. Not that Mer was trying to catch her gaze. Mer paused only to drain the last water from her flask. Trefor was beginning to weary, his tail drooping as he walked. Fane picked him up, putting the dog on his shoulder. Gryf was as calm as ever, his broad shoulders taking up too much space in the narrow cavern. And Renfrew was quiet and watchful.

They could not run. But they did move as quickly as possible.

The tunnel narrowed further, until Mer had to crawl. She moved on hands and knees, fingers seeking in the dark, hoping every moment that she wouldn't get stuck. Her heart pounded hard; she could not imagine a worse fate than being trapped, just waiting for the water to rise.

The tunnel began to wind upward, and Mer found herself half crawling, half walking up a steep incline. At least the rough stone provided natural handholds and she had yet to accidentally grab a dead fish or clump of seaweed. She was just beginning to relax, to think that their journey was almost over, when a surge of water hit her squarely in the face.

She sputtered, spat out the taste of salt, and blinked several times. The water was breath-stealingly cold. A shudder ran through her and she held on tighter, for fear of losing her balance. Someone behind her coughed raggedly—Gryf, by the sound of things.

"Mer?" That would be Renfrew. He didn't sound quite alarmed— but there was a question in his voice.

She closed her eyes, reaching out with her magic. The weight of the ocean pressed down on her, and it felt like standing in the shadow of a mountain—aware of how small and powerless she felt in comparison.

"Tide's starting to come in," she said. "We need to go faster."

She took her own advice, picking up the pace. She banged her knee against a rock and hissed, but she didn't slow down. From here, it would only get more dangerous. They had to make it to the island before the ocean reclaimed these underground caverns.

She remembered those bodies—those rotted clothes and discolored skulls, teeth broken. If they didn't find a way to the surface soon, she would be just another corpse—left to bloat and rot, and lie as a warning to those who came after. A thrill of defiance rose hot within her chest, burning away the ocean's chill. She was the last living water diviner, and she would *not* drown.

The tunnel widened, curving upward. The waves were coming faster now, flowing down the tunnel like a small river. With every wave, Mer braced herself for the icy slap and then pushed on. The third time a wave hit them, Ifanna's lantern went out.

They were plunged into darkness, and suddenly the cave felt too close. Mer forced herself to breathe. She did not need light to see by—she could sense her surroundings through the droplets of water. "Keep going up," she said to the others. "Follow my voice."

She was aware of every passing moment. Her mouth was dry, although whether it was from overuse of her powers or her own nerves, she did not know.

Something slick and slimy touched her cheek—seaweed, hopefully. She shook it off and climbed on.

She came to the edge of the steep tunnel, where it leveled out. She hauled herself up and over, breathing hard. There was sunlight ahead—the distant, wavering glow of dawn. Mussels were clumped around the walls of the cavern, and seaweed snagged on several protruding rocks.

They were so close. The waves were gathering strength, pushing against the land with ever-growing eagerness.

"Almost there," she shouted, but her voice was swallowed up by the roar of the surf.

She forced her legs through the churning water, fighting against the ocean as it sought to push her back into the cave. She wasn't sure where they would be emerging—probably the shore. She could only hope that she'd led them right, that they would come out on the island where the Well was hidden.

Mer's skin burned with the cold. Her fingers dragged through swirling sea-foam as another wave swelled into the tunnel. No matter how hard she pushed her legs, the end of the cavern grew no closer.

Salt stung her eyes, crusted into her hair. The world was being swallowed up by the spray of waves crashing against rocks.

Another swell slammed into her, far stronger than before. She slid back a few strides, and someone grabbed her by the arm. She never saw who it was that kept her upright.

The water was up to her hips. And the next wave rose up, driving the breath from her lungs. "Keep moving," she yelled.

The waves came even faster. The drag of water over land, the inevitable pull—she could feel it. Renfrew had chosen a spring tide because it had the greatest difference between the low and high waters. Which was only comforting during the low tide—now, the waves raged against the shore.

She grasped for the wall, tried to hold on while the wave surged up to her chest and neck. She rose to the tips of her feet, sucking in lungfuls of air.

It was becoming too much, even for her. They had mere moments before the force of the waves would push them all back under, down into the cavern's depths.

Gritting her teeth, Mer reached for her magic. With a snarl of contempt, she matched her will to that of the ocean.

It was a losing war—no ordinary human could stand against the ocean for long.

But she was not ordinary.

The waves stilled, retreating.

Her fingers closed around the rough edges of the wall and she pulled herself forward. Oceans were greedy, reluctant to give up their belongings; with the weight of the water in her clothes and boots, it was a struggle to lift herself up and out of the waves. She dragged herself over the rocks, scraping her forearms and knees, gasping greedily at the air. And then she was out of the cave, dragging her body onto the shore.

Ifanna came up next, bedraggled and spluttering as a half-drowned fox. Fane and Gryf pulled themselves free, and finally, Renfrew followed after. Trefor was bound up in Fane's cloak, his ears pressed low in discomfort.

They stood on a rocky shore, at the sharp edge of a cliff. With a soft groan, Mer turned and set her numb, sore fingers to the rocks. The sooner they climbed up, the sooner she could rest.

It took about ten more minutes to climb to dry land. It wasn't high, but the cliffs were treacherous and slick, with all of them exhausted. Finally, Mer sat on wind-worn yellow grasses. She dragged breath after breath into her chest, so tired that she could have simply curled up and drifted off. But instead, she forced herself to strip out of her sopping cloak and boots. She hung them over the branch of a gnarled, bent juniper. Then she sat with her back to the tree, glad for a few moments to rest.

Fane sat on the ground, Trefor panting beside him. Ifanna was wringing water from her hair while Gryf checked the contents of his pack. Renfrew alone stood on his feet, his sharp eyes sweeping their surroundings.

"Did we make it?" Ifanna said, when she could speak. "Is this the island? Because if we took the wrong tunnel and looped back around, I'm going to murder all of you. Except the dog."

Renfrew did not answer right away. He strode back toward the ledge, peering through the mists. "We're on the island," he said quietly. "I can see the shore from here." He turned to Mer. "Good work, dear child."

Mer considered replying, but the thought of forming words was far too daunting. She waggled her hand around, hoping it conveyed a nonchalant *It was nothing.*

CHAPTER 18

THE ISLAND HAD no name.

But it was quite beautiful.

The trees nearest the shore were all twisted sideways, curling around themselves like bent old crones. Amid the rocks, a few stonecrop wildflowers had managed to bloom. The grasses were yellowed, waiting for their next rainfall. The gulls were calling to one another, their wings stretched wide as they caught the morning breeze.

Mer idled beneath the foliage, enjoying the spicy scent of juniper. The ground was rocky and uneven, but succulent wildflowers had bloomed in small patches of sunlight. Trefor ambled up to Mer, sniffing at the flowers and then rolling in a patch of dried needles.

Ifanna leaned against a tree, pouring water from her boots. Fane had closed his eyes. Gryf was still rummaging through his pack. And Renfrew stood apart from the others.

Mer went to him. Despite all that had happened, he appeared

unruffled. His gaze moved across the trees, ever watchful and ever calm.

"Are you well?" he asked.

She nodded, unsure if that was a lie or not. She was shaky and cold, and a headache throbbed at the base of her neck. She would have new nightmares—of drowning in the ocean or being carried away by snarling, foaming horses.

"It will be worth it," he said.

She looked down at her hands; sunlight dappled across her bare forearms. The warmth of the morning was a comfort. "I hope so," she said. She took a breath, steadying herself. "I know I never thanked you."

He looked at her sharply. "Thanked me?"

"For getting me out of that prison wagon," she said. "For convincing me to come on this job." She gazed at the forest and its rugged beauty. Tiny birds flitted through tree branches, chirping at one another. "I spent so long running from Garanhir—I think I probably would have run until I perished from it. But now…after we get the treasure, I might have a chance at my own life." She gave a small shrug. "Thank you for that."

Renfrew remained silent. For a moment, Mer feared that she had been too free with her emotions. Renfrew had never been demonstrative. Perhaps she'd made him uncomfortable.

His mouth drew into a tight, even line. And while his eyes were always the blue of a frozen lake, now she thought she glimpsed a few cracks in that hardness. "Of all the shameful acts I have committed, you are the one I regret the most. And for that, dear child, I must apologize."

His words stunned her. Renfrew did not apologize.

"You mean taking me from my family?" she said.

He exhaled through his nose. "For all of it."

She had never thought to hear such sentiment from him. Renfrew had always told her that regrets were useless, that such thoughts only weakened a person. "It wasn't all bad," she said. "I mean—I could have done without being the prince's unwitting poisoner. And teaching me rock formations when I was ten? I forgot all of it by the next week."

That earned her the smallest of smiles, and she took pride in that. She'd always liked that she could make Renfrew smile.

"What shall you do?" she asked. "When this is all over?"

It was a question she'd never truly considered until this moment. Renfrew had always been Garanhir's spymaster—always been a fixture within Gwaelod. But with his missing index finger, his signet ring cut away and stolen treasures on his back, he would never be able to return.

"I have not given it much thought." His hand fell on her shoulder, squeezing lightly. Then he said, "Take a few minutes to rest. You'll have need of your strength." He turned and trudged away.

They could not make a fire to warm themselves. The smoke would be too visible, might alert distant watchers to the fact that people were on the island. And—although no one had said it aloud—there was the distant memory of Emrick uttering the words *chief of all boars.*

After all, there was still Ysgithyrwyn to think of.

Mer hoped that the boar was a myth. It *might* have been a

myth—propaganda was as much a weapon as any blade, and she could see Garanhir boasting of having an immortal boar guarding his treasures. It would be just like him to lie about it. And even if the boar was real, Renfrew *had* brought a magically gifted fighter with them.

Mer's eyes wandered toward Fane. He was shirtless, wringing his tunic out. His back bore as many scars as his hands. Unthinkingly, Mer came up to him. Her hand hovered over one long slash along his ribs, not quite touching. He seemed to sense the almost-touch, because he glanced over one shoulder. "Blade?" she said.

He nodded. "Thieves tried to rob me when I was sixteen. One of them had a knife."

"How many have you killed?" she asked, unable to help herself.

Fane turned toward her, his expression remote. "Less than you would suppose. More than I would have liked." He gave a little shrug. "Three, if you want to be precise about it."

There was a ragged mark beneath one collarbone. It looked as though someone had tried to slash at him with their fingernails. "That one," he said, "was a briar patch."

She blinked, then looked up and met his dark eyes. "You're jesting."

"I'm not," he said gravely. "A traveler had wandered into Annwvyn and perished—as most of them do. It had been a few years, and blackberries grew over the body. I had to cut them away to get him out—and I did not do the best of jobs." He touched the old scars. "Jabbed myself rather well there. But I got the body out of Annwvyn."

"Are there so many in search of magic?" she asked. "People just wander into Annwvyn and never return?"

He shrugged again. "Enough. People—desperate people, in particular—will risk much for…" He trailed off, searching for the right word.

"Power?" she said.

"Choices," he replied. "Those without choices are often willing to risk themselves for the chance of something better." He looked down at his own hands. "I know I did."

Sometimes Mer forgot that she was not the only person who'd had choices taken from her. Fane had lost his family, too, and not because he'd been bundled away by a spymaster.

"Well," she said. "At least we'll both have some choices when this is over."

He reached for his shirt, testing the dampness with his thumb against the shoulder seam. "You think so?"

"We'll have coin," she said. "It can buy choices—like travel and lodging and bribes. We can go anywhere we want."

"We?" he said.

The word hadn't sunk in, not until he repeated it back to her. A hot flush rose in her cheeks. "I mean—I'm leaving Gwaelod. I hadn't decided where to go. If you—you and Trefor, of course—you could always travel with me, for a time. If you wanted."

It was a nameless desire that she hadn't allowed herself to utter aloud. Ever since she'd left Ifanna and the guild, Mer had been on her own. She knew how to survive alone, how to slip in and out of villages unseen and stay unnoticed in the wilds. But in her time traveling with Fane, she thought she might have found someone she could trust. He was honest; he liked her sense of humor; they worked well as a partnership. He might not have trusted himself to fight, but she could fight well enough for both of them.

"If I wanted?" said Fane.

It was like trying to hold a conversation with an echo. She gave him a sour look. "Or maybe not. You said you enjoyed my company. And I like your dog. He's charming enough to make up for your manners."

"Forgive me," he said, the corners of his mouth quirking in a contrite smile. "I did not intend offense. It's just—it's a kind offer. And I do appreciate it. But when this is over..." He sighed. "I have somewhere I need to be."

Mer hid her disappointment behind a small, bright smile. "Ah, I see. I just thought—I mean, it would be pleasant to stop running for a while."

"You won't stop running," he said.

Her smile froze in place.

"You run," he said, "because it sates you. The way drink sates a drunk or cards soothe a gambler. You fear stillness."

She turned on him, face hard. "I'm not afraid of—"

"What was the longest you stayed in one place?" he asked. "After you left the guild, I mean."

Mer racked her memories. "The Scythe and Boot. I was there for three months."

He nodded. "As I thought."

She took another step toward him, hands clenched. "Don't talk about things you don't know."

"You fear people," he said. "Not because they might hurt you. But because they might discover your past and despise you for it."

"And why would I fear that?" she said.

His eyes were warm and dark. "Because you despise yourself."

It hurt, hearing those words. Far more than any physical blow. Mer's jaw clenched hard. There was part of her that yearned to snarl back, to deny all of it. But—but she couldn't. The truth was, there was part of her that itched to run. Even now, she wanted to turn and walk away from this conversation. To lose herself in movement and work and sleep.

She knew what it was to be haunted—not by ghosts, but by the feeling of wrongness. Perhaps it would have been easier if the spirits of those she'd gotten killed had followed her, plagued her. It would have been some kind of penance. Mer could never apologize in any way that truly mattered, could never make it right. So she'd learned to push the guilt down, to bury it deep. But like any seed given soil and time, self-loathing had grown within her, curled around her ribs like a vine, made itself part of her. She had no idea how to cut it free.

"And what of you?" she said angrily. "I see the way you cringe away from other people. You fear bumping into strangers on the street. Your only companion is a dog. Who are you to offer advice?"

"I never said I was better than you," he said. "Merely that I know what it's like. I chose this curse—I could have chosen anything, and I picked a power that no man should have. I am a murderer. I know what it is to hate yourself for past mistakes."

"Then what are people like us to do?" she said. She meant for it to sound mocking but the words came out brittle.

"I don't know," he said. "If I had answers, I wouldn't be here. I just wished for you to know that I understand." He began to turn away, to tend to Trefor. "And I do hope you'll find peace. But it won't be with me."

Mer let out a shaky breath. "You were wrong," she said. "Back at the house, when you said I wouldn't hesitate to kill you."

He went still. "You wouldn't kill me?"

"Oh, I would, if I had to," she said. "But I'd hesitate."

She turned and walked away. Ifanna was rummaging in her pack with one hand and using the other to deftly twist her hair up into a knot. She fixed it in place with a lockpick's wrench. Gryf was sitting with his back to a tree, his eyes on Mer. She gave him a forced nod of acknowledgment. Renfrew was checking his own supplies. He waved to Mer. "We should rest a little—perhaps an hour or two, at the most. But first, we need to refill the flasks," he said. "Is there fresh water nearby?"

Mer lowered herself to a crouch. This was among the first tricks she'd ever taught herself, back on the farm when she was a child. She pressed her fingers into the soil and, with a small effort of will, called her magic into the earth.

It felt like fumbling for a candle in an unlit room; everything was unknown and unseen—until it wasn't. Her magic alighted on a small trickle of moisture, even as her own tongue grew a little more parched.

There was a stream nearby. Mer could sense the fresh water moving over rock and grass.

"I'll get us some water," she said, taking Renfrew's empty flask.

She walked through the trees, along the uneven ground. Sunlight was burning away the morning mist. She pushed through the prickly branches of juniper trees bent low by the ocean winds.

Small birds chirped overhead, fluttering through the branches. One of the birds alighted on a nearby branch, cocking its head back and forth as it studied Mer. It looked a little like a finch with its sharp beak and rounded body. Light glinted from its golden feathers. "Hello, there," said Mer.

The finch startled at the sound of Mer's voice and darted away. A feather fluttered to the ground and Mer stooped to pick it up. The feather was oddly cold and heavy in her hand and she turned it over and over before she understood.

It was *gold*. The birds were spun from magic and gold.

Mer gazed up at the trees, her heart pounding. For the first time, she felt like a trespasser into lands that were not her own. This island had once belonged to the otherfolk; it still belonged to them, for all it was guarded by mortals. Mer slid the feather into her pocket and turned toward the sound of water.

The stream was small; it twined over a bed of rocks, burbling quietly. Mer knelt beside the water. One of her earliest lessons had been how to know when water was safe to drink. When she was young, she had drunk from the wrong stream and was sick for several days. After that, she'd learned the feel of still water—how it festered with dead things, and the way algae could grow, what minerals could make a person ill. It was how she'd sensed the poison in the wells that Garanhir had sabotaged.

She placed her fingers in the water and closed her eyes. The water was cool to the touch, but not unpleasantly so. Fresh water, welling up from one of the island's underground streams. Which, now that she considered it, seemed rather unlikely. They stood upon a small island; surely all of the water would have at least some traces of salt.

The water tingled against her fingers. She brought a finger to her lips and tasted a droplet. A flush of something hot ran through her, like she had swallowed a mouthful of strong drink. But it wasn't drink, it was merely water and—

A sound came from behind her. Mer whirled, a knife in hand.

Trefor stood behind her. The corgi had his head tilted, as if in question. He walked up to the stream and sniffed it. Mer slid the knife back into her belt and said, "You followed me?"

Trefor lapped at the stream. Then he let out such a sneeze that he fell onto his haunches. Perhaps he sensed it, too.

The water thrummed with quiet power. More of it than Mer had ever encountered.

"Let's see where this goes," she said, and rose to her feet.

CHAPTER 19

MER TRAILED ALONGSIDE the stream.

Perhaps she should have gone back for the others, but she did not. The presence of their stomping feet, quiet conversations, their eyes upon her—all of it would be intrusive. Mer could move more swiftly alone. Well, mostly alone. Trefor trotted alongside her, his tail waving back and forth. He smelled a little like seawater and his feet were still damp, but he was undemanding company and she found herself grateful for his presence. When this was all over, maybe she would go back for that abandoned dog at Hedd's farm.

The water twined through the forest, leading Mer farther from shore. The woods became thicker, the foliage overhead joining into a green canopy. The roar and crash of the ocean receded, giving way to birdsong and sun-warmed grasses. The small stream cascaded over rocks and curled beneath tree roots.

They journeyed in comfortable silence for perhaps a quarter of an hour. She ascended a steep hill, crossed a few large boulders, and then found herself walking into an idyllic grove. The trees parted, leaving enough sunlight for flowers to flourish—and at the center of the grove was a pool of water framed by mossy rocks. Towering over the stream was an old yew tree. The water flowed up and out of a spring—it was gloriously clear, its depths almost impossible to judge. Mer's heartbeat quickened, a strange sensation fluttering in her belly.

This place was magical. It was too pristine, too symmetrical to be anything but enchanted. Mer glanced around, every breath coming a little too fast. She was keenly aware of her solitude, that if any threat came, she would have to deal with it herself. But there was no sense of danger.

Mer held her hand over the water, not daring to touch it; even so, she felt the pulse of the magic. Her own magic rose in answer, like a hound hearing a call. This magic was alive, the water brimming with sheer, unadulterated power.

This was what they'd been searching for.

She had imagined a well built of stones, treasures tossed deep into the ground. Perhaps even a bucket and rope, like she'd seen on countless farms. But this wasn't a human well.

It was a *wellspring*.

A wellspring of magic.

She leaned over it, peering downward. The water was still and clear as glass, free of any sediment or living creatures. At the very center of the pool, she saw what lay beneath the water.

There was a sheathed sword, a mantle embroidered with golden thread, a heavy silver ring, several adder stones resting against one another, a small cooking pot, a heavy gold necklace, a drinking horn, and what looked to be a horse's bridle.

Mer's breath caught. She could sense the power emanating from the pool; it was like standing next to a bonfire, the warmth licking up her skin and threatening to burn her.

She circled the pool once, her footsteps quiet on the damp moss. There were no animal tracks, no broken undergrowth. If there was a boar, he had not been here in a long while. Trefor idly watched her, his tail thumping the ground. She knelt beside the water a second time, her own magic alive in her fingertips.

"The question is," she murmured, "if the magic from the Wellspring protects the treasures—or if the treasures are the source of the magic." She looked at the dog. "What do you think?"

Trefor sat up a little straighter. He tilted his head one way, then the other.

"Good talk," said Mer wryly. "Some otherfolk spy you turned out to be. I suppose if one of those treasures was a magical boot, you'd already have retrieved it for me."

Trefor sneezed, then began gnawing on an itchy spot on his foreleg.

"Come on," she said, giving him a nudge. "Let's go find someone who'll be more impressed with my find."

"This is it?" said Ifanna, utterly unimpressed. "*This* is the infamous Well? It's just a pool of water." She stood at the edge of the pond with a bemused smile. "I was expecting...more, somehow. Where's the boar? The otherfolk guard? The bones of trespassers?"

"Don't tell me you're disappointed," said Mer.

"Well, a little," said Ifanna. She squatted down, reaching for the water.

Renfrew seized her by the shoulder. "Ah, ah. I think it's best to leave that to Mer."

The five of them stood in the grove. Gryf halted some ways apart, seemingly uninterested in examining the water. Fane gazed into the pool while Trefor rolled in a patch of dry grass.

It was not precisely the triumphant end to their heist that Mer had been imagining.

Renfrew skirted the edge of the pond, like a carrion bird circling a fresh kill.

"There might be traps nearby," he murmured. "It was why I brought Emrick in the first place."

"And he was such a help," said Ifanna.

"No one expected the guardians in the caves," said Renfrew evenly. "Least of all you."

"I brought a crossbow," said Ifanna. "I'd say I prepared for trouble a little better."

"Both of you, hush for a moment," Mer said. "I'll examine the water. Let me see what I can find." She reached out, lightly skimming her fingertips across the surface of the pool.

The magic running through the water held more power than Mer could ever dream of. Gritting her teeth, she forced a bit more of herself into the pool, sinking her hand to the wrist. That dizzying sense of magic swam up through her arm, and she caught her breath. But she didn't pull her hand free. She needed to understand what this magic was for, what it did. If this water protected those treasures, she needed to know how.

Tell me, she thought. *Show me.*

The magic flared, and it felt for a moment as if the blood in her veins were boiling—and then Mer lost herself in it.

She wasn't just Mer.

She was water. She was all of the water, both that caged within her skin and that without. She was the pool, the droplets clinging to the forest leaves, the mist in the air. She needed to be closer to it, to lose herself beneath the surface...

Someone ripped her from the water.

She could not be sure who—it was a blur of hands and human-made fabrics and she fought them, fingers clawing at the earth. She had to get back into that pool; she belonged to that magic and that magic belonged to her.

Her back slammed into the earth.

She was gasping, her gaze gone strangely gray at the edges. She blinked at sky, at the green webwork of branches and the face peering down at her. It was Ifanna's—drawn with concern and lip bleeding sluggishly. Mer must have accidentally struck her.

"Wha—?" Mer said, and her tongue felt a little clumsy. It took a few tries to form the words in her mouth. "What happened?"

"You tried to put your head beneath the water," said Ifanna tightly. "I think we just figured out the Well's protection. Anyone who touches the water tries to drown themselves."

"Then where are the bodies?" said Renfrew. "There should be bones, at the very least."

An uncomfortable silence fell. "Maybe that's part of the magic," said Ifanna. "Or—maybe something ate them." Her gaze landed on Trefor.

"And with that comforting thought, I would like to get this over with." Mer sat up. "I'll move the water aside and then someone go in and grab them." Her head swam as if she'd had too much drink. She pressed a hand to her eyes until the dizziness passed. She had to do this—they needed to get the treasures, take away this wellspring's power, and then flee before Garanhir knew what had occurred.

She rose to her feet, both hands extended toward the pool. The water lay still and clear, innocently pristine. Mer pressed her palms together, then pushed them apart. In the movement, she infused the water with her will, guiding it away from the treasures.

The water began to part, but then Mer felt the magic shift. The pool quivered, like an animal waking from a deep sleep. Something was rousing. It felt as though Mer had awoken something cold and very ancient.

She drew in a sharp breath, a warning on her lips, when the water shivered.

"Mer," said Renfrew sharply.

"That's not me," said Mer. She retreated a step. "Get back—"

But before they could escape, the droplets flew at them, an inescapable mist, surrounding Mer. Instinctively, she clapped a hand over her nose and mouth. Her foot snagged on a root and her knees crashed into the soft earth, one hand scored against a rock. She dragged herself forward, desperate to escape the mist, but it felt as though her every movement was slowed.

Like she was crawling through deep water.

And then—

She was sinking into it.

CHAPTER 20

MER DID NOT open her eyes.

She knew where she was, even without sight.

She had been in this nightmare a hundred times before—the smell of wet stone, the dampness of the air, the chill. Her arms chained above her head, her shoulders aching as if someone had poured coals into the joints. She could not recall the last time she'd tasted water. The guards had been instructed not to give her any, regardless of the iron chains. Mer kept her eyes squeezed shut, pretending that she was asleep. Perhaps she would go unnoticed. But her attempt at trickery failed.

Nightmares were nightmares even if one never opened their eyes.

A hand seized her chin. Her eyes sprang open of their own accord and Mer found herself gazing into the face of Prince Garanhir. With his dark hair and broad shoulders, he should have been handsome. But the sight of him made Mer's stomach shrivel up.

His minstrel-soft voice spoke. "Why are you here?"

She did not answer and his grip on her chin tightened painfully.

"Why are you here?" he said again. "Answer me."

She met his eyes. She didn't want to give him the satisfaction of seeing her fear, but her voice quavered when she spoke. "Because you're a murderer."

"No," said Garanhir. "You're here because you gave intelligence to the enemy." His thumbnail bit into the soft skin beneath her jaw. "That's treachery."

"I told villagers that their wells were poisoned," she said. "That's not treachery—that's mercy."

Darkness churned deep behind his eyes like a storm gathering offshore. "Those were enemy infantry—"

"They were farmers," said Mer, "and wood-carvers and children—" She could still see their bodies; she'd sensed the tainted water in their stomachs, the poisoned berries and rotted animal carcasses the soldiers had thrown into the village wells.

He gave her jaw a shake. It made her back teeth clack painfully together and she bit her tongue. Copper flooded her mouth.

"All you had to do," he said, "was find water. That's all I've ever asked of you. And I gave you a life, an education, a home. I could have asked for so much more. You know what other princes have asked of their diviners? I could have made you an assassin, sent you into my enemies' homes and forced you to boil them alive."

She kept her mouth shut, running her tongue along the inside of her teeth.

"Renfrew thought you would be a decent spy, but he's soft," said Garanhir, "where you're concerned." He exhaled through his nose. "You're a disappointment, Mererid. What do you expect happens to people who disappoint me?"

Mer spat in his face. She had been working up a good gob of it, saliva streaked with blood. Garanhir staggered back, wiping frantically at his cheek. Mer felt a warm stab of satisfaction.

"Kill me," she said. She bared her bloodied teeth at him. "I don't care."

When he looked at her, Garanhir was pale as an old corpse. There was a grim set to his mouth that made Mer's breathing hitch.

"No," he said softly. "You wouldn't." He straightened, walked from the cell. Mer watched him go.

Garanhir was only gone for a few minutes. And when he returned, he held a long poker. Its tip glowed orange, a small sun brought into the darkness. It smelled like hot iron, like burning metal, and something terribly like old meat.

"Hold her," he said.

A guard stepped forward, taking hold of Mer's face. She kicked at him, swung in her chains as she tried to push herself backward. He cursed and seized her hair, tilting her face up.

Garanhir stepped closer. "You are mine. Do you understand me? My diviner. I think it's time you were reminded of that." He raised the poker and she saw the shape of the brand.

A twisted knot—the same emblem on the prince's signet ring,

and on the ring that had been welded to Renfrew's finger, on the fingers of all Garanhir's advisers. It was a claim, a reminder of inescapable loyalties.

"No," said Mer, her voice high and desperate. A fear like she had never known beat at the inside of her ribs and she clawed at her chains, tried to wrench free of the guard's grip. The brand edged closer, toward her left eye, so bright that it hurt to look at. Mer drew in a sharp breath, a whimper on the last gasp, and she hated that sound, hated that Garanhir and that guard heard it, hated them both—

The brand pressed hard to the corner of her left eye, against her cheek, and a scream tore from her.

Mer squeezed her eyes shut, her whole body curling off the floor, trying to pull into a tight ball.

She summoned her magic, called every bit of moisture in the air—

It shouldn't have worked; when this was real, when it was true iron around her wrists and a brand against her cheek, it had not worked. But this time, she felt the magic answer her call.

—And everything splintered apart.

Mer rolled onto her side. She was shaking so hard it felt as though her bones would come apart. She coughed, her lungs aching and overfull. A gag—and she spat water onto the ground. Her fingers sank into cold, damp earth, through grass and twigs.

She was not in a dungeon.

She was in a grove. A yew tree cast dappled shadows across her skin and midmorning sunlight warmed her arms. Her lungs felt as though they'd caught fire; she coughed again, trying to drag up any remnants of the water. She could sense it now, the magic that wasn't hers infusing her every breath. She forced another cough, pressing her hand to her lips. The droplets that came away hummed against her skin and for a moment—

For a heartbeat, she saw the dungeon again.

Mer shook her hand hard, wiping it dry on her trousers. And then she was in the grove, her stomach roiling.

It was magic. Illusions twined with water. A compulsion to sleep, to drown in nightmares. And the only reason Mer had managed to wake herself was her own magic. This was the Well's true defense, why no one had ever managed to take those treasures.

The others were fallen into the grass. Ifanna had slumped onto her stomach, cheek pressed against the dirt while Renfrew was on his back. Gryf had fallen against a tree.

Someone staggered and hit the grass beside her. Mer looked up sharply to find Fane kneeling beside her. He looked ragged and damp, but no worse for wear. His magic, she realized. Somehow, it must have protected him. "What happened?"

"It's the water," she gasped. "It's illusions—old fears. I managed to get it out of me, but I need to wake the others."

"Can you?" asked Fane.

"I have to try," said Mer. She half crawled, half shuffled to Ifanna. Mer had saved a few people after drowning, but it was a shaky thing. Water in the lungs and throat had to be carefully removed or she could risk further damage. Mer placed a hand against Ifanna's nose and mouth. She closed her eyes, reached for that well of power within herself, and gently tugged.

Ifanna spasmed, her breaths choking on a cough. Mer kept at it, pulling the water and unraveling the magic.

The water droplets flew out of Ifanna's mouth and caught between Mer's fingers and—

She stood in a man's study.

She blinked hard, as if this vision were a bit of dust to be cleared from her eyes. This was not the dungeon of her own nightmares, not the place she'd woken from a hundred times.

This was Ifanna's nightmare.

But strangely, it didn't look like one. Sunlight streamed through an open window and the air smelled pleasantly of fresh-baked bread. A man sat behind the desk; he wore armor, but it was the ornamental kind. A commander rather than a foot soldier. A plate of bread and cheese sat before him. The man lounged in his chair with indolent ease, smiling at the young woman in front of him.

Ifanna stood before the desk. Her back was straight and the corners of her smile pinched tight. "—Give them to me," said Ifanna.

The commander gave her a wide grin. "Lady ap Madyn, I don't know what you speak of. Trading in flesh's illegal." He drew out the last word with lazy enjoyment.

"I know you have them," said Ifanna. "And we can pay you."

"Like I said," the man replied, "illegal."

A muscle twitched in Ifanna's throat. Mer could see her mind racing, her eyes roaming from side to side as the thief considered her options. "What if I didn't pay the guard?" she said. "What if I paid you?"

The commander chuckled. "Mayhap you could, if I cared more for coin." He leaned forward, palms spread out on the desk. "I'm not some hound for you to snap your fingers at, girl. Your guild's been a thorn in my side for years, which is why I don't give a damn what you offer me." He nodded at the door. "Get out."

"They're mine," snarled Ifanna. "My people. What would the guard want with them?"

The man wove his fingers together, resting them beneath his chin. "They're thieves and pickpockets. The city won't miss them. And we need more hands in the quarries. You've nothing that'll interest me, girl."

Ifanna's hands twitched toward the knife Mer knew she kept on her belt. The commander's eyes fell to her hand, and his own moved to his sword.

An eternity passed in a few moments. Both commander and thief were conjuring up imagined futures, weighing their chances. Mer drew in a sharp breath. Even if this was just a nightmare, she didn't want to see Ifanna harmed.

Ifanna raised her chin. "Not coin, then," she said. "Information."

The man flicked two fingers toward the door. "Like I said, I—"

"The prince's lost water diviner."

Mer swallowed hard.

The commander's hand went still. "What did you say?"

"The diviner," said Ifanna. "The one he's been hunting for years. If I told you where to find her, you could bring her in yourself. Earn a promotion and the prince's gratitude."

The commander rose, his chair squeaking across the floor. Eagerness churned with suspicion in his eyes. He seemed to be trying to tamp it down, but he didn't hide his emotions well. "You know where she is?"

"Yes," said Ifanna, in barely a whisper. "I do."

And then the strangest thing happened—the world went still. Mer exhaled and the sound was too loud in the sudden, ringing silence.

Ifanna glanced over her shoulder. "Well, this is a change. You're never in this dream."

Mer stepped closer, eyeing the commander. He was still as a carving, his face frozen in eternal greed. Her own emotions felt like a storm in her chest. "Is this real?"

"I don't think so," said Ifanna. "Not unless the Wellspring could send me back in time."

Mer gestured at the office. "This happened. This is where you told the soldiers where to find me."

"Yes," said Ifanna.

"This is why you sold me out," said Mer.

Ifanna sat down on the desk. She looked more wearied than Mer had ever seen her. "The guards seized one of the cartwright's shipments. It wasn't gold or silver—but people being brought into the city." She lifted her gaze to the wall, her eyes distant. "There were near thirty of them. The guards took them, claimed they had come into the kingdom to spy. It was a lie, of course. They needed prisoners to work jobs that no one else would. Quarries, hard labor. Among those seized was a man—a forger. He was the best, which is why we bribed him away from the southern cities. To lose him…

would have meant losing a great advantage over the other guilds. There was no time to appeal to my mothers for help. So I offered the commander the one thing I knew he could not refuse." Her chin dropped, and it looked as though she had suddenly aged two years in as many minutes.

"Me," said Mer. All of the anger drained out of her, replaced by her own exhaustion. "That's why you told the guard where I'd be."

"Yes," said Ifanna. A muscle twitched in her cheek. "I hoped you would escape. I knew you could kill them, if you had to. I'm sorry you had to run. I'm sorry you felt betrayed. But my mothers were right. If I am going to lead the guild, I have to be seen doing what is best for everyone...not just for one person. So I sold one life for thirty. You were the only thing valuable enough to trade."

"Why didn't you tell me?" said Mer.

"Because it didn't *matter*," said Ifanna, the words tumbling out in a rush. "I chose them over you. And I knew I'd have to do it again and again if I wanted to lead the guild." She met Mer's eyes. "I couldn't make that choice a second time. It broke my heart to do it once. So I let you run. And I told anyone in the guild if they ever sold knowledge of you to the prince, I'd drown them myself."

All those years, Mer had wondered what drove Ifanna to betray her. She had thought perhaps it had been Ifanna's mothers who'd coaxed her into it or mayhap the gold reward had been too tempting. But the truth was Ifanna had chosen the guild. She had chosen her life as a thief rather than the one she could have had with Mer.

It was a hard truth to hear, but Mer hadn't realized how much she needed to hear it.

Mer remembered the stolen kisses, the interlaced fingers, the feeling of belonging to something and someone. She'd walled away those yearnings with bitterness, and now that some of that bitterness was gone, all the loss came rushing back. There was so much tangled affection and sorrow between them, Mer knew it would probably be years before she managed to sort it all out. "If you had told me…"

"There was no time," said Ifanna. "And even if I had—would you truly have taken the chance of being recaptured in exchange for thirty strangers?"

Mer did not know. She touched Ifanna's cheek. Her thumb rested at the corner of the thief's mouth, over a small freckle. "You're wrong," she said quietly. "I wasn't the only thing valuable enough to trade." She exhaled softly. "You could have offered yourself."

Ifanna jerked as if Mer had burned her. Before Ifanna could reply, Mer pressed her fingers to Ifanna's mouth, sent a pulse of power into the thief's lungs, and pulled the magicked water free.

Mer jerked out of the dream. They were back in the grove again. Ifanna rolled onto her side, retching and sputtering. Coughs racked her whole body, but Mer couldn't linger to take care of her. There were two others still drowning. She rose and hastened to Gryf. The man was slumped against a tree, his arms slack at his sides. His cheeks were rough with stubble as she touched the corner of his mouth and nose. She had never been so close to him before and it felt both intimate and awkward to reach her power into his lungs and bring up the water. She hoped this time she could do so without seeing what he did. Perhaps if she drew her hand away at the last moment—

And then she was in a house.

It was small, with a dirt floor and mended curtains waving in an afternoon breeze. It reminded Mer of her childhood home: warm and loved, without the trappings of wealth. The table and chairs looked worn and well used and there was a rocking chair in the corner.

Gryf sat in that chair, a bundle of cloth in his arms. There was a tiny hand in his—a babe's hand. His head was bowed, lips moving silently as if in prayer.

A twinge of unease shivered through Mer. If touching his cheek felt too intimate, then this was far beyond what she was comfortable with. Seeing Ifanna's memories was one thing—they'd once been close—but seeing Gryf's was too much. She wanted to retreat, to leave this place, so she turned. But as she did so, she saw the bedroom. There was no door, merely a cloth curtain that had been pulled aside.

Her stomach tightened. There was a figure lying in the bed, woven linen placed over their face. A fly landed on the white cloth, wings flickering.

Mer swallowed thickly; her throat felt too dry. She glanced back at Gryf. His expression was carved out by grief—there was a terrible emptiness in his eyes. As if he were beyond tears, beyond weeping.

The babe in his arms wasn't moving.

Mer forced herself to breathe through her mouth. She had smelled death before, knew the sickly stench of decay. This was Gryf's nightmare, the worst of his memories. A tiny, well-loved home full of corpses.

"How did they die?" she asked gently. "Sickness?"

Gryf looked up at her. The chasm of his grief seemed to crack open; his voice was unsteady when he spoke. "They drank," he said, "from a poisoned well."

For a few moments, Mer felt as if she were the one drowning.

Fallen kings.

Gwynedd. Gryf was from *Gwynedd.* Mer had known from his accent but she hadn't realized. He must have lived in one of those villages in the borderlands, one of those forsaken villages that Mer still visited in her nightmares.

With a panicked yank of her magic, Mer pulled the water from his lungs.

It wasn't gentle. But it did the trick. Both of them came out of the nightmare gasping. Mer recoiled, pushing herself back on heels and hands, as if Gryf might bite her.

He'd never said. Nothing about a poisoned family. No wonder he was so willing to risk his life to steal from Prince Garanhir. Anything to hurt the prince that had ordered corpses and poisonous berries dropped into wells and weakened his enemies by killing those who couldn't fight back.

Did he know that Mer had been the one to find those wells? That she had been part of the force sent into Gwynedd? No, he couldn't know. Not unless he had pieced things together, and if he had, then why was he here? Renfrew wouldn't have brought someone like that along on purpose, would he?

There were too many questions and no time for answers. Mer staggered upright, stumbling away from Gryf and those achingly painful memories.

Mer dropped to Renfrew's side. One more. Just one more person and she could be done with this terrible task. They would find a way to take the treasures, to remove the magic that kept the walls of Gwaelod impenetrable, and leave wealthy. All of this would be worth it. All of it had to be.

She touched Renfrew's mouth and reached into his chest with her magic.

This time she was prepared for the nightmare. She blinked and—

Renfrew stood before a map.

They were in the prince's war room, she realized. She recognized that fine oaken table, the tapestries and the smell of the ocean mists. Renfrew stood alone, dressed in the simple finery of the royal spymaster. His index finger was intact, the ring with the twisted knot upon it. His head was bowed and shoulders set in a hard line. A goblet of water sat at the edge of the map.

"We can't," Renfrew said. "I can't."

A shadowed figure stepped closer to the table. The memory came into focus and Mer recognized the broad shoulders and sleek dark hair. Garanhir gazed at Renfrew with a benevolent smile—one that set Mer's teeth on edge. "I know it will require more spies," he said. "Gwydion has promised to lend us several of his diviners. You may take them into your service. And there was a sighting of your old apprentice in a village down south. Surely you could convince her to return, given the right incentives."

Renfrew shook his head. "It's not a matter of resources."

"Then what is it?" said Garanhir, with a spark of irritation.

"There are some treaties that are too costly to break," said Renfrew. He stepped closer to the prince. "Your father understood that. Your grandfather understood. It is why he made the bargain with the Otherking in the first place. If we begin this war, I fear it will be all of humanity that pays the price."

That spark brightened into a small flame. "I am not my father," snapped Garanhir. "Nor my grandfather. I shall make my own treaties and break them when I see fit. And Gwydion has a point. The isles belong to humanity now. Why shouldn't we take what is ours?"

"Because this is a war we cannot win," replied Renfrew. "Because my spies are trained to watch and fight other humans, not to wage war against magic and myth."

"Don't tell me what we can and cannot win." Garanhir's soft voice sharpened and Renfrew bowed his head in respect. The prince gave his spymaster a hard look. "You will put together a plan and have it on my desk within the fortnight. Or I'll find someone who will follow orders. Do you understand?"

A long silence followed those words. Renfrew kept his head bowed, eyes on the stone floor. "Yes, my prince."

Garanhir straightened, his gaze sweeping over the table one last time before he turned and strode from the room. Mer watched as the humility drained out of Renfrew's posture. The moment he was alone, the spymaster's jaw tensed and his hands curled into fists.

Mer stepped closer to the map, glancing over its familiar lines. It contained all the isles, all the cantrefs sketched out. Carved metal and stone pieces were scattered on its surface. The figurines were all of Gwaelod, its armies and forces.

And they all converged on Annwvyn.

Renfrew slammed his fist into the table, knocking his goblet over. Water rolled across the map, flooding it. The parchment soaked up the water, ink bleeding forth from the lines that made up the mortal lands. Renfrew went very still, his eyes on one of the fallen figures.

It was the prince of Gwaelod. The tiny iron figure had been upended. Renfrew picked it up, held it between thumb and fore-finger, his gaze darting between the soaked map and the small figure.

His fingers wrapped around it, squeezing the metal in his palm. He looked at Mer and the blue of his eyes had never seemed more cold.

"You know why we're here, do you not?" he said. It was the same measured tone he'd used when he taught her history or letters. He was patient as a cat waiting for the prey to come to him.

Mer looked down at the soggy map. She traced one of the bleed-ing lines—the impenetrable walls of Gwaelod. She shook her head.

"Look again, dear child," he said gently.

Mer looked down at the spilled water. She ran her fingers through it, and with that gesture, she opened herself up to the magic of the Wellspring. She allowed her consciousness to sink farther into the water of the Well, into the memories of the magic.

And she saw everything. She saw the way the water had welled up from its source, descending throughout the island, flowing into the sea. Mer divined the tendrils of magic, like the roots of a tree sunk deep beneath the earth. There was power, so much power that it made her dizzy trying to comprehend it. She saw the walls of Gwaelod, impenetrable and old, standing guard against the kingdom's enemies. She saw how the magic fed into those walls—but that was not the magic's only purpose.

The magic of the Wellspring whispered to the ocean waves, sang sweetly even through the din of salt and brine. The power was not a trap—it was a wall. It was holding back the very ocean, keeping it from the lowland country.

She saw it in a flash, and for one heartbeat, it was all within her grasp. Gwaelod suddenly seemed very small. It was a kingdom built upon another kingdom, a vulture feasting upon the bones of a picked-over carcass. The land did not belong to the mortals, it had merely been borrowed. All of that fertile lowland soil, that city carved from sea cliffs, they were small and fragile as children's toys, just waiting to be swept away at a moment's notice. The tylwyth teg had coaxed the ocean back, pinned the water away from the shore with the magic of the Wellspring.

Mer opened her eyes.

She glanced up at Renfrew, at her not-father. He looked as though he were waiting for her to understand a lesson.

And she did.

She knew why they had come here—and it wasn't for treasure.

With a gasp, she reached into Renfrew's lungs and pulled the magicked waters free. They ascended the nightmarish memories together, rising up into the grove.

When Mer opened her eyes, she knelt upon the grass. Sunlight warmed her bare forearms, and the misted water was drying from her hair.

A glance at the Wellspring and she saw that it looked as though nothing had touched it. The water had returned to the pool, waiting for the next person to try and take its treasures. A golden bird chirped from the branches of the yew tree and wind whispered through the grass. All was disarmingly peaceful—but Mer knew better than to trust it.

Gryf stood ten paces away, his gaze averted. Mer wanted to say something, to apologize or explain—but she couldn't. Not now.

"What—what was that?" Ifanna said. Trefor whined softly, nudging at her ankle. She patted him, her gaze fixed on the Wellspring. "Did it…?"

"Another defense," said Mer. Her voice rasped and she tried to wet her tongue against her lips. "Anyone who tries to get at the treasures with magical means will be drowned in terrible memories and magicked water."

"All right, then how are we to get at the treasures?" said Ifanna.

Mer gazed at the water. All of those little pieces, those puzzles scattered along this journey—they had finally begun to make sense. "We aren't," she said.

Ifanna looked at her sharply.

Mer said, "The magic—it's very deep, woven through the very land itself. It's—it's not just a Wellspring." She looked up, her eyes seeking the unseen coastline through the trees. "Cantre'r Gwaelod—it's lowland country. The Lowland Hundred." She swallowed, unable to stop a slight shake in her voice. "But it wasn't always ours. It used to belong to the sea before the otherfolk worked their spells."

"What?" said Ifanna.

"The magic of the Well," said Mer, leaning forward. She saw her reflection in the glass-clear water—her face was colorless. "It protects Gwaelod—that's why no one can invade the kingdom. But that's not the Well's only purpose." She breathed raggedly. "It's holding back the ocean. Without it, all of Gwaelod would be flooded."

A shocked silence stretched between them. Ifanna looked sharply at the Wellspring, her brows drawn together. Fane gazed at the water, frowning. Only Trefor took the news without concern; he sat on his haunches watching the golden birds overhead.

"Yes," said Renfrew. "Yes, it would."

Mer looked up. Renfrew had walked to the opposite side of the pool, away from the others. Beside him, Gryf was on his knees, carefully removing jar after jar from his pack.

"What is that?" said Ifanna.

Fane drew in a breath and Mer glanced up at him. His expression, always so carefully guarded, had sharpened with an alertness she'd never seen before. All his attention was on those jars.

"You're right," said Renfrew. "With its magicked walls and old protections, Gwaelod cannot be invaded—only destroyed from within." Ifanna began to rise, but Renfrew said, "Stay down please." His voice was light and pleasant as ever—which was why Mer didn't notice the crossbow in his hands until sunlight glinted from the iron bolt.

Renfrew met Mer's gaze. There was nothing at all to those eyes: no pity, no remorse, no emotion. "Please don't move," he said.

Gryf set another jar on the ground.

"That's blasting powder," said Ifanna, her voice hushed. "I've seen shipments of it. It's used in mines."

And abruptly, Mer remembered Gryf sitting at a long table, smiling at her and quietly insisting he wasn't a hired sword. Nor was he a spy, as she'd thought.

He was a miner. His entire pack was full of blasting powder.

Numbness crept from Mer's fingertips, up her arms, stealing through her chest. She could not feel any part of herself. And part of her was grateful for it, because it meant she did not have to feel the words that left her lips.

She remembered the map in Renfrew's memories, water spilling across all of Gwaelod.

"This isn't a heist," she said. "It's a suicide mission."

CHAPTER 21

MER HAD BEEN eight years old when she'd glimpsed Renfrew for the first time. He had stood in the doorway of her home, hood drawn up over his pale blond hair, speaking quietly to her da—but all the while, his cold blue eyes had been on Mer. In all the years that followed, Mer had thought she'd known him. She'd studied under him, learned languages and history, how to slip a key from someone's pocket or memorize a map in a few moments' time. She had made him laugh and he'd made her smile. She knew how he stood, how he kept his left hand behind his back most of the time—not only because the stance made him look like a soldier, but because he always kept a knife at his back. She had learned to imitate that posture. She knew his taste for smoked fish and fresh bread. She knew more about Renfrew than perhaps anyone else alive.

But now she realized, it had not been enough. For all of their time spent together, she had never truly known him.

Not until now.

He held the crossbow easily, the tip aimed downward and his finger relaxed near the trigger. "Dear child," he said. "Please, listen to me."

Numbness gave way to anger. Mer lunged to her feet. She might have stormed around the Wellspring if not for Ifanna's hand upon her arm. The thief was frozen in place, her eyes fixed on the point of the crossbow bolt.

"No," Mer snarled. "You—you cannot. You of all people—I trusted you. You told me—"

"That we would weaken Garanhir." Renfrew's eyes flashed with cold fury. "And we will. This is the only way."

"The only way?" A terrible, bitter laugh broke free of her. "You lied to me. You lied, just like he did. You and he are exactly alike. He used me to poison innocent people, and you used me to find this place." Another terrible thought occurred to her. "Those soldiers," Mer breathed. "The ones at the Scythe and Boot. They were yours, weren't they?"

His gaze was unwavering.

"It was no mere coincidence that I was captured on the night you came to meet me," she said. "You wanted me to think this was my only way out. That I *had* to come with you. Those—those dead water diviners. It wasn't Garanhir who slew them—was it?" She took an unsteady step back. "Did you tell the guards where to find us last night?" She threw a glance at Ifanna, who still held her arm. Ifanna's gaze was moving rapidly across Gryf and Renfrew—likely calculating the odds.

"You didn't want her here, did you?" said Mer. "That's why you let slip our location. You wanted us to be attacked, so that I'd think she betrayed us. Because you knew if she came, she would side with me."

"Damned right I would," Ifanna murmured under her breath.

"Dear child," said Renfrew, and his voice was soft. "What would you like me to tell you?"

"The truth," she said. "Just for once in your life, tell me the truth."

Renfrew gazed at her, unwavering. For several long moments, she was sure he would not answer. This would be yet another secret he kept to himself. Behind him, Gryf finished placing jars of black powder on the ground. Renfrew lifted his chin. "Garanhir is going to bring the isles to war. I have seen the plans. I know of them. He has been waging the border wars against Gwynedd not just for territory, but because he intends to march into Annwvyn itself."

"So it is true," Fane said.

"That's nonsense," Ifanna said, startled. "He can't—I mean, he wouldn't—"

"He's not alone," said Renfrew. "There is a sorcerer by the name of Gwydion. His brothers. There are those who have always wished for more magic, to push into the borders of the Otherworld. Garanhir yearns for more than Gwaelod—to make himself a king like the isles have not had in centuries." He took half a step forward. "Do you understand what that means? The lives that will be lost? It will make the border skirmishes look like a tavern brawl."

Mer took half a step back. It felt as though she could not draw enough breath into her lungs.

"I protested his plan," said Renfrew. "And when I told him it was folly, he threatened to imprison me."

"So you cut off the finger bearing his signet ring," said Mer incredulously. "And then you decided to kill him?"

"No," said Renfrew. "If it were merely about killing him, I could have done that myself. Fallen kings, I could've had *you* do it, if I wanted to keep my own hands clean."

Mer's jaw clenched. Part of her wanted to protest, but truthfully, she did not know if she could. If Renfrew had come to her, coaxed her into this with kind words and poisoned promises, she might have killed Garanhir for him.

Or she might have done it for herself.

"But there are others who share his vision," said Renfrew. "They dream of a world where the otherfolk's magic is bent to their will, where diviners can be made and not simply found. They desire Garanhir's kingdom and armies to aid their cause. We must destroy all that makes him powerful—or else risk humanity going to war with the otherfolk. Humanity would not survive such a war, dear child."

"Stop calling me that," snapped Mer. "It's as much a lie as anything you've ever said."

Of all the words she'd hurled at him, these were the only ones that seemed to hurt him. His lips pulled taut for a brief moment. "Is it?"

The question made her flinch.

"If you cared about me, you wouldn't have lied to me," she said. "You wouldn't have used me."

"This is the price to be paid," said Renfrew. "For order. For survival. And if that means we die, then so be it."

"It won't just be us," said Mer. "It will be Caer Wyddno. It will be every coastal village, every home near the water, every adult and child who can't get to high ground in time." She threw a desperate look toward Gryf. "And you agreed to this? All to destroy Garanhir's power?"

Gryf had always seemed friendly, his posture relaxed and words easy—the kind of person Mer might have shared a drink and a laugh with. She had never paid much mind to him, because everything else seemed more important. Gryf's smile drained away, his affable mask fractured. And beneath it was the face of a man who'd taken his grief and used it like tinder. Fury kindled behind his eyes.

"Not all," Gryf said, and his gaze was fixed on Mer. "I came to make sure *you* died, too."

Ice seemed to form in Mer's veins. She recalled all those times she'd felt Gryf's eyes on her. She'd mistaken it for flirtation, but it had been nothing of the sort.

Which one of you is the poisoner? He had asked the question with a lazy smile, reclining in his chair. But he'd never needed the answer.

He'd known.

Mer felt the weight of his anger and she tried not to recoil. She had always known that there were deaths after Garanhir's men poisoned those wells; she had seen some of the bodies afterward.

She'd never had to confront the family of one of the victims before.

"Renfrew needed someone who knew how to handle the powder,"

said Gryf. "Told me that if I came, I'd get to witness the death of the one who helped poison my family."

"She didn't know," said Ifanna, taking half a step forward. "Fallen kings. I saw how many times she awoke from nightmares. She never meant to hurt your family."

"So that absolves her?" said Gryf. "Feeling bad?" He rose from his crouch, the jars of black powder at his feet. He stepped back, eyes always on Mer, brushing his hands on his trousers. "No. No, it doesn't."

Mer's gaze darted between Gryf and Renfrew. Renfrew had arranged all of this—he'd traded Mer's death for Gryf's black powder; he'd used Mer's weaknesses to get her help in finding the Well; he'd hired Fane and Emrick; he'd framed Ifanna and, when that hadn't worked, allowed her to accompany them.

And he'd done so knowing all of them would die here.

Mer made no attempt to hide the bitterness in her voice. "This is why Renfrew never told us the way off the island," she said. "Because there was never to be one."

"I told you not to bring anyone you cared for," said Renfrew.

"As if that was a kindness," Mer cried. "You're no better than Garanhir—treating lives like pieces on a game board. I don't care if it's true—if Garanhir wants to wage war on the tylwyth teg or Gwynedd or the continent itself. You have no right to do this. Do you know how many would die if the ocean swept inland?"

"I have *every* right," said Renfrew, his anger blazing to life. "I am the *only* one who has that right. I gave my life to this country, I gave everything—"

Mer sank to her knees, shoved her fingers into the damp earth and called to her magic.

The soil beneath Renfrew's feet suddenly turned to mud. He began to sink into it, staggered to escape the sucking mire, and nearly stepped into the jars of black powder. Gryf made a wordless sound of alarm, and Renfrew stumbled away, finally catching his balance. His arm came up, the crossbow at the ready, but Ifanna was moving, too.

Ifanna had always had good aim, whether it was tossing pebbles at a window or skipping rocks along a river. She reached down, seized a small rock the size of a child's fist, and threw it. The rock cracked into Renfrew's wrist, sending the crossbow flying. A curse ripped from his lips and he turned to retrieve it with his uninjured hand. His foot hit the muddy ground and he slipped, falling to one side.

Ifanna darted around the pool. Nimble and quick, she dug a hand into the ground and threw a fistful of mud at Gryf's eyes. It spattered across his face and he dropped a jar of powder, fingers trying to scrape the dirt from his eye and mouth.

Mer turned her attention to those jars. They were the true danger—if she could swallow them up in mud, she could stop this. She called to the water in the soil, draining it from tree roots and plants. Nothing else mattered—she had to stop Renfrew.

The ground beneath the powder jars began to bubble like that of a swamp.

Renfrew stepped forward but Ifanna slammed her fist into the back of his knee, driving him to the ground. For all that she'd disdained fighting on jobs, she did have some experience. Her mothers had insisted on it. Mer had sparred with her a few times, mostly laughing and mischievously sneaking a few kisses. Ifanna had grinned her fox's smile and stolen Mer's coin from her pocket to buy them both sweet rolls.

Now, there was nothing playful in the set of Ifanna's mouth. She lunged for the fallen crossbow.

Renfrew seized her by the ankle and gave a terrible yank. Ifanna fell, and the sound of her body slamming into the forest floor made Mer wince. A knife flicked into Renfrew's fingers and he slashed downward at the back of Ifanna's leg, likely intending to slice across muscles and tendons, rendering her unable to walk.

Ifanna kicked out, more in panic than true skill, but her heel knocked into Renfrew's elbow, deflecting the knife. She scurried backward.

Mer wished to help, but her own attention was focused on the small swamp she'd been creating. The jars were half-sunk in the mire when Gryf recovered. He threw himself flat upon the soggy ground, using the breadth of his body to keep from sinking. He plucked several jars free, even as one slipped deep into the mud. He rolled away, saving most of the them.

Mer rose to her feet, releasing her hold on the water. She seized the small throwing knife at her belt, aiming it at Gryf's face. He ducked but the blade struck him across the ear. Blood spilled down one cheek, but he didn't seem to notice.

Having shoved the jars onto solid ground, he charged toward Mer. Gryf had not been trained to fight; she could see from the way he raised his fists and how he stood that all his fights had been in tavern brawls. But he also weighed nearly twice what she did—and he stood a good head taller.

And he was rather motivated.

He threw a punch at Mer's head. She darted beneath the blow, ducking under his arm and seizing it in the same moment. Using his weight against him, she wrenched him forward and drove a second knife at the back of his arm.

Gryf turned his fall into a roll, coming up a few strides away. Mer sucked in a sharp breath as his long leg lashed out, slamming into the side of her knee with bone-jarring force. She fell, landing hard on her right hand. The blade twisted from her fingers and she snarled, scrabbling for it in the damp grass.

Gryf tried to stomp on her hand. She yanked her fingers back, but she still felt the whisper of leather across the back of her knuckles. She found the knife and lashed out with more luck than aim. The knife sliced through his trousers and he hissed in pain and stepped back. The problem with knives was that they didn't have the reach of a sword. Mer kept the point of the blade aimed at him as she rose to her feet.

"I'm sorry," she said. "If it means anything at all, I'm sorry."

"Tell it to the dead," he said coldly. He lunged for her and she darted to the left—but her foot slipped.

Gryf slammed into her. It felt like being driven to the ground by a bull. Blows rained down upon her and Mer swung out with her knife.

He seized her wrist and drove her hand into the ground once, twice, and then her numb fingers let the weapon slip free. Her ribs ached and her head throbbed from using so much magic. She needed water and rest and all she wanted was to close her eyes and be away from all of this.

Gryf picked up the knife, his knee pressing hard against her chest. She felt like a mouse, trapped beneath a cat's paw, waiting for the final blow. Sunlight glittered on the knife and he drove the point down.

Ifanna came out of nowhere.

She seized his arm, yanking him back. His weight came off of Mer and she gasped, pain flaring in her ribs. She rolled onto her side, pulling her last knife from her belt. She turned toward Gryf and Ifanna, but Renfrew's voice rang out.

"Mer, wait."

She looked at him. It took everything in her, but she looked at him. At the man who'd both been and not been her father. At the man who'd raised her, sharpened her into a weapon and turned her against Garanhir.

The knife in her hand shook. Her fury burned hot, but he was still Renfrew. Still the man who'd taught her everything—and part of her shied away from the thought of fighting him.

"Mererid," said Renfrew, and his voice was soft. Pleading. It would have been better if he'd shouted, if he'd matched her anger with his own. "You know what Garanhir has done. You've seen it. He used you to poison countless innocents—and he'll do much worse if he's allowed to invade Annwvyn. If he joins forces with other diviners, if his kingdom grows, there will be no stopping him. It has to end here." He took a step toward her. "We are the makers of order. And there will be no order, no peace, no safety if we don't take Gwaelod now."

"You're not talking about taking Gwaelod," said Mer. "You're talking about drowning it." She flung her arm out, gesturing at the Wellspring. "You knew what this did. You came here knowing. This was never about taking magical treasures from Garanhir or making ourselves rich. You're going to kill more innocents than the prince ever did."

"There is always a cost," said Renfrew urgently, as if he needed her to understand. "I wish I could pay it all myself, but I can't. We have to—"

"No." Mer gave a hard shake of her head. "We don't have to do anything."

Renfrew blew out a breath, and for a moment, his face was heavy with sadness. "All right, then. If you will not help, I ask you to at least step away."

Mer opened her mouth to retort that she would do no such thing, but then there came a rustle of bushes behind her. Mer whirled and saw Ifanna.

The thief was pressed up against Gryf's broad chest; he had one arm wrapped around her stomach and the other held a knife against her neck. Her eyes were sparking with anger, but she dared not move. One flick of Gryf's wrist would open up her throat.

"No," said Mer, stepping forward.

Gryf's fingers tightened around the blade. "You took my family," he said quietly. "I'll take yours, if you move another step."

She believed him.

"Fane," said Renfrew, his voice only slightly winded. "Please retrieve the jars. Stack them behind me."

Fane.

Mer had utterly forgotten about him. He'd been silent and not involved himself in the fighting. She cast her gaze about until she saw him. Fane stood beneath the shadow of the yew tree, Trefor by his side. His expression was remote, untouched by the violence.

Mer threw him a desperate glance that she wasn't sure he saw. She didn't know how he would react—part of her thought that he couldn't hurt her, wouldn't hurt her, but he *had* sworn to Renfrew.

"Fane," she said softly. It was as close as she would ever come to pleading.

He didn't look at her.

There was no sound, none at all. It felt as though the small forest had taken a breath and held it. Mer knew they stood balanced on the edge of another fight; all that mattered was knowing which side Fane would take.

"Fane," said Renfrew again, more sharply. "You will do as I say. I hired you. You swore to my service. You said you were bound by your word."

Fane did not move toward Renfrew. But nor did he step toward Mer. Rather, he did something that no one expected.

He stepped into the Wellspring.

Mer's mouth fell open; she began to cry out a warning, but then she saw there was no need. The water did not pull him under.

Fane stood in the Wellspring like he belonged there.

"And I would be," said Fane, "if I'd sworn to you first."

The Ironfetch

THERE WAS A BOY.

He had once been the son of a locksmith—but now, he was something else. Something with bloodstained hands and senses attuned to iron. He worked for creatures who were long-lived and magical, who wore garments woven of forest moss and crowns of poplar leaves. He had wanted to kill seven men—so he had pledged the otherfolk seven years.

But now the thought of taking seven lives made his stomach clench. So he hid himself in the forest and sifted through fallen leaves to find scraps of iron. He made himself into the perfect fetch, because it was preferable to being a murderer.

But a person could only hide for so long.

Two of the otherfolk came to him. Both women, hair woven with wildflowers and lips stained with late summer berries. They smiled at him, and he bowed his head in respect.

"We have need of your services elsewhere," the first one said.

The fetch stood straighter. "Why do you need me?"

"Because you have the best chance," the second one replied. "Because your gifts will make you valuable to the kind of people seeking what must be found."

"Who are they?" asked the fetch.

"Thieves," said the first one.

"Murderers," said the second.

"So that is why you wish to send me," said the fetch, with no small amount of bitterness. "And what must be found?"

"A piece of iron," said the first one.

"Dark iron, stained with blood," said the other.

"Some weapons cannot be allowed to remain in mortal lands," said the first one. "They know naught of its power, but that ignorance will not protect us."

"If ignorance is no protection," said the fetch, "then tell me what this weapon is for."

The otherfolk exchanged a look.

"He should know," said the second one. "If only so he will take care."

"What is this weapon?" asked the fetch. "A sword? A knife?"

"Something far more dangerous," said the first.

"Life," both said as one.

"Life," said the fetch, surprised. "How is that a weapon?"

The first merely smiled. She held out a handkerchief woven of heavy, old wool. The fetch took it, unwrapped the cloth. Nestled within was a chip of dark iron. It was old, far older than anything the fetch had ever touched. He could feel the magic humming through it, and that startled him. Iron was not supposed to be magical; iron repelled magic. Which meant this weapon was not crafted by otherhands. It had come from elsewhere.

The first one closed the fetch's fingers around the iron. "There is a mortal who seeks the place this iron can be found. He will try to hire a mercenary called the Blaidd. You will know him because he will travel with one bearing magic. Take the Blaidd's place, accompany this man. Find the weapon forged from this iron and return it to us."

The fetch bowed his head in agreement.

He had little choice—he still owed the otherfolk half a year of service. So he packed a bag with his few belongings and turned toward the west.

And he left Annwvyn for mortal lands.

CHAPTER 22

GAZING AT FANE, Mer had three realizations in quick succession.

First, only she and Ifanna—and perhaps Emrick—had come on this journey expecting a heist.

Second, Fane had not killed the Blaidd to save his friend. Or perhaps he hadn't done it simply to save his friend. He must have known that Mer and Renfrew were looking to hire the mercenary and killed the man so that they'd need to hire someone else. Him.

And lastly, Mer remembered a conversation.

Why did you leave the otherfolk, if you enjoyed working for them so much?

They had no more need of me in the mountains.

Mer had always considered herself a decent judge of liars. But she had forgotten it was possible to lie without ever uttering an untruth.

Never once had Fane stated that he'd stopped working for the otherfolk.

"You swore to the tylwyth teg," said Mer, feeling oddly detached about it all.

Fane inclined his head in acknowledgment. "Did you think the folk were unaware of Garanhir's plans?" he said. "When it became apparent that his desire for power would not be slaked with mere human quarrels, they sent me."

Several emotions flickered through Renfrew's face—disbelief, understanding, then something far colder.

"Ah," he said quietly. "Well, then." He rolled his shoulders, angling himself so that he could keep both Mer and Fane in his sights. "The otherfolk shouldn't interfere. We both wish to see Garanhir's power destroyed."

"No," said Fane. "The folk care little for human power struggles. And they know a war is coming. Which is why they did not send a spy or a soldier. They sent an ironfetch." And as Mer watched, Fane reached down into the clean water. She expected him to pick up the sword or perhaps the bridle—but instead, he chose the small, dark cooking pot.

That made her blink.

Fane tied the cooking pot to his belt, then nodded in satisfaction. "A pot?" said Renfrew with an incredulous laugh. "You came all this way for a pot?"

"You came all this way to set off a few jars of powder," said Fane. "We all have our reasons."

Renfrew's gaze narrowed. "You're safe so long as you stand in that water—none of us can touch nor enter it. But you'll not remain there forever. So you have to decide—with whom shall you stand?"

Silence fell across the grove. Mer was keenly aware of her own breath, the painful rasp of it through her dry mouth. Ifanna was behind her, a knife at her throat. Explosives were nearby, just waiting to be set alight. And now Fane—

Fane stood at the center of the Wellspring, his gaze on Mer. He had never been easy to read, but she thought she glimpsed an apology in the set of his mouth. Her heart lurched; if he did side with Renfrew, this was all for nothing. Her fingers tightened around her small knife. She'd have to move quickly: take out Gryf before he could hurt Ifanna, then disable Renfrew. She could not fight Fane, but she could use her magic to hold him in place. That iron cooking pot hanging from his belt would hinder her powers, but she would still try. She had to try.

Her weight shifted as she prepared to step forward.

But before she could move, the water in the pool *shivered*. It was a small ripple, but it drew Mer's attention.

The water quivered a second time.

There came a sound—and strangely, it reminded Mer of her childhood. She remembered the noises in the animal pens, the sound of chickens and goats and the snorting breath of pigs rustling for food.

Mer looked toward the trees. And she saw the creature rising from the undergrowth.

At first glance, she mistook it for a boulder. It was large and brown, its back rounded. It must have been asleep—or perhaps enchanted not to wake unless it was needed. Perhaps it had been the spilled blood, the iron upon the grass. Or maybe it had been Fane pulling one of the treasures from the Well.

The boar had the look of a creature from another age. An age when villagers locked their doors at night and hoped that the monsters would not find them. It could have stood shoulder to shoulder with a workhorse. Muscles rippled beneath its fur, its ears were pricked, and those eyes—those eyes were a beautiful gold, bright and intelligent.

Ysgithyrwyn.

The chief of boars.

Gryf's arm fell slack to his side as he gazed at the creature. Ifanna darted out of his grip and ran to Mer's side. The act drew the boar's attention.

Such a large creature should have lumbered, but the boar moved faster than Mer's eyes could follow.

The boar lunged forward and sank one sharp tusk into Gryf's chest.

No one moved to help him. No one dared so much as draw a breath.

Gryf opened his mouth—and blood spilled across his chin, dribbling into his shirt. His face was blanched of all color, his eyes strangely glassy. The boar had killed him—Gryf was dead, even if his heart was still beating. It was only a matter of time.

There was a terrible power and grace in the boar's movement. It gave a jerk of its head, yanking its tusk free. Gryf fell limply to the ground.

Then Ysgithyrwyn opened its mouth and *bellowed*.

The sound shattered the stunned silence; Mer's heart tore into a frenzied gallop. It was the kind of roar that sent prey scattering, that made flocks of birds take to the air, that would have had hardened soldiers quaking.

The boar charged at Renfrew. Renfrew dove, rolling out of the boar's path and coming up with the crossbow in hand. He fired off a bolt, but it glanced off the boar's heaving shoulder.

Ifanna didn't even try to fight; she leapt and grabbed a tree branch, swinging her legs and pulling herself upward and out of the boar's charge. Mer recoiled, holding her knife even as she realized it would be as useful as a twig. A small knife would not even pierce its hide.

A hand landed upon Mer's shoulder. She looked over and saw Fane, his face tight with dismay, as he pulled her out of harm's way. Spatters of the Wellspring water still clung to him, and when they touched Mer's bare skin, it felt like being struck by tiny bolts of lightning. Power surged into her, making her muscles clench up. It wasn't her magic, but it was still magic—coaxing her power to the surface, riling it up the way a person might tease a hound.

Mer squeezed her eyes shut for a heartbeat. She sensed the water in the air, the soggy soil, and the beads of foam at the boar's mouth.

It was all water. She had to use it.

The boar rounded on Renfrew, snorting as it lowered its head and charged a second time.

Mer raised her hand, called to the water in the ground, and froze it beneath the boar's cloven hooves. Renfrew lunged to one side as the boar suddenly found itself veering out of control. The creature was so large that its weight worked against it. Ysgithyrwyn slammed into the trees with such force that one of them cracked.

Ifanna let out a wordless, startled noise as the tree she'd been clinging to gave a mighty lurch. She fell to the icy ground and tried to stand, but her feet went out from under her. She shifted onto hands and knees and began trying to scurry away. Ysgithyrwyn heaved itself upright, snorting billows of steam in its fury. Pulling free of the undergrowth, the boar turned upon Ifanna. Its golden eyes were molten with fury. It lunged forward, but Ifanna rolled, her arm lashing out. Something silver glinted in her hand, and Mer realized it was the fallen crossbow bolt. Ifanna opened up a small line of blood on the boar's belly.

One of the boar's hooves stomped down so close to Ifanna's leg that for a moment Mer thought the blow connected. Such a strike would have flayed open flesh and muscle, likely to the bone. Ifanna rolled again, this time dodging a tusk. In a moment, she'd be wounded—or dead, just like Emrick and Gryf.

Mer called to the water in the boar's eyes. But this time, she did not freeze it.

She *boiled* it.

Ysgithyrwyn roared. The boar's scream was inhuman, utterly monstrous and loud enough that the birds overhead all took to the air. The boar pawed at its face, trying to rid itself of the sudden agony.

"Do something!" Mer cried, glancing at Fane.

He stood beside her, his body poised as if to fight—or run. She couldn't tell which. Trefor was at his ankles, lips peeled back and body vibrating with a growl.

"I cannot," said Fane. "If I fight that thing, I'll die. And I swore to return to Annwvyn."

"Then what good are you?" Mer turned her attention back to the boar. Ifanna scrambled away, rounding the pool and rushing toward Mer. Her hair was tangled and face bloodless, but she looked unhurt. "We have to go now!"

"I am in full support of this plan," gasped Ifanna. She leaned on her knees for support, breaths coming hard. "How?"

The boar writhed and screamed, but Mer's hold on the magic was beginning to wane. Ysgithyrwyn snorted and rubbed his face on the grass, wiping away the burning moisture. Renfrew was nearest the creature; he had gone back for the jars of black powder, and they were bundled into his cloak. He raised a crossbow with his free hand and fired.

The bolt sank into the flesh of Ysgithyrwyn's snout. He roared again, thrashing from side to side, his swollen eyes on Renfrew.

And that was when Mer realized what she had to do.

It was an unforgivable thought.

Because it was what Renfrew would have done.

"Run," said Mer urgently. "Both of you—go east, now. Don't look back. I'll catch up in a moment."

Ifanna hesitated but Mer gave her a hard shove. "Go," she snapped. "Trust me."

Ifanna turned and sprinted out of the grove. Fane lingered a heartbeat longer, his gaze heavy on Mer's. As if he knew what she intended. Then he, too, was running with Trefor at his heels and a small cooking pot bouncing at his side.

Mer turned her attention back to the spymaster and the boar.

Ysgithyrwyn had three more crossbow bolts embedded in his flesh. Blood streamed down his face, but it was like trying to take him down with bee stings. It might irritate and hurt him, but the boar would survive every one of those wounds. They would only delay the inevitable. Renfrew had his back to a tree, the jars of black powder still heavy in his cloak, pulled up tight to his chest like he was cradling an infant. He fired another shot at Ysgithyrwyn, then his weight canted forward. He was preparing to move, probably to find a safe place to set off those explosives. Something metal glinted between his teeth, and she realized it was firesteel. All he had to do was set off a single spark, and the Well would be destroyed—and Gwaelod with it.

She couldn't let him do it.

She raised her arm, fingertips reaching out as if she might take his hand from afar. And she called to her magic.

Renfrew stumbled—half his body tried to move while his feet sank deep into the muddied earth. He crouched and dug his fingers into the mud, trying to free himself. When his fingers met ice, he went still. He was ankle-deep in frozen mud. Ysgithyrwyn stepped toward him, snorting. Renfrew was trapped, unable to run or defend himself.

Renfrew met Mer's eyes. And for a heartbeat, it felt like they were back in the Scythe and Boot.

Will you kill me? he had asked.

No.

But her answer had changed since that night.

Understanding dawned in Renfrew's eyes. And he smiled.

Mer's gaze blurred with tears; the last she saw of him was that smile.

She threw herself into a sprint, tearing through the undergrowth and away from the Wellspring. Branches whipped at the bare skin of her neck and face, but she ignored them and pushed herself harder. All that mattered was escape.

Grief throbbed up through her throat, catching in the hollow spaces between her teeth. She felt it in her mouth, in the arch of her cheekbones, in the curve of her brows. It hurt to leave him to this. But she did not have the luxury of choices.

She stumbled over fallen branches and through brambles, across another stream, and then suddenly there was a dog barking nearby, and arms were flung around her. Ifanna's voice was in Mer's ear saying, "You're alive, thank goodness."

Fane stood a few strides away, Trefor beside him and the cooking pot at his belt. His shoulders sagged with something that might have been relief.

Mer opened her mouth to reply.

But then the world ripped apart.

It was as if a giant had reached down and walloped her. Pressure and force slammed into Mer's back, knocking her from Ifanna's grasp and slamming her into the ground. Everything faded away for a few heartbeats—sight and sound, breath and time. Mer blinked once, found herself looking at a tangle of buckthorn. Tiny orange berries gleamed in the morning sunlight. The world was utterly silent but for a strange ringing in her ears.

She pushed herself up onto the palms of her hands. Her lip felt swollen, and when she licked at it, the tang of blood filled her mouth. She spat, then glanced around. Acrid smoke filled the air, a plume twining toward the sky.

Fane was on his feet, checking Trefor. The corgi was whining softly, his gaze on the smoke. Ifanna rattled off a string of rather creative curses—and that was when Mer realized she could hear again.

"—was that?" Ifanna was saying. "Did the boar do something to the magic or—"

"No," Mer breathed. She turned to look at the smoke, her heart hammering. Swallowing hard, she pressed her bare fingers into the forest floor. She reached for the water that ran beneath the earth, tried to call out to the magic of the Wellspring.

The magic did not answer.

"No, no, no." The whole world was shaking—or perhaps that was Mer herself. She tried a second time, stretching out that other-sense, trying to find the deep thrum of the Well's magic.

It was gone.

"He did it," said Mer. "Renfrew managed to set off the powder before the boar could kill him." Mer squeezed her eyes shut for a moment. She should not have grieved Renfrew. She'd been the one to kill him, as surely as though she'd put a blade to his throat. It had been her choice.

Or had it? Had it really? Renfrew must have known she would never go along with his plan. It was why he'd shrouded the cost in half-truths. He would have realized that to speak it plainly would be to send Mer running. But then why had he brought her? He had killed the other water diviners when he could have used them instead. Maybe he had brought Mer because some part of him knew she would try to stop him.

She did not know what was worse: that Renfrew had taken her into this forest knowing that she would kill him or that he'd thought she would go along with his plan.

She wanted to talk to him. She wanted to tell him that she'd loved him and resented him, that he'd been the only real parent she'd ever known—that he'd shaped her in ways she still was only figuring out.

The tragedy of death was distance. Death cleaved the world in two, leaving the living and the dead standing on either side of some impassable chasm.

No more words would ever pass between them. And Mer had to find it within herself to be all right with that.

Someday she would—but for now, she had other worries.

The breath sawed in and out of her in painful heaves. She licked her lips and tasted salt water. Her own tears, although perhaps a taste of what was to come. Because the ocean was coming—she could feel the shifting of the world beneath her feet. It was a subtle thing, the winds changing direction, whispering through broken branches and stirring tall grasses. The ocean was beginning to nudge at the edges of its magical constraints, pushing at them. Soon, they would give altogether.

And the kingdom would be wholly submerged.

Ifanna rose to the balls of her feet, peering through the trees. "Is anyone following?"

"No one left to follow," replied Fane. He spoke the words matter-of-factly, with no hint of triumph. Which was a good thing, considering that if he'd sounded at all happy, Mer would have been tempted to bludgeon him over the head with a fallen branch.

"The black powder went off, but did it work?" said Ifanna. "That wellspring was other-touched, right? Could it be destroyed?"

"It worked," Mer said. "I can—I can feel it."

Ifanna and Fane stared at her—Ifanna with a rare frown, and Fane with something like consideration. Trefor merely sat on his haunches and panted.

"The Wellspring is gone?" asked Fane. His hand tightened around the belt that held that cooking pot. "The magic dispersed?"

"Yes."

Ifanna sucked a sharp breath against her teeth. "How long?"

Mer took a breath. She had no time for grief. Not with the sea slipping its leash and a forest gone silent all around her. "Half a day, perhaps. Twelve hours for the sea to gather strength."

Ifanna wrung her hands. "Half a day. We have to get back. The guild, my mothers—everyone. I have to tell them what's coming."

"Through the caves?" asked Fane.

"It would take too long," said Mer. She threw her gaze eastward. "The shoal. The sea is shallow there. I can use my power to clear enough water away that we could wade across."

"And the royal guards?" said Ifanna. "Won't they try to kill us?"

"They'll be looking for people coming toward the island, not from it," said Fane reasonably.

"They'll also probably have seen the smoke—they might even go to tell the prince that something has gone awry." Mer squared her shoulders and began walking. "We can't stay here."

"I have to get the guild out," said Ifanna. "My people—they won't be evacuated like the nobles." She pressed a hand to her blood-less mouth. "I don't know if we'll be able to get everyone out."

"You won't," said Mer grimly. "There won't be enough time, not unless…"

Not unless riders were sent out to nearby villages and all the guards were put to the task of evacuating Caer Wyddno.

And there was only one person who could do that.

Mer's fingers clenched so hard that her nails dug in. "The prince," she said. "He could save everyone."

Ifanna shook her head. "I doubt he'd even talk to me."

Mer looked at Fane. "And what of you? Where will you go?"

"I came here to retrieve a piece of iron," said Fane quietly. "To bring it to the otherfolk. This was my last task."

"Then go," said Mer. "You got what you came for."

"And so have you," Fane said. "Garanhir will no longer have the power to follow you. He likely won't even be alive in a day's time— all you have to do is run."

"I know that."

Mer *wanted* to run. She wanted to sprint across that shoal, steal a horse, and ride east. This wasn't her fault—she hadn't blown up the Wellspring. She hadn't even known what she was doing—

Tell it to the dead.

The memory of Gryf's words rang through her.

She closed her eyes, pressed a hand to her face. She tried not to remember that nightmare, that home with the empty cradle and covered figure on the bed. She didn't want to recall the flies nor the tiny figure in Gryf's arms as he sat in a rocking chair.

When Mer had discovered those poisoned wells, she had tried to run.

What if she hadn't? What if she'd stayed in that village, used her powers to try and find new water sources for them?

Her stomach churned. She had never even thought of helping those villagers, and she was pretty sure that made her a terrible person. She'd only ever thought of her own survival. She had made some exceptions: She'd fed stray dogs and given coin to beggars. But those had been passing kindnesses. She had never considered returning to those ruined villages and trying to make amends.

Could she have saved Gryf's family? She would never know.

She had to live with that.

And if she ran now, she knew she would never stop running. Because to stop would mean being alone with herself, and she couldn't live with a person who had let tens of thousands die with nothing more than a shrug and an *I didn't know.*

She thought of a young girl, eight years old, who had waded into a raging river to save a babe.

She wanted to be someone that girl could be proud of.

She couldn't run. She couldn't leave Caer Wyddno to its fate. Its prince might deserve death, but its people didn't.

"I'm going to the prince," she said. "Someone has to warn him. Someone other than a known thief."

"Thanks for that," said Ifanna, but she flashed a smile at Mer.

Mer looked up at Fane. "I have one question for you. It's more of an offer, but you don't have to take it. You're already sworn to an employer, I know."

He inclined his head. "And what would that be?"

"You said you have to return to the otherfolk." She threw her gaze northeast, toward Caer Wyddno. "But you didn't say when. You mind making a stop first?"

Fane smiled—and nodded.

CHAPTER 23

THREE STOLEN HORSES pounded up the road that led to Caer Wyddno. Early afternoon sunlight shone bright overhead and the horses panted, their sweat working into a lather around the saddles. Mer knew she should have slowed down, to let the horses cool off—but she did not have the time. They cantered past the gates, past the guards that called after them, and then Mer leapt from the saddle.

Every step felt too slow. Her fear sharpened every sense, made time feel like it dragged across her skin. Her throat and mouth were dry but not from use of her magic. It was simple terror. Part of her wanted to run, to turn and ride from the city. She could do it— she probably *should* do it. She could feel the magic leeching out of the city, leaving it unprotected. It was only a matter of time before the sea came to reclaim that which it had long been denied.

Ifanna tossed her reins to a passerby and said, "Hey, you want a horse?"

The passerby happened to be a young woman, who looked as though Ifanna had handed her a live snake.

"Take your family and valuables and ride east," said Ifanna. "City's about to be flooded."

Ignoring the gaping woman, Ifanna and Mer strode ahead. Fane swung one long leg over his own horse, taking Trefor down from where he'd been tucked into Fane's cloak. The dog had enjoyed the ride, his tongue lolling in a dog grin.

The three of them hastened farther into the city before anyone could stop them.

Ifanna's gaze kept flicking toward home; Mer knew that the thief's thoughts would be of her parents, of her friends, of all her allies in the city. Ifanna had the most to lose—which was why Mer had to let her go first.

"Hurry," she said.

Ifanna threw a glance over her shoulder. "What of you?"

Mer tried for a smile; it was more of a grimace. "You get the word out to the people. Tell everyone that they must leave the city now— that they should go east, make for higher ground. But for those outside the city, riders must be sent."

And there was only one person who could send them.

For a moment, Ifanna seemed torn. "What if he won't listen to you?"

"I won't give him a choice," said Mer.

Trefor sneezed hard, staggering back onto his hind legs. He shook his head, ears flapping.

"Wait," said Fane. He knelt beside the dog and placed a hand on his back before looking at Ifanna. "Take him with you. Take him from the city."

"Are you sure?" asked Ifanna.

"Your people will keep him safe," said Fane. "Won't they?"

Determination hardened Ifanna's face. "They will," she said. Then she turned and sprinted, light-footed and nimble, through the afternoon markets.

Trefor looked from her, then back to Fane. He whined. "Go on," said Fane softly, patting his rump. The corgi licked his hand, then ran after Ifanna and vanished from sight. Fane watched him go, his mouth tight.

"You could go with them," said Mer. "Save people with Ifanna. Where I'm going—I may not come back."

Fane rose to his full height. "I know that. Where are we going?"

It was the answer she'd both dreaded and hoped for.

She took a deep breath. It felt too tight in her lungs.

"This way," she said, and turned to the west.

The castell loomed over Caer Wyddno. It was probably by design, so the royal family could gaze down on the common people. Mer hurried toward the fortress. She dared not run, not without drawing the attention of those guarding the markets. Her hood was drawn up, her face angled down. The stakes were too high to be recognized. They had lost two hours getting back to the city—which meant perhaps only ten more to save all of Caer Wyddno.

The ocean was immortal and patient. For decades, it had waited for the magical wards to be stripped away. And now—now, it would greedily surge up, take back what rightfully belonged to the tides.

Mer hurried up a winding set of stone stairs. She did not take the main road up to the castell, instead choosing one of the routes servants used for laundry. She nearly crashed into a washerwoman who snarled and cursed at her, but Mer paid her no attention. The only thing that mattered was reaching the prince.

The sea salt seemed to catch in her throat, tickling every time she swallowed. Gritting her teeth, Mer pushed her legs even harder, taking the stairs at an all-out run once she was out of sight of the guards.

Finally, they reached the top of the stairs. The path veered left, into the servants' courtyard. There was a small sitting place, with a fountain and herb garden. Mer remembered spending a few hours with other children here, when the servants couldn't keep them out of the water. It was a calm place, where many of the seamstresses would take advantage of the sunlight to finish delicate needlework.

But now the fountain was dry. There was no water trickling down the carved stone, no children running about. There were a few servants hauling baskets of laundry to the stairs and they gave Mer and Fane startled glances.

Mer darted toward one of the doors and opened it, hastening into the kitchens.

All at once, memory slammed into her. It was not so much the sight but the smell: tea and cooking fires, steam and roasting meats. She remembered sneaking into the kitchens for sweets, lingering when the cooks asked if she could heat pots of water with a touch.

The kitchens were bustling with the preparations for supper.

One of the cooks, an older man, glanced up and did a double take. He squinted, then all the color blanched from his face.

Mer pressed a finger to her lips. She did not remember this man's name, but she knew him. He had been an apprentice when she'd left and he had been promoted to one of the cooks. "Hush," she said. "I promise I'm not here to do harm. I need to speak with the prince. It's urgent."

The man's throat moved in an audible swallow. His eyes darted between her and a rope hanging from the far wall. It was the alarm bell, meant to be rung in case of fires. His hand twitched toward it.

Mer said, "You need to leave. Everyone should—the castell isn't safe. Tell them to get out of the city."

"What?" said the cook, startled into stillness.

"There's a wave coming," said Mer. By now, several of the other servants had gone still, noticing the two strangers standing in the kitchens. "It will sweep over the city and flood it. There's no time to collect your things. Get your families and get to high ground."

Then she pushed past the cook and hurried from the kitchens. She could not stay to convince them; it was not worth risking all the lives in the city for a few people she'd known in another life. Fane followed closely.

"Come on," she said, turning down a corridor. All the hallways meant for servants were narrow, edged into the castell like an after-thought. There would be fewer guards in such places, as the nobles did not think servants merited protection. Mer remembered every hallway, every shortcut. They were carved into her memory, only waiting for the moment when she'd need them again. She ran from the kitchens, setting a hard pace up a winding set of stairs, then down another corridor through the guest wing. Mer was beginning to think that perhaps they would make it, that they'd reach the prince's chambers before anyone could think to stop them.

And then the alarm bells began to ring.

CHAPTER 24

THE DOORS OF the ap Madyn manor were always locked.

Which was why Ifanna didn't bother to use them. She hadn't, not since she was a child. Rather, she told Trefor to stay in the gardens, scaled the trellis near her bedroom, climbed through a window, and frightened a servant half to death when she rounded a corner. "Mothers," she wheezed. "Where?" Every breath felt as though someone were scrubbing her insides with fistfuls of sand.

The servant blinked twice, then pointed in the direction of the sitting room. Ifanna couldn't run—her ribs ached with exhaustion—but she managed a quick step.

Aldyth sat at her desk, a quill poised above parchment. Her golden brows swept up into her hairline. "Ifanna? I'd heard you broke out of prison. Where have you—"

Ifanna didn't stop to answer. She threw her arms around Aldyth and hugged her close for a few heartbeats.

This was what Ifanna had thought about in those moments when she'd seen the boar, when those jars of black powder had rolled across the ground: how she would never see her family again. But she'd survived—and if she acted swiftly enough, she might pull off the greatest heist of her life.

Stealing all the people from a city.

"I can't explain," said Ifanna. She stepped back. "You have to trust me. The city's going to be underwater in a matter of hours. The prince's old spymaster destroyed the magic keeping Gwaelod safe."

Aldyth's eyes flashed. "Renfrew? I thought he'd fled the city."

"He came back," said Ifanna. "Brought Mer. He's dead now. It's a whole story—I promise I'll tell it to you later, especially the part about how carrying too many books can get a person killed by water horses. Speaking of—we're not packing any books. Leave them. Just take the people."

Aldyth's gaze swept to the window. Their manor looked out across the ocean. Ifanna could see a thin line of smoke rising up from a distant island. But more than that, she saw the way the ocean was retreating from its shorelines. It looked to be a low tide, but an unnatural one.

Aldyth drew in a breath. "I'll rally the servants," she said. "You—you're going to tell Melangell to send out her birds. She's in our bedroom." She reached down, hastily scrawled a few notes, tearing them from the parchment. "Take these to her. We'll try to bring our contacts away from the shoreline."

"Or tell them to just get in boats and try to ride it out," said Ifanna.

Aldyth nodded, then wrote another note. "Not a bad plan."

Ifanna took the notes, turning away. Then she stopped and glanced over her shoulder. "We can't take the gold," she said. "The coin, the treasures—it'll slow us down."

Aldyth's face was still, the corners of her eyes hardened. "We need some of it. Our people will starve—"

"No," said Ifanna. "We can't stop for things. We have to get the people out. All of them—sick, elderly, young, I don't care. Beggars on the streets, pickpockets that don't carry our mark—we're taking them all." She swallowed; her throat was too dry. "I'm not trading any lives for gold."

Aldyth gazed at Ifanna, her eyes narrowed. "If we do this, we'll lose all our standing," she said. "The guild will be gone. The life you've worked toward your whole life—all for nothing."

Ifanna knew that. She'd known it since they rode into the city, since Ifanna had seen the beggars and refugees at the city's borders. The nobles wouldn't bother helping them; the prince wouldn't care. So Ifanna would. She wouldn't call it penance, because Ifanna didn't believe in feeling guilt. She had never been the kind of person who dwelled on past mistakes.

But she remembered Mer's hand on her cheek, the calm realization that Ifanna could have traded herself instead of selling out her first love.

No, this wasn't penance. But it was the right thing to do.

Ifanna said, "Then so be it. I'll be a pickpocket in one of the southern cities. I'll find food wherever I have to. I'll rebuild the guild from the ground up. But we're not sacrificing anyone. I'm not leaving someone behind because we needed a horse to carry sacks of silver." She smiled, but it felt more like a snarl. "Tell everyone in the guild that."

Aldyth rocked back. Ifanna waited for a flash of her cold anger, for that rationality that had helped Aldyth rule this city's criminals. But instead, her mother's posture relaxed.

"Well," she said, "it looks like you're finally ready to lead them."

CHAPTER 25

THE FIRST TIME Fane had fought another, he'd been nine years old.

It had been a scrap with a boy—one or two years older, with gangly arms and legs and a temper that flared hot. He'd said something unflattering about Fane's family, and Fane had answered with his own childish insult, and the next thing he'd known, they were grappling with each other in the muddy street.

It was no great battle; rather, Fane's mam had pulled the two apart, taken Fane by the wrist, and dragged him away. Fane's eyes were stinging from the dirt and his cheek smarted, but he'd managed to say, "Why'd you stop me?"

"Because he was shoving your face into the street, love," said Mam.

"I would have won," said Fane sulkily.

Mam had laughed—she had a merry laugh, brimming with the

kind of cheer that always made people smile. She squatted down before him, wiping the dirt from his cheek with the edge of her sleeve. "You would not have beat him."

"Are you going to tell Da I was fighting?" he asked, feeling more flattened by his mother's amusement than the implication that he would have lost the fight. Da hated fighting; he'd refused to join the cantref's armies as a lad, even when all his brothers had gone off to war.

"I think *you* should," said Mam. "Can I ask why you were fighting?"

Fane let out a breath. "He said Gethin must be a changeling because he's too quiet."

Mam's smile softened. "I know you want to stand up for your brother. But mayhap next time you just walk away, all right? Words don't always have to lead to brawling in the street."

"Then when do I fight?" he asked, frowning.

Mam's soft fingers had brushed the muddy hair from Fane's eyes. "When there's more at stake than pride."

Fane heard the iron before he saw the guards.

This iron crooned of oil, of clean cloths being moved across the breastplate and shoulders. The armor was well tended, untouched by battle. These were the royal guards, the last line of defense for Gwaelod's prince. They would be former soldiers, all chosen for their skill and experience. Fane closed his eyes for a moment, trying to reach out, to count how many armored pairs of feet were pounding toward them.

Mer glanced at Fane and he saw the question in her eyes. "At least five," he said curtly. "Maybe eight."

Mer spat out a curse, reaching for the flask at her belt. She put it to her lips and drank deeply, then flung the last of the water to the stone floor. A twist of her fingers and the puddles froze on the spot.

The first guard rushed around the corner. His heel hit the frozen water and he lost his balance. Under the weight of his armor, there was no stopping his fall. He tumbled over backward, crashing into the guard behind him. "Come on," Mer snapped, and ducked through a doorway to their left. Fane followed, taking a moment to pull the door shut behind them. He gave the latch one hard yank and felt something snap. Hopefully that would delay the guards, if only for a few moments.

"They'll be taking the prince to his chambers," said Mer grimly. "Now the alarm's been raised."

"I assume that's bad," said Fane. They'd run into a bedroom; it was empty, the bed mussed and a gown thrown over the back of a chair. Fane glanced around for another door, but he did not see one.

"No way in once the doors shut," said Mer. "The hinges are reinforced with iron. I can't break them. It would take a stone diviner to do so." She went to the window—glass, far more expensive than Fane was used to—and pushed it open. She took a breath and said, "How are you with heights?"

He blinked. "Fine?" It came out as a question.

"Good." Mer put one foot on the windowsill, grimaced, then

crept out onto the ledge. It was narrow, winding around the circular wall of the tower. Mer crawled nimbly as a spider, her gaze kept straight ahead.

For Fane, getting out of the window took a little more maneuvering. He bruised a knee and banged one elbow, but then he was on the narrow ledge. One glance down and—

He had meant what he said. Fane had never had a problem with heights. But then again, he had never crouched on the edge of a sea cliff before. The world fell away beneath him. Distant waves crashed into the rocks below. His heart thumped unsteadily and sweat broke out across his neck.

He had always thought his death would arrive on the point of a knife or tip of a sword. Gazing down at the jagged rocks, the wind tugging at his shirt and whispering through his hair—it was a stark reminder that a fall could kill him just as easily. He swallowed—his throat suddenly parched—and forced himself not to look down. Mer was ahead of him, moving slowly but steadily. He crawled after.

It felt as though the journey took an hour, but it was likely only five minutes. Fane was aware of every passing moment until Mer reached up and grabbed another window. It did not budge. With a scowl, Mer reached into her belt and withdrew a knife. She cracked the hilt hard against the glass, sending a spiderweb of cracks across it. Another strike and—

Mer wobbled dangerously. Without thinking, Fane grabbed her ankle. It was all he could seize, and he knew that if she did fall, she would pull them both down.

He held on, nonetheless.

Steadying herself, Mer lifted her arm a third time and smashed her knife into the glass. Then she fumbled about, found the latch, and swung the frame open. Mer scrambled inside. Fane followed, a throb of relief accompanying every heartbeat. Glass crunched beneath his boots as he followed Mer to the door. They had entered what seemed to be an old study—there was a desk, wrought of heavy oak, and stacks of books were piled atop it.

For a moment, Mer went utterly still. Her gaze went elsewhere— a memory he could not follow.

"What is it?" he asked quietly.

Mer blinked, then shook her head. "This was Renfrew's study. Where—where he taught me. I thought the prince would have cleared it all out." Taking a shaky breath, she said, "We have to keep moving. The prince's room is at the end of this hallway. If we can reach it before he does…" She trailed off, as if this was where her plans had ended. Her brows pulled together and she gave a sharp jerk of her head, like a dog shaking off water. "We need to keep moving."

She put her hand on the door's latch, then she tilted her head. It took Fane a moment to realize why.

The bells had stopped. A silence had swelled up to fill their place—and that silence chilled him far more than the sounds of alarm. It was the kind of quiet that felt like a drawn breath, like the moment of stillness before everything fell apart.

Mer tried the latch, but it snagged. "Locked," she murmured. "Of course he locked it. Probably threw the key into the ocean."

"We're locked in Renfrew's office?" said Fane. The door had the heavy, solid appearance of a well-made barrier. But he could still try to break it.

"Give me a moment." Mer reached into her boot and withdrew two slips of metal. He recognized one as the lockpick's wrench. She knelt before the door and slid both tools into the lock.

A restless shiver ran through Fane; part of him yearned to spend that energy on pacing. But that might distract Mer. Instead, he tried to focus his attention on the study. It was a small room, but even so, it held all the luxurious splendor of the rest of the castell. Caer Wyddno was by no means a poor city; the markets were bustling and trade was brisk. Fane had seen the cities bordering the edge of Gwaelod and Gwynedd, where the fields had been burned and farmers driven out.

Fane gazed about the study, untouched by poverty and strife. It had rows of books and expensive glass inkwells. Feather quills and rolls of parchment had been left to molder, when a family could have sold such valuables and eaten for a month. There was a map on the wall, marked by colored pins.

Fane felt disgust rise in his throat like bile. Renfrew had worked and plotted and studied here. And it was no wonder he'd seen the lives of so many people as disposable—he was so far removed from suffering that it was a theoretical concept. From a high tower, he could have counted lives the way a banker counted coin.

A click came from the locked door. "There we go," muttered Mer. She shoved the tools back into her boot, reached for the latch and—

Fane heard it too late.

There was iron in the door, on the window ledge, in the wrench, in the heavy keys hanging off a bookshelf. There was iron all around him, which was his only excuse for not noticing the iron just beyond the door.

"Wait," he began to say. Mer had the door half-open as she glanced over one shoulder. It only meant she didn't see the guard's heavy gauntlet reach for her.

The man seized Mer around the throat. She made a choked sound, moving with admirable speed as she grabbed for the man's wrist. A knife was in her fingers, and she shoved it between the joints of his armor. The guard bellowed with pain, releasing her at once and stumbling away.

A second guard struck her across the face, then seized her by the hair. Her face was forced up, her brand bared for all to see.

Fane rushed forward, every instinct screaming to help, but then he halted.

He had killed three times: those two robbers on the road and then the Blaidd. The first two had been an accident and the latter was at the behest of the otherfolk. He'd sworn never to use his magic for his own gain. He wouldn't be like those mercenaries who had slain his family. He wouldn't kill because it was easy or simple. He wouldn't be the reason a child grew up an orphan. That was what he told himself every time he avoided a conflict, cringed away from physical contact, and spent his nights alone.

The hesitation cost him. A third guard seized Fane, painfully wrenching his arms up behind his back. Fane made a soft sound of protest, but he dared not struggle. To do so would call upon the magic.

Two guards held Mer. One had Fane.

Three people. All it had taken to doom a kingdom was three people.

"Hari was right," said the first guard, astonished. "She's here. I never thought—"

"I have to see Garanhir," said Mer tightly. The muscles strained in her neck; she was forced up onto her toes by the guard's grip on her hair. "He has to know—"

"Oh, you'll see him." The guard gave her a shake, the way a hound might have shaken a rat. "He'll come see your body. To make sure we've done our job."

"You're all fools," snarled Mer. "This isn't some assassination attempt. Renfrew's dead and the whole city is in danger."

The second guard slipped a knife from his belt. "None of that now."

"We have to get to the prince," said Mer, her voice fraying with panic.

She had not panicked once since Fane first met her. Not when water horses slaughtered a man standing an arm's length from her, not when Renfrew betrayed her, not when a giant boar attacked, nor even when she told them all that the sea would come for them.

But caught in these guards' armored hands, her eyes were wide as a snared hare's. She threw her body against them, clawing and fighting to free herself, but the iron in the guards' gloves kept her magic at bay.

She was no longer the water diviner who had confidently led them through sea caves and found an age-old wellspring of magic. Her face looked younger, tight with terror. And Fane knew who she was in that moment: She was the girl who'd been tortured and branded at the behest of a prince. The memories held her as securely as the grip of iron.

Fane couldn't watch Mer die.

She was stubborn and angry, capable of drowning a man without so much as blinking. But she was also kind and good and braver than anyone he'd ever met. She had risked her life and freedom to save the lives of everyone in Caer Wyddno.

There was a single guard behind him, keeping Fane's arms at his back. Were he to struggle, Fane knew that his curse would take control of him. All those years of restraint, of keeping himself at a distance— they would be rendered meaningless. He would become the very killer he promised himself he'd never be.

Fane wanted to say he made the choice because it was the only thing to do. If they did not reach the prince, thousands would perish. And if that meant that a few lives had to be forsaken, then someone had to do it.

But in his heart of hearts, Fane did not choose the city. He did not choose a kingdom.

He chose her.

This was why death should not have loved ones.

Because this was what came of it.

Fane threw his head back. He felt the back of his skull crack into the guard's nose and heard a sickening crunch. The guard staggered back, but it was far too late. Fane felt the change, the shift in his perception as the blow connected. He closed his eyes, took a breath, then reopened them.

And he let the magic have him.

CHAPTER 26

WHEN THE FIGHT broke out, Mer could not turn her head. A guard had a painful grip on her hair, craning her neck back. But Mer saw the flicker of movement from the corner of her eye.

Fane drove the back of his head into his captor's nose, breaking bone and cartilage with a stomach-churning crack. The guard cried out, releasing him. Fane whirled, and in one easy movement, pulled the guard's sword from his scabbard.

Fane opened the guard's throat with a slash of the blade, then turned on the two guards who held Mer. One of them shoved her into a wall, knocking the breath from her. There was a whisper of metal as they drew their own weapons. Fane flicked the blood from his sword in a contemptuous whirl, resting the flat of the blade against his forearm, the tip at eye level and pointed at his enemies.

"Run," he snarled.

It took a heartbeat for her to realize that he spoke not to the guards, but to her.

One of the guards brought his sword down, and Fane parried the strike, only to turn and catch another on his blade. Every movement was fluid, as practiced as though he had been sword fighting for all of his life. It was the magic, taking hold within him as swiftly as a fire invaded dry tinder. He would not escape it until all of his enemies were dead—or he was. She wanted to thank him and to tell him she wasn't worth it all in the same breath. But there was no time.

Mer scrambled to her feet, her heart hammering painfully against her breastbone. She threw herself in a clumsy sprint, hurtling around corners and colliding with walls when she could not slow herself. Her palms ached as she used her hands to haul herself up a circular stairway.

Another guard stepped in front of her, but Mer ducked under his arm and threw a kick at the back of his knee. His leg went out from under him and Mer bolted out of reach. She was so close. She could see the heavy double doors of the prince's chambers. She had never been inside, but she had stood in the hallway as Renfrew conversed with Garanhir.

The doors were closing.

Mer snarled a wordless curse, raising one hand. Those wooden doors had traces of water in them—all wood did. The locks were reinforced with iron; once they were shut, she'd never get them open. So she couldn't let them shut. She ignored the parched ache of her tongue and the sudden throb in her temples as she pulled at the water in the wood, holding the doors still.

She would not let all of this be for naught.

She *wouldn't*.

The doors went still. There was a startled noise, and then Mer felt the wood give a sudden yank. Someone was trying to push them shut from the inside.

Mer held on with all of her will. She was perhaps twenty paces from them, her legs suddenly wobbly. So close. She was so close.

The doors twitched and Mer's jaw ached with the exertion of holding them open.

Ten paces. Eight—then five. And finally—

Mer raised both hands and urged all of her magic, every droplet of water, into those wooden doors, and then she slammed them open.

The doors collided with the two guards who had been desperately trying to close them. They went down hard, knocked senseless.

Garanhir stood in the center of his bed chambers, his last line of defense on the floor. The room was beautiful—a bed draped in soft, embroidered fabrics; a table spread with cheeses and a pitcher of wine. A tall chair stood in the corner. It was a room meant for royalty and no one else. Mer strode inside like it was hers.

Garanhir had aged in the time she'd been away. His hair had not grayed but dulled like dark metal too long without a polishing. The years of war sagged on a face that should have otherwise been youthful. But his eyes were narrow and sharp as a snake's. He gazed upon Mer like he could rend her apart with his bare hands.

"Your Majesty," said Mer. Her voice was cold and steady—and she was glad for it. She'd feared perhaps this would be like a nightmare in which she would never manage to utter the words she so desperately needed to. "You have to evacuate the city."

Garanhir gazed at her, seemingly startled out of his anger. "What?"

"You need to act now," she said. "Send out riders—warn the coastal villages. You have hours, perhaps half a day at most."

She watched as walls were erected behind his eyes; his mouth pursed and arms pulled tight against his sides. She might have startled him at first, but whatever advantage she'd had was rapidly draining away.

"Diviner," he said. His voice was soft, too melodious to come from such a hard mouth. And at once, Mer was a child and standing in that dungeon, listening to Garanhir speak to a spy mere moments before thrusting a knife into his eye. "You should never have come here."

Quicker than she would have expected, Garanhir's hand flashed toward the table. Amidst the cheeses was a small, wicked knife. His arm pulled back, muscles coiling as he readied himself to slam the blade into Mer's stomach. She sidestepped the strike, catching his arm. He'd been trained to defend himself—perhaps even by his own spymaster.

Mer did not have time for this. With a snarl, she curled her fingers into a fist. She found the water in his body and held it tight. The cheese knife fell from his grip, clattering to the floor.

Garanhir choked on his own words. Then he was stumbling back, forced against a wall by his own traitorous body. It was blunt, clumsy magic and Mer only managed it because the prince wore no armor. The only metal upon him was silver signet rings, and those were no protection.

The prince's head thunked against the stone wall. Mer stalked toward him. She did not care that Garanhir was the prince, that he'd had her branded, that he had sent men after her, that he would see her killed or imprisoned and had the coin and power to do so.

She had never been brave—but she'd always been angry. It would have to be enough.

Garanhir bared his teeth in defiance, waiting for the final blow.

And there was a large part of Mer that yearned to do it. She had spent four years running from this man, always looking over her shoulder, never able to stay in one place. He had taken Mer from her family, replaced a kindly father with one who had molded Mer into a weapon. And when she had questioned the prince, he'd marked her as property.

She could quash her nightmares by ending him.

But it would have been a selfish decision, one made in a moment of childish spite. It would have been the actions of someone still bound up in Renfrew's desires. He would have killed the prince.

"Do it," said Garanhir. He was many things, but none could call him a coward. "I know you want to."

But Mer still needed him. Only a prince could evacuate the city and surrounding countryside in time.

This was her choice—to save those that Renfrew had deemed dispensable. Renfrew and the prince had both used her, tried to sharpen her into a weapon, but both had failed.

She belonged to herself.

"No," she said. "I'm not here to kill you, Garanhir."

Confusion flickered through his eyes. And she could see why—her invasion of the castell, using her knowledge of the passageways to get this far, her companion attacking the guards. Her actions weren't those of a woman who desired a peaceful conversation.

"You are going to listen to me," she said, and she barely recognized her own voice. Her anger was cold and even as a frozen lake. Renfrew, she realized. She sounded like her mentor, even now. "Renfrew destroyed the Well."

It took a few heartbeats for the words to sink in. She watched as Garanhir's pupils dilated, his mouth falling open. "That is—that's not possible. That Well is protected, my grandfathers made sure—"

"He used black powder," said Mer. "He brought in a miner from Gwynedd who helped him do it. The boar is dead, the Well is gone, and the magic that came from the spring is draining away."

Red spilled across his face in a furious flush. "Gwynedd? Those damned—"

"Everyone is going to die," she snarled. She slammed her hand against the wall and he flinched. "Stop thinking about your damned wars. Gwaelod will be flooded. The Lowland Hundred will be no more, do you understand me? Everyone in the farmlands is going to die unless you send out riders right now to warn them. Tell them to get to high ground, now. This city will be little more than an underwater ruin in ten hours."

"That's why you came here?" said Garanhir with an incredulous bark of laughter. "You came to warn me?"

"Not you," she said. "I'd not lose a moment's sleep if you were to drown. But the city—I couldn't watch it happen to them."

He gazed at her, several expressions crossing his face in quick succession. "You were Renfrew's diviner," he said. "Why should I believe you?"

It was disconcerting to speak to him like this. To her, Garanhir had always been an impressive figure—Renfrew's master, a prince, and then later, a terror that loomed over her every nightmare. But now she saw a man. Fallible, graying, and his breath smelling of wine.

"Because all I want," she said, "is for you to save as many as you can. For once in your life, act as a ruler should."

A bit of hardness returned to his face. "And if this is a lie? What if you're trying to spread my forces thin?"

She shook her head. She was too weary to argue. "Look out your window." She stepped back and released her grip on the magic. It was a relief; her head throbbed.

Garanhir rolled his shoulders, then pushed himself away from the wall. There was a pitcher on a small table and Mer went to it. Hands shaking, she poured herself a cup and threw it back. Now that her message had been delivered, now that all of this was out of her hands, she felt utterly exhausted. Her legs trembled beneath her and she forced herself to drink another cup, then another.

The prince did not move for a heartbeat, as if to prove that glancing out the window was his choice and not hers. Then he took a few steps and looked out.

She knew what he would be seeing. She could feel the ocean

pulling away from the shore, like a person drawing in a deep breath. It could only be held so long before that breath would gust free.

"What—what is that?" said Garanhir. "The sea is—"

"Retreating," said Mer. "Within hours, it will surge back, higher than you can imagine. Only the last remnants of Caer Wyddno's magic is keeping it at bay. Those will fail and soon." Legs unsteady, she sank into the tall-backed chair. All at once, everything seemed to crash down upon her: the lies and betrayals, the realization that everything she'd been fighting for had come to naught. She had returned for her freedom, and instead she'd helped destroy a kingdom.

Garanhir's face had gone bone white. He turned to glance at her, then back at the window.

"But you—" He seemed to struggle for words. "You've power over water. Can't you stop it?"

"Stop the sea?" She let out a terrible, incredulous laugh. "I may as well try to carry the moon on my back. I could not stop—"

Her voice died in her throat.

Because it was true—she could not stop the sea.

But she could delay it for a time.

He saw the change in her face. Garanhir took a step toward her. "What is it?"

The clang of armored footsteps made her tense. There were more soldiers coming—and her time had run out. She could have fought, but there was little point. Her message had been delivered.

"Another thing," she said. "There's a man being attacked by your guards. Dark hair and eyes, tall. He helped me. You need to call off your soldiers, right now. Those who haven't attacked him yet may live." She didn't allow herself to consider that Fane might have already fallen.

Garanhir's mouth tightened, but his reply was swallowed up by a man bursting through the door. He wore armor that was unbuckled, pulled on in haste. He looked wildly about the room, likely expecting to see a battle.

But there was just the prince, standing in the middle of the room unharmed. Two guards knocked senseless. And a young woman dressed in dark clothing, sitting quietly. The guard's gaze lingered on Mer, and she couldn't quite decipher his expression. It was not precisely fear, not confusion, but some mingling of both.

Garanhir stepped forward and spoke to the guard. Mer could have listened, but she did not. If the prince was taking her advice, then good. And if he was not, she would prefer not to know. Garanhir's choices were not her responsibility.

Mer thought of Ifanna. Dear, pragmatic Ifanna, who had sold Mer to save the lives of thirty people.

Mer had forgiven Ifanna for that—and part of her regretted not telling Ifanna so. Because this was the one thing about herself she could not escape, the one lesson that Renfrew had managed to impress upon her: Not everyone had choices. Mer's magic had cost her family and her chance at a normal life. Her decision to run had cost her freedom. And her decision to trust Renfrew might have cost the people of Gwaelod everything.

Choices and cost. It felt like the weighing of scales, trying to balance it all.

Mer closed her eyes, her fingers tight on the arms of the chair.

The magic of the city was dwindled to near nothing; there was no pulse of warmth, of life and heat. Everything she had loved and hated about this place would soon be underwater—the markets brimming with caught fish and mussels, the bathhouse with its sweet drinks, the noble houses and the poor districts. Stray dogs and orphaned children. High-born ladies and servants alike.

Water did not care for rank nor wealth. It would sweep in, drown all.

Unless someone stood in its path.

She opened her eyes, her body tight as a drawn bowstring. A tremor ran through her—just the once.

She had helped drown a kingdom. She had done so without knowing she was doing it, but she bore that responsibility nonetheless. Just like those poisoned villages.

If she left now, she would live. But she did not know how she would live with herself.

Mer rose from the chair. She wished she could say her decision was easy, but things were not that simple. Her heart lurched in her chest; her fingers felt unsteady and cold; when she spoke, her voice was almost too quiet to hear.

"Evacuate the city," she said. "I'll give you as much time as I can."

When she looked up, Garanhir's gaze was on her. His face was still starkly pale, but at least his shoulders were straight. The guard gave Mer another questioning glance.

Garanhir nodded at the other man. "Do it," he said. "Send the riders now. Tell all that they're to leave their homes, no exceptions, and to go east."

"Help people," said Mer. "Those who cannot go on foot, find them wagons. Use your own horses. I don't care what it costs."

The guard looked at her incredulously but Garanhir held up a hand. "Do as she says," he murmured.

The guard snapped a bow, then hastened from the room.

Garanhir exhaled hard. "I suppose I should thank—"

"Don't," said Mer sharply. "I don't want your gratitude. Only your promise that you'll get the people out."

There was a moment of quiet. Then Garanhir inclined his head. "I will."

Mer pressed her lips tight, to keep herself from saying more. She did not trust herself to keep silent otherwise. One last glance at the room and—

And she saw why the guard had looked at her so oddly.

The chair Mer had been sitting in was no chair at all. It was a makeshift throne, carved from dark wood. Meant for a prince holding court in his own chambers.

Mer dragged her attention from that throne, then straightened her shoulders and strode from the room.

CHAPTER 27

THE WORLD BEGAN and ended with iron.

It was in his mouth—a lucky strike, when a soldier's fist struck Fane's jaw—and scattered along the floor, armored figures still where they had fallen. Iron was in his hand; a sword rested in his palm like the weight was part of him. Iron was in every breath. Iron was in the cauldron still hanging from the strap at his belt.

All Fane knew was iron and magic.

He sensed more than heard the approach of more soldiers. He had killed the three that tried to stop him. He stepped over them, his breaths ragged and muscles aching.

He wanted to stop. He wanted all of this to end.

"Please," he said, when another guard stepped around the corner and saw him. This one was a woman, her hair drawn back in a hasty knot. Her eyes widened at the sight of him, then she retreated. When another man tried to step around her, a crossbow in hand and a snarl on his face, the woman said, "No! The prince told us to leave him. We're to round up the scholars."

The man grimaced, but the two of them hurried on.

Leaving Fane alone in the hallway.

His chest rose and fell, rose and fell. He was the only living thing here, and as he caught his breath, the magic began to recede.

He felt it drain out of him, and his knees wobbled. He caught himself on the wall, his palm against the stone.

The sword clattered to the floor.

All around him, there was movement. Footsteps, shouts, the sounds of things being hauled away. But no one touched him; no one even went near him. Which could only mean one thing.

Mer found the prince. She had succeeded.

That thought made him breathe a little easier. All of this—it was for something.

It didn't make him feel any less stained. He had taken lives, chosen to take them. Because the kingdom needed him to. Because countless people were going to perish. Because he couldn't watch Mer be killed.

Fane forced himself to stand. His whole body ached and there was blood dripping down his back from some unseen wound.

"Fane!"

He turned at the familiar sound of Mer's voice.

She was unhurt—and that realization made him relax. She hastened toward him, hands extended. Her fingers hovered over his chest without quite touching. He understood her hesitation; blood spattered most of his clothing. "You made it," she said. "I—I wasn't sure…"

Fane let out a breath. "I killed the three guards. Turns out my curse is good for something."

"You saved hundreds of lives today," she said. "Don't ever forget that. Without you, the prince would never have gotten word."

"No," he said. "That was you. I just—cleared the way a little."

He swayed on his feet and her hand came up to grasp his arm. He felt the touch even through his cloak.

"Listen," she said. "Go with the prince's guards. They're taking him out a side door, through a passageway used by the royal family. It'll be the fastest way out of the city."

He blinked at her. "And what of you?"

She smiled, but it was forced and faltering. "You need to—go with the prince's men. Get out of the city, Fane." She turned to leave.

Fane sidestepped so that he stood before her. A terrible, creeping realization stole through him. "Mer. Where are you going?"

She would not meet his eyes.

"Tell Ifanna she was right," she said. "One life for thirty—it's not a bad bargain."

Abruptly, he understood. Part of him wished he hadn't.

"Mer," he said again.

Neither spoke for a few moments. Mer kept her gaze averted, but he saw the exhaustion and pain hang heavy on her shoulders.

He could not go with her. He was bound to bring the cauldron back to the otherfolk. He could not break his oaths.

For a moment, he was overwhelmed by helplessness. All this blood—all this iron singing around him—and he still couldn't save her.

"Can I do anything?" he asked.

She finally met his eyes. "Just—tell me you'll remember this. Everything that's happened. Someone should, and Ifanna will embellish the details."

"I will," he said, and she smiled again. This time it was smaller and sadder, but more honest.

Silence fell between them. Fane did not know what to say. He considered and discarded several meaningless comforts; he knew she wouldn't appreciate them. If he'd learned one thing about her, it was that she valued the truth. "I wanted to say yes," he said. "When you asked me to go with you, after the heist."

"But you couldn't," she said. Her gaze flicked down to the pot tied to his belt.

"No," he agreed. "I couldn't."

His hand came up—slowly, ever so slowly—and brushed her jaw. His thumb swept across her cheek, his eyes on hers, trying to drink in every detail. He tilted her face up and her hair fell back, away from the brand. This was how he wanted to remember her: brilliant and angry and so very alive.

She leaned into the touch. He watched her lips part, a breath dragged against her teeth.

"Can I ask one thing?" she said.

He nodded.

"If you hadn't sworn to the otherfolk," she said, "if you'd been free to choose. Who would it have been?"

He knew of what she spoke. That moment in the grove, magic at his feet and blades scattered in the grass, and those quiet heartbeats when Fane had been balanced between Renfrew and Mer.

"When I met you," he said, "you and Renfrew—only one of you bent down to greet my dog." It felt as though there were a snare around his throat. He had to swallow a few times. "I would've chosen that woman, if I could."

She smiled. And then she fisted her hand in his shirt, hesitated, then drew him down.

Her mouth pressed against his, lightly, and then with more ferocity. She kissed him hard, pouring every bit of fear and longing into that kiss. And he drank it down, welcomed all of it, because he knew this was his only chance.

She had stopped running.

And for a moment, everything was still.

She pulled away quickly, as if she needed to. "Live well, fetch," she said.

It took a few tries for him to muster a reply. "Farewell, diviner," he said.

She took a step back, then another, her eyes on his. Then she turned and slipped through a doorway. The wind caught in her hair—and that was the last Fane saw of her.

CHAPTER 28

IFANNA'S LEGS WERE leaden with exhaustion.

She stood at the top of a hill, gesturing others on. The wagons were too slow for her tastes, but there was no other way to get everyone out. There were those who could not run—children, the elderly, and those with injuries from the war. Everyone who owned a horse, goat, cow, or sheep was currently herding them up the road, sheepdogs barking madly at anyone who strayed from the path. Trefor was among them, seemingly having taken on the role of honorary herd dog.

People streamed out of the city like ants escaping a collapsing hill. The roads were clogged, but at least Ifanna and the guild had managed some kind of order. One of the guild's riders had gone on ahead, warning nearby travelers not to approach the coastline.

The people left Caer Wyddno with only what they could carry. Ifanna knew how much people would lose. Fortunes, family heirlooms, homes. The guild had left behind its manor house with all its treasures, save for a few trinkets that could be shoved into pockets. Ifanna knew that all she'd worked for, all the power and the coin she had spent years accumulating, was gone.

But still—at least people would live.

Ifanna stood by the road, watching people pass by: families, beggars, merchants, cartwrights, bakers, members of the guild, those who worked for the guards, the old and the young. Ifanna searched their faces—and finally, she found one she recognized.

It was Fane. She called out to him, but he didn't hear her above the din of rolling wagons and bleating sheep. It was Trefor who met him, his tail wagging so hard that he nearly toppled over. Fane picked him up, holding the wriggling dog to his chest. He caught sight of Ifanna and approached, putting Trefor down along the way. The dog leapt around his ankles.

"How many did we save?" he asked, his eyes drifting over the line of people.

Ifanna grimaced. "I don't know. I saw riders—I assume that Mer got to Garanhir?"

He nodded.

"Where's Mer?" she asked. She turned to glance behind him, as if Mer would be there.

Fane did not answer. A shaky breath escaped him, and he pressed a hand to his eyes.

And she understood.

Ifanna looked out to the ocean. It had begun to come in, the waves pushing up against the rocks. It *should* have come in—but it hadn't. Because, she realized, someone was holding it back.

"She said you were right," he said. "One life for thirty. It was the right choice."

Ifanna watched the ocean. She didn't know if she hoped to see a lone figure there or not. Grief and frustration roiled within her and she clenched her hands so hard her nails bit deep into her skin.

Ifanna had always loved risk and reward, danger and beauty. But a person couldn't win every coin toss, succeed in every job, take every stolen treasure. And she had always known that, one day, it might be her turn to lose.

She just hadn't considered that Mer would be the one to pay the price.

"All the times she could've listened to me," Ifanna said, "and she chose now." Her smile ached at the edges.

She turned back to the people. *Her* people, the ones she had sworn to protect. She had to keep looking at them, to remind herself what could be protected with one life.

Trefor whined softly and Fane reached for the dog, stroking his ears.

And the roar of the sea grew louder.

CHAPTER 29

T HE LAST LIVING water diviner stood on a rocky outcropping.

Her feet were bare, boots discarded. The sharp crags bit into her skin, but she was so cold that she hardly felt the discomfort. Ocean mist blew against her legs and arms, whipped her hair into her face. Her arms were held out, fingers spread and muscles straining.

The power of the ocean welled up beneath her like the deep thrum of thunder. She felt it tremble through her bones, but she did not let it frighten her.

The sea yearned to take that lowland country.

Mer wouldn't let it. She closed her eyes, dug deep into that well of power she carried, and held the sea back. The ocean raged at her, trying to escape the boundaries of her magic.

She thought of her family. Of her mam and da, her sisters and brother. Perhaps the story of Gwaelod's diviner would reach them. Perhaps they'd be proud of her.

And she thought of Renfrew. Renfrew, who was both family and not family, who had taught Mer that they were the agents of order. That it was their job to do the terrible things, if it meant others would be safe. But he had been wrong.

One could not save a land by destroying its people.

She held on for hours. Past the point where her mouth had gone dry and her temples ached. She felt blood trickle from her nose, felt the dryness behind her own eyes. Her magic sapped the water from her own body. Standing against the ocean was folly; it was like trying to hold the moon in place. Her power had granted her far more sway than anyone else, but even she had her limits.

Her magic faltered for a heartbeat. A wave spattered against the rocks, spray misting into the wind. Long had magic held it at bay—first the Wellspring and now a diviner.

But oceans were patient things, and they would not be denied.

Mer staggered to one knee, every breath scraping in and out of her. There was salt on her lips, on her cheeks, all around her. Blood spilled from her nose and stained her shirt. Her eyes blurred and her whole body ached. She did not even have the water to cry. Surely, she had held the ocean back long enough for the others to escape. She hoped so, because she had nothing left.

She lifted her face to the waves. She was a water diviner, an unwitting poisoner, a former spy, and a thief. She'd almost forgotten that little farm girl who had made puddles dance for her siblings.

All those parts of herself—and she chose that one.

She chose the little girl who had waded into a river to save a child.

"Well," she rasped, "come on, then."

And the sea swept in.

CHAPTER 30

THE NEW SHORELINE was illuminated by flecks of fire.

The camps were scattered across the cliffs. Some were larger than others—noble houses had banded together with their stewards and servants and a few private soldiers. However, even the nobles' tents were simple canvas and rope, pulled taut across wind-gnarled trees. Those who had made it out of the city were people who'd known better than to linger for their valuables.

Smaller camps had sprung up; families huddled together around fires and ate handfuls of hard cheese and freshly caught fish. A few traveling merchants had seen opportunity and halted their wagons to sell the survivors blankets and provisions at painfully high prices...that was until a young woman from the thieves' guild spoke to one of them. Word swiftly spread that those who tried to gouge the refugees for coin would swiftly find themselves an enemy of the infamous thief who'd once ransomed a nobleman's son.

"I thought he wasn't a ransom," said Fane.

Ifanna shrugged. The firelight caught in her tawny-brown hair. "Sometimes one has to bow to rumor. It sounds better than truth."

They sat around a small fire. Night had fallen some time ago, and a chill settled into the air. Fane gave Trefor his cloak and the dog curled up beneath it. His ears twitched in dreams.

Ifanna had a fresh bruise along one cheek and what appeared to be a bandaged wound along her forearm. When asked, she had simply shrugged and said, "A few people got in my way."

They hadn't spoken much since Fane found her amidst the other refugees. Ifanna and her mothers had been rounding up members of the guild, trying to keep things organized. The two noblewomen leading the guild were nothing like Fane expected—one of them was fair-haired and short, her hands heavy with rings. The other was willowy and stern-faced, but she still took a moment to clasp Fane's hands and thank him for getting Ifanna safely home. Then they marched into the crowds like generals, sifting order from the chaos.

Fane didn't know what story Ifanna had given them, only that he'd played a far more heroic role than he deserved. But Ifanna had waved off his skeptical glance and told him there was a blanket and a bowl of cawl awaiting him.

The fire sent sparks into the dark night sky. He watched them billow upward, caught on a warm updraft. The sound of the ocean lapping at rocks kept drawing his attention. They had made camp on high ground, but even now, he could hear the waves.

He wasn't sure there would ever be a time he would forget that sound.

"Bae Ceredigion," said Fane. "That's what they're calling it." He nodded down at the waters.

"A new bay," murmured Ifanna. She was chewing on a piece of dried apple. "I don't envy any mapmakers right now. Imagine having to correct every map you came across."

"I imagine those killed by the floods are probably having a worse time of it," said Fane.

There were so many dead. Even with the warnings, Fane knew they hadn't managed to evacuate all of the city. And then there were all those who'd lived along the shore that the riders hadn't managed to warn.

But rather than look chastened, Ifanna snorted. "Doubt that. The dead have very few worries, far as I can tell. The living, though. We'll be the ones with starving children come winter." She looked away from the water. "My mothers and I are planning on taking our people south."

"Start a new guild?" asked Fane.

Ifanna shrugged. "We've no coin, not at the moment. Our legacy is underwater. We'll have to rebuild from scratch—and it takes generations to establish a guild as deeply as the one in Caer Wyddno. I'll likely be working as a regular thief for many years to come. No infamy, no glory."

"Yet you chose to leave the coin behind," said Fane. "I saw those wagons you used to cart out some of the sick—you might have used them for gold."

"Don't remind me." She stretched, rolling her shoulders. "And what about you?"

He looked down at his hip. He'd tied the cauldron to his belt; the folk had told him never to let it leave his sight. While other iron objects hummed to him, this one seemed to wail. It was beautiful and unsettling, and he yearned to be rid of it. He gazed down at the dark iron. It was smudged with something that might have been rust, but he knew must be blood.

"What is that thing?" asked Ifanna. "You never did tell us."

Fane exhaled. "A weapon. One that the otherfolk could not allow to be used against them."

"Does it make magic soup or something?" asked Ifanna, smiling incredulously. "Or perhaps you just hit your enemies over the head with it?"

Fane shook his head. "Trust me. It's best you not know. You'll sleep better."

"Now I have to know," she wheedled. "Does it vomit boiling water at advancing armies? Mayhap make a terrible poison? Or maybe a very awkward battle helmet?"

A startled laugh rolled up and out of him. It was the first time he'd uttered such a noise since they'd found the Wellspring—and he realized, with a glance at Ifanna's satisfied expression, that was her intent all along.

And abruptly, the loss seemed to well up anew. The grief between them was different—Ifanna mourned something she'd once had and Fane mourned something that had never begun. Ifanna had lost a former thief, a young woman who'd helped her smuggle goods and run with criminals. And Fane had lost a young woman who greeted dogs with a wide smile, who'd been angry and a little lost, and had understood Fane in a way he'd never found in anyone else.

"Mer thought of you at the end," he said.

Ifanna laughed, but it sounded forced. "Of course, she did. I'm unforgettable." She leaned forward, her fingers touching her mouth as she gazed into the fire. "I'll miss her."

Fane did not reply. His own pain was a numb throbbing somewhere in his chest. He hadn't examined the extent of it yet, not truly, for fear of what he'd find when he did.

When Fane woke, it was an hour before dawn.

And somewhere nearby, iron was singing. It was a drumbeat of human blood, a soft song that reminded Fane of a crooning lullaby.

It wouldn't have woken him, but it was an iron that his body knew, thus, the magic within him prodded and poked until he lifted his head. Trefor was asleep under his arm; Ifanna had curled up beside the waning coals of the fire.

Fane sat up, his blanket falling away. Early morning mist dewed upon the wool, catching on his fingers as he gently placed the blanket over Trefor. Fane stood, silent amidst the sleeping figures, then made his way out of the camp.

The iron was like a siren's call that drew him to the sea. Fog hung heavy along the shore and part of him regretted not taking that blanket, draping it across his shoulders to ward off the chill.

He picked his way toward the shore, where the waves were lapping grasses and small, gnarled trees.

There was a body in the water. Caught in the waves, tossed about like a piece of driftwood.

Fane waded in before he made the decision to do so. The world felt dreamlike—time fragmented into heartbeats. One moment, the waves were splashing against his ankles and then the next, he was up to his waist. The current tugged at his trousers, rough rocks and grass against his bare feet. This place was not meant to be a shore, but it would be one nonetheless. Nothing could remain unchanged.

Another wave broke across his forearms as he leaned down. Honey-blond hair spilled through the water like sunlight. Fane managed to hook both arms beneath the figure and lifted. It took most of the strength he had; the figure's clothes were soaked through with seawater.

The one mercy was that the cold ocean had kept death's grasp at bay. Rot and bloat had yet to set into the flesh.

Fane carried her from the water, placing her beneath one of the gnarled trees. Her face had gone pale, her lips still. If it were not for the unnatural pallor, he might have thought her sleeping.

"Fallen kings."

There came a sharp intake of breath behind him.

Ifanna stood an arm's length away, her feet and ankles bare, her hair unbound. Her eyes were on the still figure that had once been the last living water diviner. Ifanna took half a faltering step, then sank into an unsteady crouch, wrapping her arms around her own head as if she could not bear to look any longer. Trefor had come with her; he looked at Mer and gave a low, questioning whine.

Fane reached down, brushed a strand of sodden hair from Mer's face. The brand was there, still visible against her pale skin. His thumb ran across it.

His grief felt distant, like the rumblings of a storm that had yet to reach shore. It had been the iron in her blood that had called to him. He had sensed it when she'd been injured in the caves, and that iron-sense of his had latched on without his knowing. It had led him to her, just like it had led him to—

His breath snagged in his throat.

Seven years of service for seven human lives.

He had killed six people. Those two robbers on the road when he was sixteen, the Blaidd, and the three guards in the castell.

He was still owed one life.

Surely the otherfolk would allow him this.

It was a risk. The folk had told him to return the cauldron to their lands. But then again, they had never told him not to *use* it.

He pulled her close again, then rose to his feet. Ifanna looked up. Her eyes were red-rimmed and her face gone blotchy. "You want to bury her?"

"No," said Fane, then hesitated. The cauldron was still tied to his belt. He pulled the cauldron free, setting it on the ground. Ifanna watched him, confusion written across her face.

"Make a fire," he said. "Please."

"You want to burn her?" asked Ifanna.

He shook his head. "You wish to know what that cauldron does?" he said. "I cannot tell you—they bound me to silence. But I can show you."

Ifanna regarded him with that confused frown. But she shrugged and rose to look for dry wood.

It took the better part of an hour. Once the fire was burning, Fane filled the cauldron with what little fresh water he could find. The water boiled, then cooled. Fane tipped some of it into Mer's mouth. Ifanna made a soft noise of protest, but she let him. She must have thought him mad, but Fane did it a second time. And then he waited.

For several long minutes, nothing happened. Fane thought that perhaps he must have done this wrong, or that the otherfolk had been wrong about this cauldron.

The color returned to her cheeks first. A soft flush, like the pink light of dawn creeping over a horizon. Then she drew in a shattered little breath, gagged, and vomited hard. It was all Fane could do to roll Mer onto her side. He barely heard Ifanna cursing or Trefor barking and then sneezing so hard he fell back onto his haunches.

Mer coughed raggedly.

Ifanna squatted down beside Mer, gaping at Fane as if she'd never seen him before.

Mer's hand came up, rubbed blearily at her eyes. Like she was awakening from a night of bad sleep.

"Fallen kings," said Ifanna faintly. "Oh. That's—that's what the otherfolk wanted?"

Fane nodded.

"No wonder they couldn't let it stay in human lands," said Ifanna. "I mean, imagine what I could do with that—"

"No," said Fane.

"Unkillable thieves—"

"No," said Fane again, but he was smiling.

Mer groaned and tried to sit up.

"Mer." Ifanna took her hand and squeezed. "Are you all right? Do you remember what happened? Who we are?"

Mer blinked at them both. She looked as though she'd been dunked in a river; she kept shivering and Ifanna tugged off her cloak, wrapping it around Mer's shoulders. Fane helped her nearer the fire. For a few long moments, Mer did not speak. Her gaze darted between Fane and Ifanna, uncomprehending. Fane's heart fell. What if the magic had gone awry?

Mer held up a hand, gesturing at Ifanna. Her voice was rusted as old iron. "Lady thief." Her hand twitched toward Fane. "Ring fighter." A wave at Trefor. "Otherfolk spy?"

Ifanna made a sound that could have been a laugh or a sob. She reached forward and tugged Mer into a hug. When they parted, Ifanna's cheeks were damp with more than seawater.

Fane exhaled hard. He hadn't let himself hope it would work.

"You all right?" he said quietly.

"What did you do?" she asked. She coughed, then cleared her throat.

"Magic," he said simply. "The otherfolk owed me seven lives for seven years of service. I had only claimed six."

Mer shook her head ruefully. "Seven years. I hope it was worth it."

Fane looked out across the camp—at the small fires, the sleeping figures, and the remnants of Gwaelod. The lands were forever changed, but they had saved some of its people. His gaze drifted to the west, to the place where the island had hidden a wellspring of magic. It was swept out to sea.

Cold fingers wove through his. He startled, then glanced down. Mer was smiling with one corner of her mouth and the sight made his heartbeat quicken. Ifanna was petting Trefor and the dog lolled on his back, feet waving in the air.

"Yes," Fane said. "It was."

THERE WAS ONCE *a kingdom called Cantre'r Gwaelod. It was full of rich farmland and crowned with a city carved from sea cliffs. The lowland kingdom should have been swept out to sea, but a magical well kept the waves at bay.*

According to a wandering bard, there was a girl who tended the well. But one day, she saw a lovely young lad and abandoned her responsibilities. The well was destroyed and the kingdom flooded.

That bard had a piece of rotten fruit thrown at him by a girl with tawny-brown hair and a fox's keen eyes. He would later amend his song to say that the kingdom had actually been quite corrupt, a rogue spy had destroyed the Wellspring, and a noble water diviner, an ironfetch, and the land's most skilled thief all banded together to save Gwaelod's people. The diviner had been many things: a farmer's daughter, a spymaster's apprentice, and a server of drinks. She had fought the ocean itself and lost—but in the fighting, she saved many lives.

As far as the world was concerned, the diviner drowned. The fetch vanished into the wilds. And the thief went southward to take up her trade in a port city.

It was almost the truth.

There once was a kingdom called Gwaelod.

The kingdom drowned.

But some of its people didn't.

Among those who survived were a young man with scarred hands and a young woman with hair that fell across her left eye. They stayed with the other refugees for a time, helping any who needed it.

The young man set up shelters and scavenged broken parts of houses that washed ashore. The young woman had a knack for finding fresh water.

One night, the two of them vanished from the camp. Their tent was empty, the dog gone. No one ever saw them again.

And to most, that is where their story ended.

Here is where another began.

A young woman, a young man, and a corgi traversed the cantrefs. They drew little attention; they were simply two more refugees from the flooded lowland kingdom. They stopped by a small farmhouse where an old sheepdog had been abandoned. The dog recognized the woman and came when she called out. Together, they crossed fields and farms, rivers and streams, forest and meadow.

They came upon the forests of Annwvyn. Waiting at the edge of the wood were the emissaries of the otherfolk. Folk crowned with poplar leaves and blackberry brambles greeted them. The sheepdog shrank back, but the corgi bounded up to meet them.

The young man pulled a small cauldron from a strap on his belt. The iron was cold to the touch and the folk who took it wore heavy gloves.

"You have succeeded," said one of the folk. "The cauldron of rebirth has long been lost to mortal lands." She knelt before the dog and gave him a gentle pat. The corgi grinned up at them and barked once.

"I believe I carried the cauldron, at least," said the young man with a dry smile.

"And so you did." The lady of the folk stepped forward. "You have done all that we asked and more."

"A favor is owed," said another.

The young man hesitated, then gestured the woman forward. "Can you heal a scar?" He pointed to a brand at the corner of her eye.

"We could, if that is what you wish," said one of the folk.

The woman shook her head. "No," she said quietly to the young man. "It's all right." She spoke to the folk. "I would ask two things."

The folk nodded.

"First," said the young woman, "this one has completed his service to you. He has served seven years and claimed seven lives, which means he no longer has need of your magic. Any of it."

The man drew in a sharp breath.

The lady of the folk said, "There is balance in that. We shall take his magic. And what is your other favor, diviner?"

"A home," said the young woman. "A safe place where we won't have to hide."

The folk smiled. And then she gave the woman an acorn and told her to plant it beside their house.

"We don't have a house," said the woman, confused.

"You will," said the second of the folk.

"Follow the edge of the forest around our lands," said the first. "Go to the east of the mountains. There is a small village—still growing. Its people would welcome you." She placed her hand on the man's forehead, and drew the magic from him. He shuddered and looked down at his hands.

"What of you?" said the folk, speaking to the dog. "Shall you return home?"

The corgi wagged his tail, then walked to the man's side and sat down beside his ankle. He looked up, tongue lolling.

"I see," said the second of the folk, smiling. "Farewell." And then they vanished into the wood, leaving the mortals behind.

The man and the woman journeyed with their hounds, skirting the edges of Annwvyn. And near the eastern footholds of the mountains, they found a fledgling village. They stayed a night in the tavern, listening to the villagers discuss the fresh vein of copper they'd found and how the town would surely be prosperous.

The young man and young woman found a place on the edge of town, near the forest. There would be timber to build a home, if that was what they chose. The two sat upon a grassy hill, fingers tangled together as they gazed at the countryside. Their corgi napped in a patch of wildflowers, the sunlight warming his fur. The sheepdog fell asleep beside him.

"Do you want to stay here?" asked the woman. "It's beautiful, but I've never stayed in one place before. At least, one place that wasn't a fortress or a thieves' guild. What would we do here?"

The young man shrugged. "I heard the villagers say they don't have a gravedigger yet. I've enough experience dragging corpses out of woods—might prove a decent occupation. This place looks like a nice one for a graveyard."

"We're going to need a well," she said. "If you want to build a house nearby."

"Then tell me where to dig one," he said, nudging her shoulder. He had little fear of touching her now that the magic had been taken from him. It made her smile.

She sank her fingers into the damp soil and called to the water below.

And the water answered.

ACKNOWLEDGMENTS

Writing a book feels a little like planning a heist. And like every heist, it cannot be accomplished without a good crew.

Firstly, to my agent, Sarah Landis. Thank you for your guidance, your keen eye for edits, and your hard work. And to everyone at Sterling Lord Literistic, I appreciate you so much.

To the team at Little, Brown Books for Young Readers—you're all amazing and I am so lucky to be counted among your authors. To the accomplished and dedicated editors who helped this story take shape: Hannah Milton, Hallie Tibbetts, and Alexandra Hightower. A big thank-you to my publicist, Sydney Tillman, and the marketing team: Stefanie Hoffman and Shanese Mullins. To Savannah Kennelly, whose Instagram Stories always make me smile. To Victoria Stapleton, for all her hard work with School & Library. To the art director, Sasha Illingworth, and designer Jenny Kimura, for creating a cover that made me gasp aloud when I first saw it. (That tree! So pretty!) To Brittany Groves, Marisa Finkelstein, and Virginia Lawther, for keeping everything smoothly on track. To Kathryn Carroll, for the lovely audiobook. And of course, the biggest of thank-yous to Alvina Ling and Megan Tingley, for continuing to give my characters a home.

To my fantastic team at Hodder & Stoughton—I'm so glad to be working with you. Thank you to my brilliant editor, Molly Powell. To the talented and tireless Natasha Qureshi. To proofreader Liz Ward, thank you for catching any mistakes. To my publicist, Kate Keehan, and Callie Robertson in marketing. And a huge shout-out to Lydia Blagden, for making the UK edition so beautiful.

To some of this book's earliest readers: Kailey Steward, Billie Bloebaum, Kalie Barnes-Young, Sami Thomason-Fyke, Katie Bircher, Cody Roecker, and Gabrielle Belisle.

To all the booksellers and librarians who have supported me over the years—I wouldn't be here without you.

To all the book boxes, bloggers, tweeters, Instagrammers, BookTubers, TikTokers, and anyone who has ever recommended my books to a friend. I appreciate you more than you will ever know.

To my friends, thank you for listening to me ramble about characters, plots, and the industry. You know who you are.

To the family, who has been with me since the beginning. Particularly my mother, without whom I couldn't have weathered the last two and a half years. If I had to be trapped inside a house with anyone, I am glad it was you.

And lastly—thank you, dear reader.